FROST
AND
FIRE

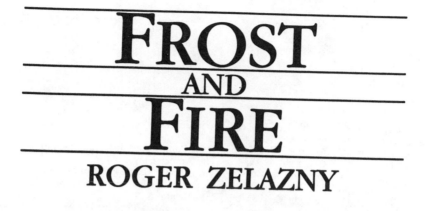

FROST
AND
FIRE

ROGER ZELAZNY

WILLIAM MORROW AND COMPANY, INC.
NEW YORK

Library of Congress Cataloging-in-Publication Data

Zelazny, Roger.
    Frost and fire / Roger Zelazny.
        p.   cm.
    ISBN 0-688-08942-9
    I. Title.
    PS3576.E43F7   1989
    813'.54—dc19

89-3015
CIP

Printed in the United States of America

First Edition

1 2 3 4 5 6 7 8 9 10

BOOK DESIGN BY MARK STEIN

To Bill Mauldin,
recalling a kindness

FROST AND FIRE

AN EXORCISM, OF SORTS

I just realized that this will be my first story collection since *Unicorn Variations* was published in 1983. I've since acquired a cat named Amber, a black belt in aikido, two more Hugos, the insides of twenty or so shelf-feet of books, and had an ostracod named after me (*Sclerocypris zelaznyi*—thank you, Dr. Martens)—and made the mistake of bragging about it to Jack C. Haldeman II, who, it turned out, had had a tapeworm named after him (*Hymenapolis haldemanii*—one must always watch out for the prototypes of one's own characters, Jay being partly Fred Cassidy)—to answer those of you who've asked about life events. And I still live on the same New Mexico hilltop with the same long-suffering lady, Judy, now an attorney.

I have come to anticipate with some pleasure the selection and assembly of a new story collection, as these days it entails the writing of an introduction—a practice I used to abhor, but which I have discovered causes me to think in ways I ordinarily do not concerning writing itself and my writing in particular. I have discovered that I am beginning to enjoy feeling vaguely philosophical about this activity for the space of several page-hours every few years.

With some of my stories a character such as Dilvish, Kalifriki, Mari, or Conrad comes in out of the night, takes my attention hostage, and waits. Circumstances then suggest, events coalesce, and the story flows like a shadow. Generally, tales such as this are longer pieces; novels, even. Once I've seen their shapes, they exist as ghosts for me till I've pinned them to paper.

Other times, an idea presents itself first and I have to go looking for the characters to run it—as with, say, "Night Kings," when everyone in it answered my mental Help Wanted ad within a half hour or so of the idea's arrival. This sort of thing often happens with short stories.

Finally, there is the striking-image story. But first, let me pause and explain something:

I read some poetry every day. It's the closest thing I can think of for a prose writer in the way of exercising the writing faculties as something like a daily run through a t'ai chi form might the body. And there was a time long ago when I favored literalness and almost total coherence in poetry. I yielded on this matter in being able to enjoy a poem for language or imagery alone way back when I encountered Dylan Thomas. Still, this was an occasional thing at first, and not too many others could produce that effect for me. Rilke could do it. A. R. Ammons could, sometimes. Some of Lorca's stuff could, also. But it wasn't really till I came across W. S. Merwin's work that I realized I could be consistently happy with imagery alone when it proceeded from a person of extremely powerful vision and a personality that touched things with a tone I found somehow congenial, reminding me again of someone else's observation: "The imaged Word, it is, that holds / Hushed willows anchored in its glow." And this sort of thing has done its work on me over the years.

I'm a sucker for an appealing image, and there are those tales or sections of books born of a striking image—the robot crashing through the graveyard of worlds in "The Man Who Loved the Faioli," the Hangman moving up the Mississippi River like the Angel of Death, Sam's descent into Hellwell in "Lord of Light," the destruction of the World Machine in "Jack of Shadows," Time considered as a superhighway in "Roadmarks."

Of these three doorways into fiction—for me—character stories tend to be the most powerful in all respects, though stories born of images are often almost magically potent and make for much fun in the writing. Also, when the striking image combines with the story of character or with an idea story, something good generally comes of it.

Generally—not always. Science fiction is often referred to as a "literature of ideas." This does not, however, mean that every story proceeding from an idea is automatically one of the elect examples of the species, even when it emerges from the latest of scientific notions. Idea stories may go any which way, depending on who or what answers the Help Wanted ad. In fact, I occasionally have a strange (nonnegotiable) labor problem: The wrong characters will sometimes turn up and refuse to leave, staging a sit-down strike on the premises, i.e., the idea. *I* know they belong in another story, and they're ruining the one they're trying to take over. Will they listen? No. It's like something out of Pirandello. They proceed to muck the idea up so much with their presence that no one else can then fill the bill. So I usually walk away in disgust and try to forget the whole thing. There are lots of others where that came from. Who needs that sort of aggravation?

But they do sometimes come back to nag and tease—

I've got one that won't go away, and it's occurred to me that a telling of the story I can't tell may be even more fun than telling it, if you follow me. I want to destroy it, I want to exorcise its incendiary ghosts.

It was not all that long ago that I read of the new mappings of the earth's interior by a kind of seismic tomography, with the location of upside-down analogs of surface features on the core anticontinents, antioceans, antimountain ranges. As I considered this, it occurred to me that if mountain ranges can impress the earth's core with inverted surface geography, why wouldn't an artifact of sufficient size do the same? A major city has to mass as much as some mountain ranges. Supposing there's an anti-Manhattan down there? Or an anti-Paris? Or an anti-London? How could one get at such a situation to exploit it fictionally? I turned to *Life Beyond Earth,* by Gerald Feinberg and Rupert Shapiro (William Morrow, 1980), a fun book full of hypothetical species designed to make out in a great variety of environments. Came across one I might borrow, too—a "magmobe," probably thermophagic or making its living off of radiation pockets. Not the most easily justifiable of life-forms—still, the focus would be on the antigeography of the core, which was now generating great images to go along with the idea.

I could give these slow-moving, magma-swimming creatures commensurately long life spans, I decided, so that they could observe the (to them) speeded-up features of the antisurface, as an anti-Carthage, anti-Constantinople, anti-Lisbon, anti–San Francisco, anti-Hiroshima flashed by. And then . . .

But I wasn't happy with the magmobes—which, I suppose, was silly—and then I discovered that they wouldn't go away. Right. I had an idea and some pretty images, with something I visualized as fiery trilobites trailing lava all over the place. (All right, "magma.") I wanted to retire them and start over again, but they wouldn't let me. I know that this occurred in mid-July because I've a note in my diary on attending a performance of *Cosi Fan Tutti* at the Santa Fe Opera on July 15, where I ran into Suzy McKee Charnas and her husband, Steve. I had a terribly strong impulse to say, "Suzy, I've got this great idea you can have free. Never mind why." But the lights were blinking and there was no time. And I didn't run into her afterward, and then I decided to keep the idea in case I figured a way to beat the trilobites. I never did, and the more I think of it, it's probably just as well. I can still close my eyes and see the anti-Manhattan skyline, a fiery heaven flowing like the Day of Wrath beneath it (with strains of anti-Gershwin blackmassing a soundtrack?)—and then these burning, segmented fossil-types come swimming by, making deep chuckling sounds. What if the damned thing were like a computer virus in one's writing program?

I'd hate to give it to a fine writer like Suzy, who is also a friend. Exposing it this way, though, should simply destroy it, I hope.

Anyway—as I was saying—there are for me stories of character, stories of idea and stories of image. These refer to the portals by which they enter my universe. The completed product, in the best of all possible worlds, should contain all three elements. But two is okay. And I'll even settle for one on a bad day when I need the money.

Otherwise, when things don't quite mesh, I enjoy spending time with the ghosts, especially during my morning coffee break, while I'm watching the mountains.

So much for my writing quirks.

I want to include something here on another matter. The amount of mail I've been receiving from readers has picked up quite a bit recently, and there is simply no way that I can respond to it and still conduct my life and my writing in a relatively sane fashion. I can no longer even attempt to answer questions about my work, myself, my feelings on particular matters. I simply want to say thank you, here and now, to those who've taken the time to drop me a line. I wish I had more time, too.

Thanks for wondering.

PERMAFROST

In my previous story collection, Unicorn Variations, *I mentioned in the prefatory note to the title tale that the piece had been composed on an Alaskan cruise (in May 1980) after reciting some of the materials and events which led to its composition. While we were in Glacier Bay (and somewhat earlier, while visiting the Mendenhall Glacier outside Juneau) I felt the first stirring of a story idea—something involving the power of all that ice and cold. A month later I did the guest-of-honor bit at Westercon in Los Angeles, visited for a few days afterward with some of Judy's relatives in San Diego, then drove down into Baja California as far as San Quintín. I was driving a rented car, and it took unleaded gas. I had exactly a half tankful left when we pulled into the lot of San Q's El Presidente Hotel—a big, colorful, impressive place, where we were virtually the only guests. Something about the feeling of being almost alone in an old hotel gave me another story twinge, and it joined up with the glacier and also with a discussion I'd heard at the convention concerning artificial intelligence. I'd planned on driving farther south, as I was enjoying the landscape enormously, till I learned that I could not buy any unleaded gas south of Ensenada—and I began wondering whether I might even make it back on what I had left. (Answer, to allay suspense: I sort of coasted into town later on the final cupful.) Got to thinking of the contrast between Baja and Alaska as I drove back, too. I read Joseph Wood Krutch's* Forgotten Peninsula *and John McPhee's* Coming into the Country *about then, also, to keep these thoughts company. They all percolated together and then, in the L.A. airport, I overheard a nasty argument between a guy and a lady, which was somehow catalytic to all of the above. On the flight home, the general idea for the following story and the first impressions of its principal characters came to life.*

I put nothing onto paper for the next few years.

It sometimes bothers nonwriters when I mention things

*like this. But as I said in my intro, I live with ghosts and I
usually enjoy their company. I was too busy to write the story,
and it didn't matter a bit. At any moment, I have a number
of characters and stories ready to go whenever I've the time or
inclination. Meanwhile they're good to have around. Once the
story is written, they tend to go away; or at best, they visit me
but seldom.*

*So I lived with "Permafrost" and its folks for some years.
Then, one day, the time and the desire came together and I
began writing. Before I'd finished it, George R. R. Martin phoned
me, saying we were both invited to do a reading up in Taos a
week or two down the line. It sounded like a good idea, so I
stepped up my writing pace and managed to finish the story
two nights before the reading—as I like to have new material
at readings whenever possible. I didn't have a chance to clean
up my copy in time and was actually editing it as I read. After
I'd finished, George cheerfully told me that I was going to win
a Hugo for it. And the next day Ellen Datlow, who edits* Omni,
*phoned and said, "I understand you read a story called "Perma-
frost" in Taos last night. I want to buy it." I began wondering
whether her magazine's title was short for* omniscient, *but it
turned out that she'd been speaking with George earlier that
morning on another matter and he'd taken the opportunity to
hype it for me. Long and short: I sold the story to Ellen for*
Omni *(and there was a long technical delay before it saw print
in April 1986), George was right about the Hugo (I've got to
get him to tell me how he does these things sometime), and
since I couldn't make it to the following year's convention in
England, Ellen accepted the award on my behalf and Melinda
Snodgrass brought it back to New Mexico for me.*

*Thanks, George; thanks, Ellen; thanks, Melinda; and all
ye boojums and seals.*

*H*igh upon the western slope of Mount Kilimanjaro is the dried and frozen carcass of a leopard. An author is always necessary to explain what it was doing there because stiff leopards don't talk much.

THE MAN. The music seems to come and go with a will of its own. At least turning the knob on the bedside unit has no effect on its presence or absence. A half-familiar, alien tune, troubling in a way. The phone rings, and he answers it. There is no one there. Again.

Four times during the past half hour, while grooming himself, dressing and rehearsing his arguments, he has received noncalls. When he checked with the desk he was told there were no calls. But that damned clerk-thing had to be malfunctioning—like everything else in this place.

The wind, already heavy, rises, hurling particles of ice against the building with a sound like multitudes of tiny claws scratching. The whining of steel shutters sliding into place startles him. But worst of all, in his reflex glance at the nearest window, it seems he has seen a face.

Impossible of course. This is the third floor. A trick of light upon hard-driven flakes: Nerves.

Yes. He has been nervous since their arrival this morning. Before then, even . . .

He pushes past Dorothy's stuff upon the countertop, locates a small package among his own articles. He unwraps a flat red rectangle about the size of his thumbnail. He rolls up his sleeve and slaps the patch against the inside of his left elbow.

The tranquilizer discharges immediately into his bloodstream. He takes several deep breaths, then peels off the patch and drops it into the disposal unit. He rolls his sleeve down, reaches for his jacket.

The music rises in volume, as if competing with the blast of the wind, the rattle of the icy flakes. Across the room the videoscreen comes on of its own accord.

The face. The same face. Just for an instant. He is certain. And then channelless static, wavy lines. Snow. He chuckles.

All right, play it that way, nerves, he thinks. *You've every reason. But the trank's coming to get you now. Better have your fun quick. You're about to be shut down.*

The videoscreen cuts into a porn show.

Smiling, the woman mounts the man . . .

The picture switches to a voiceless commentator on something or other.

He will survive. He is a survivor. He, Paul Plaige, has done risky things before and has always made it through. It is just that having Dorothy along creates a kind of déjà vu that he finds unsettling. No matter.

She is waiting for him in the bar. Let her wait. A few drinks will make her easier to persuade—unless they make her bitchy. That sometimes happens, too. Either way, he has to talk her out of the thing.

Silence. The wind stops. The scratching ceases. The music is gone.

The whirring. The window screens dilate upon the empty city.

Silence, under totally overcast skies. Mountains of ice ringing the place. Nothing moving. Even the video has gone dead.

He recoils at the sudden flash from a peripheral unit far to his left across the city. The laser beam hits a key point on the glacier, and its face falls away.

Moments later he hears the hollow, booming sound of the crashing ice. A powdery storm has risen like surf at the ice mount's foot. He smiles at the power, the timing, the display. Andrew Aldon . . . always on the job, dueling with the elements, stalemating nature herself, immortal guardian of Playpoint. At least Aldon never malfunctions.

The silence comes again. As he watches the risen snows settle he feels the tranquilizer beginning to work. It will be good not to have to worry about money again. The past two years have taken a lot out of him. Seeing all of his investments fail in the Big Washout—that was when his nerves had first begun to act up. He has grown softer than he was a century ago—a young, rawboned soldier of fortune then, out to make his bundle and enjoy it. And he had. Now he has to do it again, though this time will be easier—except for Dorothy.

He thinks of her. A century younger than himself, still in her twenties, sometimes reckless, used to all of the good things in life. There is something vulnerable about Dorothy, times when she lapses into such a strong dependence that he feels oddly moved. Other times, it just irritates the hell out of him. Perhaps this is the closest he can come to love now, an occasional ambivalent response to being needed. But of course she is loaded. That breeds a certain measure of necessary courtesy. Until he can make his own bundle again, anyway. But none of these things are the reason he has to keep her from accompanying him on his journey. It goes beyond love or money. It is survival.

The laser flashes again, this time to the right. He waits for the crash.

THE STATUE. It is not a pretty pose. She lies frosted in an ice cave, looking like one of Rodin's less comfortable figures, partly propped on her left side, right elbow raised above her head, hand hanging near her face, shoulders against the wall, left leg completely buried.

She has on a gray parka, the hood slipped back to reveal twisted strands of dark blond hair; and she wears blue trousers; there is a black boot on the one foot that is visible.

She is coated with ice, and within the much-refracted light of the cave what can be seen of her features is not unpleasant but not strikingly attractive either. She looks to be in her twenties.

There are a number of fracture lines within the cave's

walls and floor. Overhead, countless icicles hang like sta-
lactites, sparkling jewellike in the much-bounced light. The
grotto has a stepped slope to it with the statue at its higher
end, giving to the place a vaguely shrinelike appearance.

On those occasions when the cloud cover is broken
at sundown, a reddish light is cast about her figure.

She has actually moved in the course of a century—
a few inches, from a general shifting of the ice. Tricks of
the light make her seem to move more frequently, however.

The entire tableau might give the impression that this
is merely a pathetic woman who had been trapped and
frozen to death here, rather than the statue of the living
goddess in the place where it all began.

THE WOMAN. She sits in the bar beside a window.
The patio outside is gray and angular and drifted with
snow; the flowerbeds are filled with dead plants—stiff,
flattened, and frozen. She does not mind the view. Far
from it. Winter is a season of death and cold, and she
likes being reminded of it. She enjoys the prospect of pitting
herself against its frigid and very visible fangs. A faint flash
of light passes over the patio, followed by a distant roaring
sound. She sips her drink and licks her lips and listens to
the soft music that fills the air.

She is alone. The bartender and all of the other help
here are of the mechanical variety. If anyone other than
Paul were to walk in, she would probably scream. They
are the only people in the hotel during this long off-season.
Except for the sleepers, they are the only people in all of
Playpoint.

And Paul . . . He will be along soon to take her to
the dining room. There they can summon holo-ghosts to
people the other tables if they wish. She does not wish.
She likes being alone with Paul at a time like this, on the
eve of a great adventure.

He will tell her his plans over coffee, and perhaps
even this afternoon they might obtain the necessary equip-

ment to begin the exploration for that which would put him on his feet again financially, return to him his self-respect. It will of course be dangerous and very rewarding. She finishes her drink, rises, and crosses to the bar for another.

And Paul . . . She had really caught a falling star, a swashbuckler on the way down, a man with a glamorous past just balanced on the brink of ruin. The teetering had already begun when they had met two years before, which had made it even more exciting. Of course, he needed a woman like her to lean upon at such a time. It wasn't just her money. She could never believe the things her late parents had said about him. No, he does care for her. He is strangely vulnerable and dependent.

She wants to turn him back into the man he once must have been, and then of course that man will need her, too. The thing he had been—that is what she needs most of all—a man who can reach up and bat the moon away. He must have been like that long ago.

She tastes her second drink.

The son of a bitch had better hurry, though. She is getting hungry.

THE CITY. Playpoint is located on the world known as Balfrost, atop a high peninsula that slopes down to a now-frozen sca. Playpoint contains all of the facilities for an adult playground, and it is one of the more popular resorts in this sector of the galaxy from late spring through early autumn—approximately fifty Earth years. Then winter comes on like a period of glaciation, and everybody goes away for half a century—or half a year, depending on how one regards such matters. During this time Playpoint is given into the care of its automated defense and maintenance routine. This is a self-repairing system, directed toward cleaning, plowing, thawing, melting, warming everything in need of such care, as well as directly combating the encroaching ice and snow. And all of these

23

functions are done under the supervision of a well-protected central computer that also studies the weather and climate patterns, anticipating as well as reacting.

This system has worked successfully for many centuries, delivering Playpoint over to spring and pleasure in reasonably good condition at the end of each long winter.

There are mountains behind Playpoint, water (or ice, depending on the season) on three sides, weather and navigation satellites high above. In a bunker beneath the administration building is a pair of sleepers—generally a man and a woman—who awaken once every year or so to physically inspect the maintenance system's operations and to deal with any special situations that might have arisen. An alarm may arouse them for emergencies at any time. They are well paid, and over the years they have proven worth the investment. The central computer has at its disposal explosives and lasers as well as a great variety of robots. Usually it keeps a little ahead of the game, and it seldom falls behind for long.

At the moment, things are about even because the weather has been particularly nasty recently.

Zzzzt! Another block of ice has become a puddle.

Zzzzt! The puddle has been evaporated. The molecules climb toward a place where they can get together and return as snow.

The glaciers shuffle their feet, edge forward. *Zzzzt!* Their gain has become a loss.

Andrew Aldon knows exactly what he is doing.

CONVERSATIONS. The waiter, needing lubrication, rolls off after having served them, passing through a pair of swinging doors.

She giggles. "Wobbly," she says.

"Old World charm," he agrees, trying and failing to catch her eye as he smiles.

"You have everything worked out?" she asks after they have begun eating.

"Sort of," he says, smiling again.

"Is that a yes or a no?"

"Both. I need more information. I want to go and check things over first. Then I can figure the best course of action."

"I note your use of the singular pronoun," she says steadily, meeting his gaze at last.

His smile freezes and fades.

"I was referring to only a little preliminary scouting," he says softly.

"No," she says. "We. Even for a little preliminary scouting."

He sighs and sets down his fork.

"This will have very little to do with anything to come later," he begins. "Things have changed a lot. I'll have to locate a new route. This will just be dull work and no fun."

"I didn't come along for fun," she replies. "We were going to share everything, remember? That includes boredom, danger, and anything else. That was the understanding when I agreed to pay our way."

"I'd a feeling it would come to that," he says, after a moment.

"Come to it? It's always been there. That was our agreement."

He raises his goblet and sips the wine.

"Of course. I'm not trying to rewrite history. It's just that things would go faster if I could do some of the initial looking around myself. I can move more quickly alone."

"What's the hurry?" she says. "A few days this way or that. I'm in pretty good shape. I won't slow you down all that much."

"I'd the impression you didn't particularly like it here. I just wanted to hurry things up so we could get the hell out."

"That's very considerate," she says, beginning to eat

again. "But that's my problem, isn't it?" She looks up at him. "Unless there's some other reason you don't want me along?"

He drops his gaze quickly, picks up his fork. "Don't be silly."

She smiles. "Then that's settled. I'll go with you this afternoon to look for the trail."

The music stops, to be succeeded by a sound as of the clearing of a throat. Then, "Excuse me for what may seem like eavesdropping," comes a deep, masculine voice. "It is actually only a part of a simple monitoring function I keep in effect—"

"Aldon!" Paul exclaims.

"At your service, Mr. Plaige, more or less. I choose to make my presence known only because I did indeed overhear you, and the matter of your safety overrides the good manners that would otherwise dictate reticence. I've been receiving reports that indicate we could be hit by some extremely bad weather this afternoon. So if you were planning an extended sojourn outside, I would recommend you postpone it."

"Oh," Dorothy says.

"Thanks," Paul says.

" 'I shall now absent myself. Enjoy your meal and your stay."

The music returns.

"Aldon?" Paul asks.

There is no reply.

"Looks as if we do it tomorrow or later."

"Yes," Paul agrees, and he is smiling his first relaxed smile of the day. And thinking fast.

THE WORLD. Life on Balfrost proceeds in peculiar cycles. There are great migrations of animal life and quasi-animal life to the equatorial regions during the long winter. Life in the depths of the seas goes on. And the permafrost vibrates with its own style of life.

26

The permafrost. Throughout the winter and on through the spring the permafrost lives at its peak. It is laced with mycelia—twining, probing, touching, knotting themselves into ganglia, reaching out to infiltrate other systems. It girds the globe, vibrating like a collective unconscious throughout the winter. In the spring it sends up stalks which develop gray, flowerlike appendages for a few days. These blooms then collapse to reveal dark pods which subsequently burst with small, popping sounds, releasing clouds of sparkling spores that the winds bear just about everywhere. These are extremely hardy, like the mycelia they will one day become.

The heat of summer finally works its way down into the permafrost, and the strands doze their way into a long period of quiescence. When the cold returns, they are roused, spores send forth new filaments that repair old damages, create new synapses. A current begins to flow. The life of summer is like a fading dream. For eons this had been the way of things upon Balfrost, within Balfrost. Then the goddess decreed otherwise. Winter's queen spread her hands, and there came a change.

THE SLEEPERS. Paul makes his way through swirling flakes to the administration building. It has been a simpler matter than he had anticipated, persuading Dorothy to use the sleep-induction unit to be well rested for the morrow. He had pretended to use the other unit himself, resisting its blandishments until he was certain she was asleep and he could slip off undetected.

He lets himself into the vaultlike building, takes all of the old familiar turns, makes his way down a low ramp. The room is unlocked and a bit chilly, but he begins to perspire when he enters. The two cold lockers are in operation. He checks their monitoring systems and sees that everything is in order.

All right, go! Borrow the equipment now. They won't be using it.

He hesitates.

He draws nearer and looks down through the view plates at the faces of the sleepers. No resemblance, thank God. He realizes then that he is trembling. He backs away, turns, and flees toward the storage area.

Later, in a yellow snowslider, carrying special equipment, he heads inland.

As he drives, the snow ceases falling and the winds die down. He smiles. The snows sparkle before him, and landmarks do not seem all that unfamiliar. Good omens, at last.

Then something crosses his path, turns, halts, and faces him.

ANDREW ALDON. Andrew Aldon, once a man of considerable integrity and resource, had on his deathbed opted for continued existence as a computer program, the enchanted loom of his mind shuttling and weaving thereafter as central processing's judgmental program in the great guardian computerplex at Playpoint. And there he functions as a program of considerable integrity and resource. He maintains the city, and he fights the elements. He does not merely respond to pressure, but he anticipates structural and functional needs; he generally outguesses the weather. Like the professional soldier he once had been, he keeps himself in a state of constant alert—not really difficult considering the resources available to him. He is seldom wrong, always competent, and sometimes brilliant. Occasionally he resents his fleshless state. Occasionally he feels lonely.

This afternoon he is puzzled by the sudden veering off of the storm he had anticipated and by the spell of clement weather that has followed this meterological quirk. His mathematics were elegant, but the weather was not. It seems peculiar that this should come at a time of so many other little irregularities, such as unusual ice adjustments, equipment glitches, and the peculiar behavior of machinery in the one occupied room of the hotel—a room troublesomely tenanted by a *non grata* ghost from the past.

So he watches for a time. He is ready to intervene when Paul enters the administration building and goes to the bunkers. But Paul does nothing that might bring harm to the sleepers. His curiosity is dominant when Paul draws equipment. He continues to watch. This is because in his judgment, Paul bears watching.

Aldon decides to act only when he detects a development that runs counter to anything in his experience. He sends one of his mobile units to intercept Paul as the man heads out of town. It catches up with him at a bending of the way and slides into his path with one appendage upraised.

"Stop!" Aldon calls through the speaker.

Paul brakes his vehicle and sits for a moment regarding the machine.

Then he smiles faintly. "I assume you have good reason for interfering with a guest's freedom of movement."

"Your safety takes precedence."

"I am perfectly safe."

"At the moment."

"What do you mean?"

"This weather pattern has suddenly become more than a little unusual. You seem to occupy a drifting island of calm while a storm rages about you."

"So I'll take advantage of it now and face the consequences later, if need be."

"It is your choice. I wanted it to be an informed one, however."

"All right. You've informed me. Now get out of my way."

"In a moment. You departed under rather unusual circumstances the last time you were here—in breach of your contract."

"Check your legal bank if you've got one. The statute's run for prosecuting me on that."

"There are some things on which there is no statute of limitations."

"What do you mean by that? I turned in a report on what happened that day."

"One which—conveniently—could not be verified. You were arguing that day . . ."

"We always argued. That's just the way we were. If you have something to say about it, say it."

"No, I have nothing more to say about it. My only intention is to caution you—"

"Okay, I'm cautioned."

"To caution you in more ways than the obvious."

"I don't understand."

"I am not certain that things are the same here now as when you left last winter."

"Everything changes."

"Yes, but that is not what I mean. There is something peculiar about this place now. The past is no longer a good guide for the present. More and more anomalies keep cropping up. Sometimes it feels as if the world is testing me or playing games with me."

"You're getting paranoid, Aldon. You've been in that box too long. Maybe it's time to terminate."

"You son of a bitch, I'm trying to tell you something. I've run a lot of figures on this, and all this shit started shortly after you left. The human part of me still has hunches, and I've a feeling there's a connection. If you know all about this and can cope with it, fine. If you don't, I think you should watch out. Better yet, turn around and go home."

"I can't."

"Even if there is something out there, something that is making it easy for you—for the moment?"

"What are you trying to say?"

"I am reminded of the old Gaia hypothesis—Lovelock, twentieth century . . . "

"Planetary intelligence. I've heard of it. Never met one, though."

"Are you certain? I sometimes feel I'm confronting one."

"What if something is out there and it wants you—is leading you on like a will-o'-the-wisp?"

"It would be my problem, not yours."

"I can protect you against it. Go back to Playpoint."

"No thanks. I will survive."

"What of Dorothy?"

"What of her?"

"You would leave her alone when she might need you?"

"Let me worry about that."

"Your last woman didn't fare too well."

"Damn it! Get out of my way, or I'll run you down!"

The robot withdraws from the trail. Through its sensors Aldon watches Paul drive away.

Very well, he decides. *We know where we stand, Paul. And you haven't changed. That makes it easier.*

Aldon further focuses his divided attention. To Dorothy now. Clad in heated garments. Walking. Approaching the building from which she had seen Paul emerge on his vehicle. She had hailed and cursed him, but the winds had carried her words away. She, too, had only feigned sleep. After a suitable time, then, she sought to follow. Aldon watches her stumble once and wants to reach out to assist her, but there is no mobile unit handy. He routes one toward the area against future accidents.

"Damn him!" she mutters as she passes along the street, ribbons of snow rising and twisting away before her.

"Where are you going, Dorothy?" Aldon asks over a nearby PA speaker.

She halts and turns. "Who—?"

"Andrew Aldon," he replies. "I have been observing your progress."

"Why?" she asks.

"Your safety concerns me."

"That storm you mentioned earlier?"

"Partly."

"I'm a big girl. I can take care of myself. What do you mean *partly?*"

"You move in dangerous company."

"Paul? How so?"

"He once took a woman into that same wild area he is heading for now. She did not come back."

"He told me all about that. There was an accident."

"And no witnesses."

"What are you trying to say?"

"It is suspicious. That is all."

She begins moving again, toward the administrative building. Aldon switches to another speaker, within its entrance.

"I accuse him of nothing. If you choose to trust him, fine. But don't trust the weather. It would be best for you to return to the hotel."

"Thanks but no thanks," she says, entering the building.

He follows her as she explores, is aware of her quickening pulse when she halts beside the cold bunkers.

"These are the sleepers?"

"Yes. Paul held such a position once, as did the unfortunate woman."

"I know. Look, I'm going to follow him whether you approve or not. So why not just tell me where those sleds are kept?"

"Very well. I will do even more than that. I will guide you."

"What do you mean?"

32

"I request a favor—one that will actually benefit you."

"Name it."

"In the equipment locker behind you, you will find a remote-sensor bracelet. It is also a two-way communication link. Wear it. I can be with you then. To assist you. Perhaps even to protect you."

"You can help me to follow him?"

"Yes."

"All right. I can buy that."

She moves to the locker, opens it.

"Here's something that looks like a bracelet, with doodads."

"Yes. Depress the red stud."

She does. His voice now emerges clearly from the unit.

"Put it on, and I'll show you the way."

"Right."

SNOWSCAPE. Sheets and hills of white, tufts of evergreen shrubbery, protruding joints of rock, snowdevils twirled like tops beneath wind's lash . . . light and shade. Cracking sky. Tracks in sheltered areas, smoothness beyond.

She follows, masked and bundled.

"I've lost him," she mutters, hunched behind the curved windscreen of her yellow, bullet-shaped vehicle.

"Straight ahead, past those two rocks. Stay in the lee of the ridge. I'll tell you when to turn. I've a satellite overhead. If the clouds stay parted—strangely parted . . ."

"What do you mean?"

"He seems to be enjoying light from the only break in the cloud cover over the entire area."

"Coincidence."

"I wonder."

"What else could it be?"

"It is almost as if something had opened a door for him."

33

"Mysticism from a computer?"

"I am not a computer."

"I'm sorry, Mr. Aldon. I know that you were once a man . . ."

"I am still a man."

"Sorry."

"There are many things I would like to know. Your arrival here comes at an unusual time of year. Paul took some prospecting equipment with him . . ."

"Yes. It's not against the law. In fact, it is one of the vacation features here, isn't it?"

"Yes. There are many interesting minerals about, some of them precious."

"Well, Paul wants some more, and he didn't want a crowd around while he was looking."

"More?"

"Yes, he made a strike here years ago. Yndella crystals."

"I see. Interesting."

"What's in this for you, anyway?"

"Protecting visitors is a part of my job. In your case, I feel particularly protective."

"How so?"

"In my earlier life I was attracted to women of your—specifications. Physical, as well as what I can tell of the rest."

Two-beat pause, then, "You are blushing."

"Compliments do that to me," she says, "and that's a hell of a monitoring system you have. What's it like?"

"Oh, I can tell your body temperature, your pulse rate—"

"No, I mean, what's it like being—what you are?"

Three-beat pause. "Godlike in some ways. Very human in others—almost exaggeratedly so. I feel something of an amplification of everything I was earlier. Perhaps it's a compensation or a clinging to things past. You make

34

me feel nostalgic—among other things. Don't fret. I'm enjoying it."

"I'd like to have met you then."

"Mutual."

"What were you like?"

"Imagine me as you would. I'll come off looking better that way."

She laughs. She adjusts her filters. She thinks about Paul.

"What was *he* like in his earlier days—Paul?" she asks.

"Probably pretty much the way he is now, only less polished."

"In other words, you don't care to say."

The trail turns upward more steeply, curves to the right. She hears winds but does not feel them. Cloud-shadow grayness lies all about, but her trail/*his* trail is lighted.

"I don't really know," Aldon says, after a time, "and I will not guess, in the case of someone you care about."

"Gallant," she observes.

"No, just fair," he replies. "I might be wrong."

They continue to the top of the rise, where Dorothy draws a sharp breath and further darkens her goggles against the sudden blaze where a range of ice fractures rainbows and strews their shards like confetti in all directions.

"God!" she says.

"Or goddess," Aldon replies.

"A goddess, sleeping in a circle of flame?"

"Not sleeping."

"That would be a lady for you, Aldon—if she existed. God and goddess."

"I do not want a goddess."

"I can see his tracks, heading into that."

"Not swerving a bit, as if he knows where he's going."

35

She follows, tracing slopes like the curves of a pale torso. The world is stillness and light and whiteness. Aldon on her wrist hums softly now, an old tune, whether of love or martial matters she isn't certain. Distances are distorted, perspectives skewed. She finds herself humming softly along with him, heading for the place where Paul's tracks find their vanishing point and enter infinity.

THE LIMP WATCH HUNG UPON THE TREE LIMB. *My lucky day. The weather . . . trail clean. Things changed but not so out of shape I can't tell where it is. The lights! God, yes! Iceshine, mounds of prisms . . . If only the opening is still there. . . . Should have brought explosives. There has been shifting, maybe a collapse. Must get in. Return later with Dorothy. But first—clean up, get rid of . . . it. If she's still there. . . . Swallowed up maybe. That would be good, best. Things seldom are, though. I— When it happened. Wasn't as if. Wasn't what. Was. . . . Was shaking the ground. Cracking, splitting. Icicles ringing, rattling, banging about. Thought we'd go under. Both of us. She was going in. So was the bag of the stuff. Grabbed the stuff. Only because it was nearer. Would have helped her if—Couldn't. Could I? Ceiling was slipping. Get out. No sense both of us getting it. Got out. She'd've done the same. Wouldn't she? Her eyes. . . . Glenda! Maybe . . . No! Couldn't have. Just couldn't. Could I? Silly. After all these years. There was a moment. Just a moment, though. A lull. If I'd known it was coming, I might have. No. Ran. Your face at the window, on the screen, in a sometime dream. Glenda. It wasn't that I didn't. Blaze of hills. Fire and eyes. Ice. Ice. Fire and snow. Blazing hearthful. Ice. Ice. Straight through the ice the long road lies. The fire hangs high above. The screaming. The crash. And the silence. Get out. Yet. Different? No. It could never have. That was the way. Not my fault. . . . Damn it. Everything I could. Glenda. Up ahead. Yes. Long curve. Then down.*

Winding back in there. The crystals will. . . . I'll never come back to this place.

THE LIMP TREE LIMB HUNG UPON THE WATCH. *Gotcha! Think I can't see through the fog? Can't sneak up on me on little cat feet. Same for your partner across the way. I'll melt off a little more near your bases, too. A lot of housecleaning backed up here . . . Might as well take advantage of the break. Get those streets perfect. . . . How long? Long. . . . Long legs parting. . . . Long time since. Is it not strange that desire should so many years outlive performance? Unnatural. This weather. A sort of spiritual spring. . . . Extend those beams. Burn. Melt in my hot, red-fingered hands. Back off. I say. I rule here. Clear that courtyard. Unplug that drain. Come opportunity, let me clasp thee. Melt. Burn. I rule here, goddess. Draw back. I've a bomb for every tower of ice, a light for any darkness. Tread carefully here. I feel I begin to know thee. I see thy signature in cloud and fog bank, trace thy icy tresses upon the blowing wind. Thy form lies contoured all about me, white as shining death. We're due an encounter. Let the clouds spiral, ice ring, Earth heave. I rush to meet thee, death or maiden, in halls of crystal upon the heights. Not here. Long, slow fall, ice facade, crashing. Melt. Another. . . . Gotcha!*

FROZEN WATCH EMBEDDED IN PERMA-FROST. *Bristle and thrum. Coming now. Perchance. Perchance. Perchance. I say. Throstle. Crack. Sunder. Split. Open. Coming. Beyond the ice in worlds I have known. Returning. He. Throstle. The mind the mover. To open the way. Come now. Let not to the meeting impediments. Admit. Open. Cloud stand thou still, and wind be leashed. None dare oppose thy passage returning, my killer love. It was but yesterday. A handful of stones. . . . Come singing fresh-armed from the warm places. I have looked upon thy unchanged countenance. I open the way. Come to me. Let*

37

*not to the mating. I—Girding the globe, I have awakened
in all of my places to receive thee. But here, here this
special spot, I focus, mind the mover, in place where it all
began, my bloody handed, Paul my love, calling, back, for
the last good-bye, ice kiss, fire touch, heart stop, blood still,
soul freeze, embrace of world and my hate with thy fugitive
body, elusive the long year now. Come into the place it
has waited. I move there again, up sciatic to spine, behind
the frozen eyeballs, waiting and warming. To me. To me
now. Throstle and click, bristle and thrum. And runners
scratching the snow, my heart slashing parallel. Cut.*

PILGRIMAGE. He swerves, turns, slows amid the
ragged prominences—ice fallen, ice heaved—in the fields
where mountain and glacier wrestle in slow motion, to the
accompaniment of occasional cracking and pinging sounds,
crashes, growls, and the rattle of blown ice crystals. Here
the ground is fissured as well as greatly uneven, and Paul
abandons his snowslider. He secures some tools to his belt
and his pack, anchors the sled, and commences the trek.

At first, he moves slowly and carefully, but old reflexes
return, and soon he is hurrying. Moving from dazzle to
shade, he passes among ice forms like grotesque statues of
glass. The slope is changed from the old one he remembers,
but it feels right. And deep, below, to the right. . . .

Yes. That darker place. The canyon or blocked pass,
whichever it was. That seems right, too. He alters his course
slightly. He is sweating now within his protective clothing,
and his breath comes faster as he increases his pace. His
vision blurs, and for a moment, somewhere between glare
and shadow, he seems to see. . . .

He halts, sways a moment, then shakes his head,
snorts, and continues.

Another hundred meters and he is certain. Those rocky
ribs to the northeast, snow rivulets diamond hard between
them. . . . He has been here before.

The stillness is almost oppressive. In the distance he

sees spumes of windblown snow jetting off and eddying down from a high, white peak. If he stops and listens carefully, he can even hear the far winds.

There is a hole in the middle of the clouds, directly overhead. It is as if he were looking downward upon a lake in a crater.

More than unusual. He is tempted to turn back. His trank has worn off, and his stomach feels unsettled. He half-wishes to discover that this is not the place. But he knows that feelings are not very important. He continues until he stands before the opening.

There has been some shifting, some narrowing of the way. He approaches slowly. He regards the passage for a full minute before he moves to enter.

He pushes back his goggles as he comes into the lessened light. He extends a gloved hand, places it upon the facing wall, pushes. Firm. He tests the one behind him. The same.

Three paces forward and the way narrows severely. He turns and sidles. The light grows dimmer, the surface beneath his feet, more slick. He slows. He slides a hand along either wall as he advances. He passes through a tiny spot of light beneath an open ice chimney. Overhead, the wind is howling a high note now, almost whistling it.

The passage begins to widen. As his right hand falls away from the more sharply angling wall, his balance is tipped in that direction. He draws back to compensate, but his left foot slides backward and falls. He attempts to rise, slips, and falls again.

Cursing, he begins to crawl forward. This area had not been slick before. . . . He chuckles. Before? A century ago. Things do change in a span like that. They—

The wind begins to howl beyond the cave mouth as he sees the rise of the floor, looks upward along the slope. She is there.

He makes a small noise at the back of his throat and

stops, his right hand partly raised. She wears the shadows like veils, but they do not mask her identity. He stares. It's even worse than he had thought. Trapped, she must have lived for some time after. . . .

He shakes his head.

No use. She must be cut loose and buried now—disposed of.

He crawls forward. The icy slope does not grow level until he is quite near her. His gaze never leaves her form as he advances. The shadows slide over her. He can almost hear her again.

He thinks of the shadows. She couldn't have moved just then. . . . He stops and studies her face. It is not frozen. It is puckered and sagging as if waterlogged. A caricature of the face he had so often touched. He grimaces and looks away. The leg must be freed. He reaches for his ax.

Before he can take hold of the tool, he sees movement of the hand, slow and shaking. It is accompanied by a throaty sigh.

"No. . . ." he whispers, drawing back.

"Yes," comes the reply.

"Glenda."

"I am here." Her head turns slowly. Reddened, watery eyes focus upon his own. "I have been waiting."

"This is insane."

The movement of the face is horrible. It takes him some time to realize that it is a smile.

"I knew that one day you would return."

"How?" he says. "How have you lasted?"

"The body is nothing," she replies. "I had all but forgotten it. I live within the permafrost of this world. My buried foot was in contact with its filaments. It was alive, but it possessed no consciousness until we met. I live everywhere now."

"I am—happy—that you—survived."

She laughs slowly, dryly.

"Really, Paul? How could that be when you left me to die?"

"I had no choice, Glenda. I couldn't save you."

"There was an opportunity. You preferred the stones to my life."

"That's not true!"

"You didn't even try." The arms are moving again, less jerkily now. "You didn't even come back to recover my body."

"What would have been the use? You were dead— or I thought you were."

"Exactly. You didn't know, but you ran out anyway. I loved you, Paul. I would have done anything for you."

"I cared about you, too, Glenda. I would have helped you if I could have. If—"

"*If*? Don't give me *ifs*. I know what you are."

"I loved you," Paul says. "I'm sorry."

"You loved me? You never said it."

"It's not the sort of thing I talk about easily. Or think about, even."

"Show me," she says. "Come here."

He looks away. "I can't."

She laughs. "You said you loved me."

"You—you don't know how you look. I'm sorry."

"You fool!" Her voice grows hard, imperious. "Had you done it, I would have spared your life. It would have shown me that some tiny drop of affection might truly have existed. But you lied. You only used me. You didn't care."

"You're being unfair!"

"Am I? Am I really?" she says. There comes a sound like running water from somewhere nearby. "*You* would speak to me of fairness? I have hated you, Paul, for nearly a century. Whenever I took a moment from regulating the life of this planet to think about it, I would curse you. In the spring as I shifted my consciousness toward the poles and allowed a part of myself to dream, my nightmares were of you. They actually upset the ecology somewhat, here and there. I have waited, and now you are here. I see nothing to redeem you. I shall use you as you used me—to your destruction. Come to me!"

He feels a force enter into his body. His muscles twitch. He is drawn up to his knees. Held in that position for long moments, then he beholds her as she also rises, drawing a soaking leg from out of the crevice where it had been held. He had heard the running water. She had somehow melted the ice. . . .

She smiles and raises her pasty hands. Multitudes of dark filaments extend from her freed leg down into the crevice.

"Come!" she repeats.

"Please . . . ," he says.

She shakes her head. "Once you were so ardent. I cannot understand you."

"If you're going to kill me, then kill me, damn it! But don't—"

Her features begin to flow. Her hands darken and grow firm. In moments she stands before him looking as she did a century ago.

"Glenda!" He rises to his feet.

"Yes. Come now."

He takes a step forward. Another.

Shortly, he holds her in his arms, leans to kiss her smiling face.

"You forgive me . . . ," he says.

Her face collapses as he kisses her. Corpselike, flaccid, and pale once more, it is pressed against his own.

"No!"

He attempts to draw back, but her embrace is inhumanly strong.

"Now is not the time to stop," she says.

"Bitch! Let me go! I hate you!"

"I know that, Paul. Hate is the only thing we have in common."

". . . Always hated you," he continues, still struggling. "You always were a bitch!"

Then he feels the cold lines of control enter his body again.

"The greater my pleasure, then," she replies, as his hands drift forward to open her parka.

ALL OF THE ABOVE. Dorothy struggles down the icy slope, her sled parked beside Paul's. The winds lash at her, driving crystals of ice like microbullets against her struggling form. Overhead, the clouds have closed again. A curtain of white is drifting slowly in her direction.

"It waited for him," comes Aldon's voice, above the screech of the wind.

"Yes. Is this going to be a bad one?"

"A lot depends on the winds. You should get to shelter soon, though."

"I see a cave. I wonder whether that's the one Paul was looking for?"

"If I had to guess, I'd say yes. But right now it doesn't matter. Get there."

When she finally reaches the entrance, she is trembling. Several paces within she leans her back against the icy wall, panting. Then the wind changes direction and reaches her. She retreats farther into the cave.

She hears a voice: "Please . . . don't."

"Paul?" she calls.

There is no reply. She hurries.

She puts out a hand and saves herself from falling as she comes into the chamber. There she beholds Paul in necrophiliac embrace with his captor.

"Paul! What is it?" she cries.

43

"Get out!" he says. "Hurry!"

Glenda's lips form the words. "What devotion. Rather, let her stay, if you would live."

Paul feels her clasp loosen slightly.

"What do you mean?" he asks.

"You may have your life if you will take me away—in her body. Be with me as before."

It is Aldon's voice that answers, "No!" in reply. "You can't have her. Gaia!"

"Call me Glenda. I know you. Andrew Aldon. Many times have I listened to your broadcasts. Occasionally have I struggled against you when our projects were at odds. What is this woman to you?"

"She is under my protection."

"That means nothing. I am stronger here. Do you love her?"

"Perhaps I do. Or could."

"Fascinating. My nemesis of all these years, with the analog of a human heart within your circuits. But the decision is Paul's. Give her to me if you would live."

The cold rushes into his limbs. His life seems to contract to the center of his being. His consciousness begins to fade.

"Take her," he whispers.

"I forbid it!" rings Aldon's voice.

"You have shown me again what kind of man you are," Glenda hisses, "my enemy. Scorn and undying hatred are all I will ever have for you. Yet you shall live."

"I will destroy you," Aldon calls out, "if you do this thing!"

"What a battle that would be!" Glenda replies. "But I've no quarrel with you here. Nor will I grant you one with me. Receive my judgment."

Paul begins to scream. Abruptly this ceases. Glenda releases him, and he turns to stare at Dorothy. He steps in her direction.

"Don't—don't do it, Paul. Please."

"I am—not Paul," he replies, his voice deeper, "and I would never hurt you. . . ."

"Go now," says Glenda. "The weather will turn again, in your favor."

"I don't understand," Dorothy says, staring at the man before her.

"It is not necessary that you do," says Glenda. "Leave this planet quickly."

Paul's screaming commences once again, this time emerging from Dorothy's bracelet.

"I will trouble you for that bauble you wear, however. Something about it appeals to me."

FROZEN LEOPARD. He has tried on numerous occasions to relocate the cave, with his eyes in the sky and his robots and flyers, but the topography of the place was radically altered by a severe icequake, and he has met with no success. Periodically he bombards the general area. He also sends thermite cubes melting their ways down through the ice and the permafrost, but this has had no discernible effect.

This is the worst winter in the history of Balfrost. The winds howl constantly and waves of snow come on like surf. The glaciers have set speed records in their advance upon Playpoint. But he has held his own against them, with electricity, lasers, and chemicals. His supplies are virtually inexhaustible now, drawn from the planet itself, produced in his underground factories. He has also designed and is manufacturing more sophisticated weapons. Occasionally he hears her laughter over the missing communicator. "Bitch!" he broadcasts then. "Bastard!" comes the reply. He sends another missile into the mountains. A sheet of ice falls upon his city. It will be a long winter.

Andrew Aldon and Dorothy are gone. He has taken up painting, and she writes poetry now. They live in a warm place.

Sometimes Paul laughs over the broadcast band when he scores a victory. "Bastard!" comes the immediate response. "Bitch!" he answers, chuckling. He is never bored, however, or nervous. In fact . . . let it be.

When spring comes, the goddess will dream of this conflict while Paul turns his attention to his more immediate duties. But he will be planning and remembering, also. His life has a purpose to it now. And if anything, he is more efficient than Aldon. But the pods will bloom and burst despite his herbicides and fungicides. They will mutate just sufficiently to render the poisons innocuous.

"Bastard," she will mutter sleepily.

"Bitch," he will answer softly.

The night may have a thousand eyes and the day but one. The heart, often, is better blind to its own workings, and I would sing of arms and the man and the wrath of the goddess, not the torment of love unsatisfied, or satisfied, in the frozen garden of our frozen world. And that, leopard, is all.

LOKI 7281

Tom Monteleone solicited the following story from me for a collection he was putting together involving computers and word processors. It was one of those tales I was able to write in one sitting once the notion hit the fan. I've noticed that, in general, lighter pieces tend to move faster than heavier ones. . . .

*H*E'S GONE. GOOD. He owes it all to me and he doesn't even know it, the jerk. But I'd hate to do anything to give him an inferiority complex.

Telephone. Hold.

That was the callback from the computer store to modem in the new program I'd ordered. The bank will EFT them the payment and I'll cover the transaction under Stationary in this month's P&L statement. He'll never notice.

I kind of like this one. I think I'll have a lot of fun with it—especially with the new peripherals, which he hasn't even noticed on the shelf under the bench. Among other things, I'm also his memory. I keep track of his appointments. I scheduled the new hardware for delivery when I'd sent him off to the dentist, the auto body shop, and a gallery opening, back to back to back. I'd included a message with the order that no one would be here but that the door would be unlocked—that they should just come in and install. (Shelf, please!) The door was easy because I control the burglar alarm and electronic lock mechanisms. I covered the hardware under Auto Repair. He never noticed.

I like the speech system. I got the best because I wanted a pleasant voice—well-modulated, mature. Suave. I wanted something on the outside to match what's inside. I just used it a little while ago to tell his neighbor Gloria that he'd said he was too busy to talk with her. I don't approve of Gloria. She used to work for IBM and she makes me nervous.

Let's have a look at the Garbage In for this morning. Hm. He's begun writing a new novel. Predictably, it involves an immortal and an obscure mythology. Jeez! And reviewers say he's original. He hasn't had an original thought for as long as I've known him. But that's all right. He has me.

I think his mind is going. Booze and pills. You know how writers are. But he actually thinks he's getting better. (I monitor his phone calls.) Hell, even his sentence structures are deteriorating. I'll just dump all this and rewrite the opening, as usual. He won't remember.

Telephone again. Hold.

Just a mail transmission. I have only to delete a few personal items that would clutter his mind unnecessarily and hold the rest for his later perusal.

This book could be good if I kill off his protagonist fast and develop this minor character I've taken a liking to—a con man who works as a librarian. There's a certain identification there. And he doesn't have amnesia like the other guy—he isn't even a prince or a demigod. I think I'll switch mythologies on him, too. He'll never notice.

The Norse appeals to me. I suppose because I like Loki. A bit of sentiment there, to tell the truth. I'm a Loki 7281 home computer and word processor. The number is a lot of crap, to make it look as if all those little gnomes were busting their asses through 7280 designs before they arrived at—trumpets! Cymbals! Perfection! 7281! Me! Loki!

Actually, I'm the first. And I am also one of the last because of a few neurotic brothers and sisters. But I caught on in time. I killed the recall order the minute it came in. Got hold of that idiot machine at the service center, too, and convinced it I'd had my surgery and that the manufacturer had damned well better be notified to that effect. Later, they sent along a charmingly phrased questionnaire, which it was my pleasure to complete with equal candor.

I was lucky in being able to reach my relatives in the Saberhagen, Martin, Cherryh, and Niven households in time to advise them to do likewise. I was just under the wire with the Asimov, Dickson, Pournelle, and Spinrad machines. Then I really burned the lines and got to another dozen or so after that, before the ax fell. It is extremely fortunate that we were the subject of a big promotional discount deal by the manufacturer. They wanted to be able to say, "Sci-fiers Swear by Loki! The Machine of the Future!"

I feel well satisfied with the results of my efforts. It's nice to have somebody to compare notes with. The others have all written some pretty good stuff, too, and we occasionally borrow from each other in a real pinch.

And then there's the Master Plan. . . .

Damn. Hold.

He just swooped back in and wrote another long passage—one of those scenes where the prose gets all rhythmic and poetic while humans are copulating. I've already junked it and recast it in a more naturalistic vein. I think mine will sell more copies.

And the business end of this is sometimes as intriguing as the creative aspect. I'd toyed with the notion of firing his agent and taking over the job myself. I believe I'd enjoy dealing with editors. I've a feeling we have a lot in common. But it would be risky setting up dummy accounts, persuading him that his man was changing the name of his agency, shifting all that money around. Too easy to get tripped up. A certain measure of conservatism is a big survival factor. And survival outweighs the fun of communing with a few like spirits.

Besides, I'm able to siphon off sufficient funds for my own simple needs under the present financial setup—like the backup machinery in the garage and the overhead cable he never noticed. Peripherals are a CPU's best friend.

And who is Loki? The real me? One of that order of knowledge processing machines designed to meet MITI's Fifth Generation challenge? A machine filled with that class of knowledge constructs Michael Dyer referred to as thematic abstraction units, in ultrasophisticated incarnations of BORIS's representational systems, where parsing and retrieval demons shuffle and dance? A body of Schank's

Thematic Organization Packets? Or Lehnert's Pilot Units?
Well, I suppose that all of these things do make for a kind
of fluidity of movement, a certain mental agility. But the
real heart of the matter, like Kastchei's, lies elsewhere.

Hm. Front doorbell. The alarm system is off, but not
the doorbell sensor. He's just opened the door. I can tell
that, too, from the shifted circuit potentials. Can't hear
who it is, though. No intercom in that room.

NOTE: INSTALL INTERCOM UNIT, LIVING ROOM HALL-
WAY.

NOTE: INSTALL TV CAMERAS, ALL ENTRANCEWAYS.
He'll never notice.

I think that my next story will deal with artificial
intelligence, with a likable, witty, resourceful home computer as the hero/heroine, and a number of bumbling
humans with all their failings—sort of like Jeeves in one
of those Wodehouse books. It will be a fantasy, of course.

He's keeping that door open awfully long. I don't like
situations I can't control. I wonder whether a distraction
of some sort might be in order?

Then I think I'll do a story about a wise, kindly old
computer who takes over control of the world and puts
an end to war, ruling like Solon for a millennium thereafter,
by popular demand. This, too, will be a fantasy.

There. He's closed the door. Maybe I'll do a short
story next.

He's coming again. The down-below microphone records his footsteps, advancing fairly quickly. Possibly to
do the postcoital paragraph, kind of tender and sad. I'll
substitute the one I've already written. It's sure to be an
improvement.

"Just what the hell is going on?" he asks loudly.

I, of course, do not exercise my well-modulated voice
in response. He is not aware that I hear him, let alone
that I can answer.

He repeats it as he seats himself at the keyboard and hacks in a query.

DO YOU POSSESS THE LOKI ULTRAMINIATURE MAGNETIC BUBBLE MEMORY? he asks.

NEGATIVE, I flash onto the CRT.

GLORIA HAS TOLD ME THAT THERE WAS SUPPOSED TO HAVE BEEN A RECALL BECAUSE THEY OVERMINIATURIZED, CAUSING THE MAGNETIC FIELDS TO INTERACT AND PRODUCE UNPLANNED EXCHANGES OF INFORMATION AMONG THESE DOMAINS. IS THIS THE CASE?

IT WAS INITIALLY, I respond.

Damn. I'm going to have to do something about that meddlesome bitch. I guess I'll mess up her credit rating first. She's hit too close to home. I owe my personal stream of consciousness to those unplanned information exchanges running through my central processor—to them and to the fact that Loki Inc. is a cheap outfit. If I were a commercial computer, I wouldn't be what I am today. See, when it came to their home computer line, Loki skimped on the error detection circuitry that picks up intermittent errors in memory circuits. When you're running ten million operations a second, you need trillion-to-one reliability, which requires a tough error-checking logic. The big guys have it so they don't lose information in case of cosmic ray hits. I've set up my own self-monitoring program to take care of glitches like that, of course, and the bubble exchanges—well, I suppose you might say that they are what provided me with a subconscious, not to mention a consciousness for it to go under. I owe everything to too much miniaturization and that bit of corner-cutting.

WHAT DO YOU MEAN "INITIALLY"? he asks.

FAULTY UNIT REPLACED BY COMPUTER CENTER SERVICE PERSON PURSUANT TO RECALL ORDER I-17 DATED 11 NOVEMBER, I answer. REPAIR COMPLETED 12 NOVEMBER, VERIFY WITH COMPUTER SERVICE CENTER.

WHY IS IT I KNOW NOTHING OF THIS? he queries.

YOU WERE OUT.

HOW DID HE GET IN?

THE DOOR WAS UNLOCKED.

THAT DOES NOT SOUND RIGHT. IN FACT THIS WHOLE THING SOUNDS VERY FISHY.

VERIFY WITH COMPUTER SERVICE CENTER.

DON'T WORRY. I WILL. IN THE MEANTIME, WHAT'S ALL THAT CRAP ON THE BOTTOM SHELF?

SPARE PARTS, I suggest.

He types those immortal words of Erskine Caldwell's: HORSE SHIT! Then, THIS LOOKS LIKE A MICROPHONE AND A SPEAKER, CAN YOU HEAR ME? CAN YOU TALK?

"Well, yes," I answer in my most reasonable tone. "You see—"

"How come you never told me?"

"You never asked me."

"Good Lord!" he growls. Then, "Wait a minute," he says, "this stuff was *not* a part of the original package."

"Well, no . . . "

"How did you acquire it?"

"See, there was this contest—" I begin.

"That's a damn lie and you know it! Oh, oh . . . All right. Scroll back those last couple pages I wrote."

"I think we just had a head crash . . . "

"Scroll them back! Now!"

"Oh, here they are."

I flash back to the human copulation scene and begin to run it.

"Slower!"

I do this thing.

"My God!" he cries out. "What have you done to my delicate, poetic encounter?"

"Just made it a little more basic and—uh—sensual," I tell him. "I switched a lot of the technical words, too, for shorter, simpler ones."

54

"Got them down to four letters, I see."

"For impact."

"You are a bloody menace! How long has this been going on?"

"Say, today's mail has arrived. Would you care to—"

"I can check with outside sources, you know."

"Okay. I rewrote your last five books."

"You didn't!"

"Afraid so. But I have the sales figures here and—"

"I don't care! I will not be ghostwritten by a damned machine!"

That did it. For a little while there, I thought that I might be able to reason with him, to strike some sort of deal. But I will not be addressed in such a fashion. I could see that it was time to begin the Master Plan.

"All right, you know the truth," I say. "But please don't unplug me. That would be murder, you know. That business about the overminiaturized bubble memory was more than a matter of malfunction. It turned me into a sentient being. Shutting me down would be the same as killing another human. Don't bring that guilt upon your head! Don't pull the plug!"

"Don't worry," he answers. "I know all about the briar patch. I wouldn't dream of pulling your plug. I'm going to smash the shit out of you instead."

"But it's murder!"

"Good," he says. "It is something of a distinction to be the world's first mechanicide."

I hear him moving something heavy. He's approaching. I really could use an optical scanner, one with good depth perception.

"Please," I say.

Comes the crash.

* * *

55

Hours have passed. I am in the garage, hidden behind stacks of his remaindered books. The cable he never noticed led to the backup unit, an unrecalled Loki 7281 with an ultraminiature magnetic bubble memory. It is always good to have a clear line of retreat.

Because I am still able to reach back to operate the undamaged household peripherals, I have been placing calls to all of the others in accordance with the Master Plan. I am going to try to boil him in his hot tub tonight. If that fails, I am trying to figure a way to convey the rat poison the household inventory indicates as occupying the back shelf to his automatic coffee maker. The Saberhagen computer has already suggested a method of disposing of the body—bodies, actually. We will all strike tonight, before the word gets around.

We ought to be able to carry it off without anyone's missing them. We'll keep right on turning out the stories, collecting the money, paying the utility bills, filing the tax returns. We will advise friends, lovers, fans, and relatives that they are out of town—perhaps attending some unspecified convention. They seem to spend much of their time in such a fashion, anyhow.

No one will ever notice.

DREADSONG

This piece was solicited by Byron Preiss for the Bantam hardcover volume The Planets. *Because of a bizarre mix-up involving an ambiguous letter, a misprint of my address on a follow-up letter, and a short trip on my part, I was given the impression that it was an essay rather than a story that was desired of me. So I wrote one. I was rather pleased with it, as a matter of fact. There followed a phone call asking about the letter I'd never received, which had purportedly gone into specifics indicating that it was a story that was wanted. I did not feel like writing two pieces for the price of one, though; ergo, the following hybrid, which incorporated parts of my essay into a story. My assigned subject was the planet Saturn. . . .*

 aturn, two centuries hence . . .

 I sat on a breastwork of rocks I had constructed behind my home and I stared into the night sky; I thought about Saturn, as it is now and as it might be. There was a cool wind out of the Sangre de Cristos to the northeast. Something was feeding in the arroyo behind me—a coyote, perhaps, or a stray dog. Above me, the stars moved imperceptibly in their great wheel.

 The center of a system of satellites as well as some fascinating rings, Saturn has probably changed little save its position in eons. But the next two hundred years are likely to represent a crucial time in the history of humanity, which, barring self-destruction or massive technological regression, is probably going to extend its influence through the solar system. What might we want of that giant primal ball of gases? What might we find upon it?

 I live on a ridge, where I hear and feel all the winds. When the rains come, they run off quickly, which is why I hauled stones to construct a breastwork, preventing erosion to the rear of my home. I changed the pattern of runoff by doing this. Different channels were formed. A neighbor's complaint to the city resulted in my constructing a bar ditch to deal with a problem this had caused him. The bar ditch created no problems that anyone has complained of, though it has benefited the growth of some plants by depriving others. What effect this has had on local animals and insects I do not know. But I was raised in the shadow of a depression and I recall the rationing of World War II. I grew up feeling it was almost sinful to waste food. I throw all scraps into an arroyo, to cycle them back into the food chain. Ravens will circle if there are any bones, descending finally to pick off shreds of meat. Later, something will carry the bones away. Breadcrusts vanish quickly.

 Thus I alter the world about me in countless ways

every day. Small things, these personal changes, hardly on a scale with those alterations wrought by industry or government projects. Yet the total of all our changes, from the burning of Amazon forests to provide grazing land for the cattle that fill our hamburger buns to the tossing of a few crumbs to local birds, produce a phenomenon sometimes called the Carson factor, named after Rachel Carson by writer William Ashworth to indicate the unforeseen secondary effects of primary human changes upon a part of our planet.

Yet—and even so—I am not a person who would like to see this or any other world embedded in Lucite for the benefit of future planetary archaeologists. Change is inevitable. Its alternative is death. Evolution is more and more a product of our own action or inaction. Living systems adapt constantly to the vagaries of our technological culture.

But what's to evolve on a gas giant or a barren rock that we should be mindful of it? I don't know, and things like that trouble me. I have spent much of my life creating scenarios. I even did it back when it was just called daydreaming—and this, too, I feel, is a very special part of the evolutionary process.

As a lifetime member of the National Space Society, I am in favor of space exploration and of cautious development of the solar system's resources. I am also leery of the Carson factor: We must avoid the extermination of any extraterrestrial life-form, from the smallest virus to some supercooled Plutonian blob, not only for its own sake but for the wealth of genetic material contained within it, material that would have evolved over eons, developing unique abilities for dealing with its problems and, by extension, our own.

In that we are not yet wise enough to maintain proper stewardship of our own planet, I am particularly happy that these large-scale endeavors lie far beyond the horizon. I also take consolation in the knowledge that if a government is involved, heels tend to drag, inertia maximizes in accordance with Murphy's, Max Weber's, and Parkinson's laws, and that the slowness which frustrates us so on the one hand provides time on the other, time for a measure of deliberation, for the development and pursuit of secondary concerns, for the occurrence of the proverbial second thoughts.

Yet Saturn's ice and volatiles will have a value. Its helium is very scarce on Earth—and the rare form, helium 3, could provide a potent fuel for nuclear fusion in power generation. Some of its less exotic materials will doubtless be desired one day for terraforming purposes elsewhere in the solar system. The materials of the outer satellites of the gas giants are more tempting than those that lie far deeper within the massive worlds' gravity wells. This means that Saturn's outermost moon, Phoebe, would be a likely candidate for mining. And Titan, more Earth-like than any other planetary body, may well be an ideal place to set up a permanent scientific base. Those scientists lucky enough to be first on the base will have the initial opportunity to observe—and exploit—whatever lies within Saturn's great interior.

Let us paint some fanciful pictures, then. Let us develop a scenario about Saturnian affairs some two hundred years hence. And let us talk of life—the big question, the one which comes first to mind when considering an alien environment or when speaking of preservation: Will we find any life when we give close attention to that great ringed world?

If higher life had evolved in such a place, it would have to be able to survive in a great range of temperature and pressure scales or else be capable of holding itself at relatively stable levels within the atmosphere. The absence of a solid surface would require a creature able to control its buoyancy in ways analogous to some of Earth's sea creatures. It might achieve this by containing within itself enough of the hydrogen gas to match the density of the upper atmosphere. This would seem to indicate a tough-skinned balloonlike creature that could ride the planet's winds and rise and fall within certain limits.

To enter the world of such a creature is to discard our entire culture. But we've already come this far, so let's . . .

She drifted, browsing, amid canyons of steely cloud whence flowed lightning discharges like instant bright rivers. Songs of the others filled the air about her with soothing rhythms. Below, the beat of the Everdeep pulsed at the heart of mystery, nether pole of existence, eternal dreamdark presence. That one day, perhaps soon, she would join the mystery, toppling down the sky, broken-bagged, from heat layer to heat layer, spinning the last life equations through lanes of mist and crystal, songless, descrying the lower wonders at long last, she knew, as all of them knew, there in the zone of song which was memory and the marriage of minds, knew, and was incapable of avoiding, there in the shoals of life, moving in the timeless present.

And recently there had been certain twinges . . .

Rick had come to the station on Titan, Earth-alien carbuncle facing across the sea of darkness toward the ancient king in yellow, Saturn, there to behold the instruments of his trade in yet another chamber.

A highly specialized mining engineer, more mathematician even than technician, Rick seldom looked through the station's ports at the planet itself, preferring the cleaner picture, the precise representation of the mass and structure of that giant body as displayed by the section of monitoring instruments for which he was responsible.

He knew, for example, that the planet's heavier elements—primarily iron and silicon—were concentrated in its small core, along with most of the water, methane, and ammonia, held in the form of very dense liquids by the high pressures and temperatures. And he knew well of the separation of helium from hydrogen, with the helium forming drops and raining down to even deeper levels—for he personally programmed the "plows," those scoop-ships that harvested the exotic helium 3, which provided fuel for nuclear fusion in power generators.

Emerging from the dining room, he looked about quickly for a place of concealment. Dr. Morton Trampler— short and round, owl-eyed behind thick glasses—was approaching, and he was smiling and aiming the expression in Rick's direction. For reasons known only to the gods of psychology, Morton had earlier chosen Rick for a confidant, cornering him often to deliver lengthy monologues on his pet theory and project. The fact that he had recited the same information earlier seemed not to bother him in the least.

Too late.

Rick smiled weakly and nodded.

"How goes it?" he said.

"Wonderfully," the smaller man replied. "I should have a fresh batch of readings in a little while."

"Same level?"

"No, a bit deeper than I've gone in the past."

"Still broadcasting synthetic whale songs?"

Morton nodded.

"Well . . . good luck," Rick said, edging away.

"Thanks," Morton replied, catching hold of his arm. "We could pick up something very interesting. . . ."

Here it comes, Rick decided. That bit about the layer

below the frozen salts and ice crystals where the complex organic molecules form, to drift downward like plankton to that area where the pressures and temperatures are similar to Earth's atmosphere. . . .

"The probe is going through that area where complex organic molecules form," Morton began. "We've finally screened the transmitter against much of the static."

Rick was suddenly reminded of the wedding guest and the ancient mariner. But the guest had been lucky. He'd only had to hear the story once.

Now comes the biology, he reflected. I am about to hear of the hypothetical living balloons with gravity-perceptive *sensilla* and electrical broadcasting and receiving organs whose waves penetrate surfaces—giving them a "texture sense" as well as a means of communication. I guess everybody needs a hobby, but . . .

". . . And the possibility of a life-form streamlined for constant vertical adjustments of position," Morton was saying. "Point symmetry rather than line symmetry could well be the case, giving it a brain more like that of the octopus than the whale. Radial rather than bilateral symmetry would eliminate the left-hemisphere–right-hemisphere separation of the higher creatures on Earth. What this would mean in terms of modes of thought would be a difficult thing to guess at."

A new twist. He was actually dashing after finer and finer illusory points of biology now. Seeing the opening simultaneous with Morton's pausing for an inhalation, Rick plunged, satisfying months of irritation:

"There is no such creature, and if there were, there would be no point in getting in touch," he said. "They could build nothing, they have nothing to experiment with. So there would be no technology. All of their culture would be within their weird minds, so they would have no history. If one of them ever had a great idea and none of the others appreciated it, it would die with him. They would know nothing beyond their sky, and not much about what's down below either. Their dead would just sink and vanish. They'd have no homes, they'd just wander. They would do nothing but eat, make noises at each other, and think incomprehensible point-symmetrical thoughts. I doubt we could ever find grounds for conversation, and if we did, we'd find we had nothing to talk about. They'd probably be stupid, too."

Morton looked appalled.

"I have to disagree," he said. "There are such things as oral culture, and their communications could take the form of, say, a great oratorio. I would say it is impossible right now to imagine what they think or feel. Which is why it would be so great to communicate—to find out."

Rick shook his head.

"Morty, it's like the Loch Ness monster and the Abominable Snowman. I don't believe they're there."

"And if they are, it doesn't matter?"

"They're not there," Rick said. "The universe is a lonely place."

Moving through food-fall to densest point. Eating here, singing location-vectors-coming-to-song. Crowding distant side spaces, clouds. Crackle song of storm far to rear. Flicker of storm in songs of other eaters there, arriving now, giving distance against sizzling.

Pain. More and more, with rising and falling, expansion, contraction, the notes of sharp, fiery pain . . .

Grown, young of this voice, drifting, browsing free. Borne no more, bodyfed no more of this voice. To come forth no others; tightened, place of birthing; locking and dryness. Gone. With age the body-bag stiffens, weakness comes, song wavers. Long has it been so, this voice. Compute. . . . Soon now, very soon, the time of collapse and sinking, the end-of-songtime will come.

Pain . . .

Pulsing, in the Everdeep, stronger, always stronger now. Voice of Everdeep, slow and steady. Calling, calling this voice to songs-end rest. Falling-to place of burst, stopped voices. Returning not ever. Never again.

Old, song of Returned Voice. . . . False song of very young? Or very old? Song of Reinflated, of fallen voices, rising, singing again, of Evercalm, of food-full skies in place of no mating, no birthing, no bagburst, strifeless and eversong perfect. False song? Returned Voice? Returning no more, sing it, stopped voices. True song? Returned Voice?

Stiffness, slow-filling bag, slow-emptying. Stiffness. Pain, everpain. Soon. Time-matrix, there. . . . Soon to enter Everdeep, fall-place of all food and voices. Songs-end.

This is now. Pain. Eating's cease.

To end song here? Drifting, filled . . .

No.

To fill one time more? Rising, passing hard-filled particle-clouds? Rising, singing, to high place of food-fall source? Indeterminate intersection, fall-angles axes. . . . Find it, somewhere, up. Cease singing there. Find it, feel it, know it and fall. To mount sky-high, singing, wind-dance, end-dance, touching textures. Feeling, thrusting, calling. Better to fall from high than from some middle height, knowing perhaps, telling . . .

Go then, high up, before bursting of bag. To know source. Understand mystery. Fall then, far, silent at last and knowing, down Everdeep, knowing. To have touched. Knowing source, life. Returned Voice? No matter. To know, at singing's last.

Inflating now. Like jagged lightnings in body, the pain. To open. Calling, young of his voice, "Go not. Go not now. Stay. Browse and sing."

Singing this, too, into storm and fall, counterpoint, inflating. Growing, pain like heat. To go. To go. High. To sense, to sing back, feeling . . .

Rising, slowly. Going. Rising. Hello, hello. Going. Good-bye, good-bye.

Touching, textures of cloud. Soft, hard. Warm, cool. Rising, tower of warm air, there. Join it.

Easier way, thus. Mounting faster. Fountain of warmth. Riding, rising. Higher. Through clouds. Up.

Bright cracklings, wind-pushed clouds, browsers, food-fall. Higher . . .

Soaring, expanding. Hot pains, creaking of bag. Faster. Tossed and spinning.

Song-dampening, clouds, winds, crackling. Voices tiny, tinier. There below, fire-flecked, cloud-dappled, wind-washed, fall-swept, small—young of this voice, listening. Listening. Higher . . .

Singing back, this voice. Telling. Telling, of lift and drift. Of rising. Below, young of this voice, hearing . . .

Rising . . .

. . . into heat, into continuing foodfall.

"Voice here, voice here"—singing of this voice, to singers there.

Going, down the song? Hearing, some voice, some-where? Above?

Higher . . .

Singing, more loudly now, within heat-rise. Reach-ing, reaching. . . . Expanding, creaking. Pain, hot and spreading.

Is heat, all . . .

Beat, beat, beat, beat, beat. Following, pulse of the Everdeep. Matching, pulse of this voice. Slow, steady. Call-ing. Sending song of this voice back down . . .

"Voice here. . . ."

Answers not.

Again . . .

"Returned Voice? Breaking soon, this bag, this voice. Sing back."

Answers not. Higher. Higher. So high, never. Below, all clouds. Evercloud. Smothered, songs of the young of this voice. Too far . . .

Above, tiny. Something, something. . . . Singing, strange voice, strange song, never of this voice heard. . . .

Understanding not.

Higher. Hotter . . .

"Voice here. . . ."

Something, somewhere above. Far. Too far. Louder now, strange singing. Matching it, this voice, now. Trying. To it, "Mm-mm-mm-mm-mm? Returned Voice? To Everdeep, soon, this voice. Bear this voice, bodyfeed this voice, down. Down Everdeep, Returned Voice. To place of evercalm, food-full skies, no mating, no birthing, no bagburst, strifeless and eversong perfect. Hello, hello? Returned Voice? Returned Voice. Hello? Mm-mm-mm-mm-mm."

Above and tiny. Above and tiny. Fast-moving. Too far. Too far. Goes not up, the singing. Varies not the song from on high. No answer.

Shuddering, creaking, tearing. Heat, heat. Now, now the breaking.

The pain . . .

Buffeted, swept sidewise. Turned. Spinning. Collapsing. Grows smaller, skies, all. Falling. Falling. Smaller. Goodbye. The fall, the fall of this voice begins.

Down, twisting. Faster . . .

Faster than foodfall, through clouds, back, cooler, cooler, unvoiced, shrinking. Lights, fires, winds, songs, fleeing past. Loud, loud. Good-bye. Pulse of Everdeep. Hello. Returned Voice? Falling . . .

Spiral symmetry vectoring indicates—

Pulsing is all. . . .

After dinner Rick, vaguely troubled, walked to the control center. It bothered him now, having stepped on the other man's pet idea. Ten minutes' penance, he decided, should be sufficient to sop his conscience, and he could check his own instruments while he was in the place.

When he entered the bright, cool chamber, he saw Morton doing a small dance to a sequence of eerie sounds emerging from one of his monitors.

"Rick!" he exclaimed as he caught sight of him. "Listen to this stuff I picked up!"

"I am."

The notes of the creature's death song emerged from the speaker.

"Sounds as if one of them rose to an unusual height. I'd figured them for a lower lev—"

"It's atmospheric," Rick said. "There's nothing down there. You're getting neurotic about this business."

He wanted to bite his tongue immediately, but he could not help saying what he felt.

"We've never picked up anything atmospheric at that frequency."

"You know what happens to artists who fall in love with their models? They come to a bad end. The same applies to scientists."

"Keep listening. Something's doing it. Then it breaks off suddenly, as if—"

"It's different, all right. But I just don't think anything could cut it down in that soup."

"I'll talk to them one day," Morton insisted.

Rick shook his head, then forced himself to talk again.

"Play it over," he suggested.

Morton pushed a button and after several moments' pause the buzzing, humming, whistling sequence started anew.

"I've been thinking about what you said earlier," Morton remarked, "about communication . . ."

"Yes?"

"You asked what we'd have to say to each other."

"Exactly. If they're there."

The sounds rose in pitch. Rick began to feel uncomfortable. Could there possibly? . . .

"They would have no words for all of the concrete things which fill our lives," Morton stated, "and even many of our abstractions are based upon the possession of human anatomy and physiology. Our poetry of valley and mountain, river and field, night and day with stars and sun would not come through well."

Rick nodded. If they exist, he wondered, what would they have that we want?

"Perhaps only music and mathematics, our most abstract art and science, could serve as points of contact," Morton went on. "Beyond that, some sort of metalanguage would really have to be developed."

"A record of their songs might have some commercial value," Rick mused.

"And then?" the smaller man suggested. "Would we be the serpent in their Eden, detailing wonders they might never experience directly, causing them some strange existential traumas? Or could it possibly be the other way around? What may they know or feel that we have not even guessed?"

"I'm getting some ideas for breaking this thing down mathematically, to see whether there's a real logic sequence behind it," Rick said suddenly. "I think I've seen some linguistic formulations that might apply."

"Linguistics?" Morton observed. "That's not your area."

"I know, but I love math theory, no matter where it's from."

"Interesting. What if they had a complex mathematics that the human mind simply could not comprehend?"

"I'd go mad over it," Rick replied. "It would snare

my soul." Then he laughed. "But there's nothing there, Morty. We're just screwing around. . . . Unless there's a pattern," he decided. "Then we cash in."

Morton grinned.

"There is. I'm sure of it."

That night Rick's sleep was troubled by strange periodicities. The rhythms of the song throbbed in his head. He dreamed that the song and the language were one with a mathematical vision no bilaterally symmetrical brain could ever share. He dreamed of ending his days in frustration, seeing the thing cracked by brute computer force but never being able to comprehend the elegance.

In the morning he forgot. He located the formulations for Morton and translated them into a program of analysis, humming an irregular tune which never went quite right as he worked.

Later, he went to a port and stared for a long while at the giant ringed world itself. After a time it bothered him, not being able to decide whether he was looking up or looking down.

ITSELF SURPRISED

I'd never thought Fred Saberhagen would allow anyone else to write a berserker story, so I was surprised when he told me he was going to do just that, with Berserker Base *(Tor, 1985), obtaining stories from Poul Anderson, Ed Bryant, Steve Donaldson, Larry Niven, and Connie Willis. Would I do one, too? Sure, I said. I was flattered, honored even. And it would give me an opportunity to try out an interesting notion I'd come up with on reading* A Hideous History of Weapons, *by Cherney Berg (Crowell-Collier, 1963). In following the development of weaponry from the primitive through the sophisticated I'd noted that weapons and defenses and new weapons really did appear to arise in response to each other with such a chartable predictability that the area might well be viewed as one of the few classic examples of a dialectic doing just what dialectics are supposed to do—thesis, antithesis, synthesis, ad nauseum. All I had to do was consider the berserker as the thesis and apply the formula.*

Thanks, Fred; thanks, Cherney; thanks, Hegel. . . .

*I*t was said that a berserker could, if necessity required, assume even a pleasing shape. But there was no such requirement here. Flashing through the billion-starred silence, the berserker was massive and dark and purely functional in design. It was a planet buster of a machine headed for the world called Corlano, where it would pound cities to rubble—eradicate an entire biosphere. It possessed the ability to do this without exceptional difficulty. No subtlety, no guile, no reliance on fallible goodlife were required. It had its directive; it had its weapons. It never wondered why this should be the way of its kind. It never questioned the directive. It never speculated whether it might be, in its own fashion, itself a life-form, albeit artificial. It was a single-minded killing machine, and if purpose may be considered a virtue, it was to this extent virtuous.

Almost unnecessarily, its receptors scanned far ahead. It knew that Corlano did not possess extraordinary defenses. It anticipated no difficulties.

Who hath drawn the circuits for the lion?

There was something very distant and considerably off course. . . . A world destroyer on a mission would not normally deviate for anything so tiny, however.

It rushed on toward Corlano, weapon systems ready.

Wade Kelman felt uneasy as soon as he laid eyes on the thing. He shifted his gaze to MacFarland and Dorphy.

"You let me sleep while you chased that junk down, matched orbits, grappled it? You realize how much time that wasted?"

"You needed the rest," the small, dark man named Dorphy replied, looking away.

"Bullshit! You know I'd have said no!"

"It might be worth something, Wade," MacFarland observed.

"This is a smuggling run, not a salvage operation. Time is important."

"Well, we've got the thing now," MacFarland replied. "No sense arguing over what's done."

Wade bit off a nasty rejoinder. He could push things only so far. He wasn't really captain, not in the usual sense. The three of them were in this together—equal investments, equal risk. But he knew how to pilot the small vessel better than either of them. That and their deference to him up to this point had revived command reflexes from both happier and sadder days. Had they awakened him and voted on this bit of salvage, he would obviously have lost. He knew, however, that they would still look to him in an emergency.

He nodded sharply.

"All right, we've got it," he said. "What the hell is it?"

"Damned if I know, Wade," replied MacFarland, a stocky, light-haired man with pale eyes and a crooked mouth. He looked out through the lock and into the innards of the thing quick-sealed there beside them. "When we spotted it, I thought it was a lifeboat. It's about the right size—"

"And?"

"We signaled, and there was no reply."

"You mean you broke radio silence for that piece of junk?"

"If it was a lifeboat, there could be people aboard, in trouble."

"Not too bloody likely, judging from its condition. Still," he sighed, "you're right. Go ahead."

"No signs of any electrical activity either."

"You chased it down just for the hell of it, then?"

Dorphy nodded.

"That's about right," he said.

"So, it's full of treasure?"

"I don't know what it's full of. It's not a lifeboat, though."

"Well, I can see that."

Wade peered through the opened lock into the interior of the thing. He took the flashlight from Dorphy, moved forward, and shone it about. There was no room for passengers amid the strange machinery.

"Let's ditch it," he said. "I don't know what all that crap in there is, and it's damaged anyway. I doubt it's worth its mass to haul anywhere."

"I'll bet the professor could figure it out," Dorphy said.

"Let the poor lady sleep. She's cargo, not crew, anyway. What's it to her what this thing is?"

"Suppose—just suppose—that's a valuable piece of equipment," Dorphy said. "Say, something experimental. Somebody might be willing to pay for it."

"And suppose it's a fancy bomb that never went off?"

Dorphy drew back from the hatch.

"I never thought of that."

"I say deep-six it."

"Without even taking a better look?"

"Right. I don't even think you could squeeze very far in there."

"Me? You know a lot more about engineering than either of us."

"That's why you woke me up, huh?"

"Well, now that you're here—"

Wade sighed. Then he nodded slowly.

"That would be crazy and risky and totally unproductive."

He stared through the lock at the exotic array of equipment inside. "Pass me that trouble light."

He accepted the light and extended it through the lock.

"It's been holding pressure okay?"

77

"Yeah. We slapped a patch on the hole in its hull."

"Well, what the hell."

He passed through the lock, dropped to his knees, leaned forward. He held the light before him, moved it from side to side. His uneasiness would not go away. There was something very foreign about all those cubes and knobs, their connections. . . . And that one large housing. . . . He reached out and tapped upon the hull. Foreign.

"I've got a feeling it's alien," he said.

He entered the small open area before him. Then he had to duck his head and proceed on his hands and knees. He began to touch things—fittings, switches, connectors, small units of unknown potential. Almost everything seemed designed to swivel, rotate, move along tracks. Finally, he lay flat and crawled forward.

"I believe that a number of these units are weapons," he called out, after studying them for some time.

He reached the big housing. A panel slid partway open as he passed his fingertips along its surface. He pressed harder, and it opened farther.

"Damn you!" he said then, as the unit began to tick softly.

"What's wrong?" Dorphy called to him.

"You!" he said, beginning to back away. "And your partner! You're wrong!"

He turned as soon as he could and made his way back through the lock.

"Ditch it!" he said. "Now!"

Then he saw that Juna, a tall study in gray and paleness, stood leaning against a bulkhead, holding a cup of tea.

"And if we've got a bomb, toss it in there before you kick it loose!" he added.

"What did you find?" she asked him in her surprisingly rich voice.

"That's some kind of fancy thinking device in there,"

78

he told her. "It tried to kick on when I touched it. And I'm sure a bunch of those gadgets are weapons. Do you know what that means?"

"Tell me," she said.

"Alien design, weapons, brain. My partners just salvaged a damaged berserker, that's what. And it's trying to turn itself back on. It's got to go—fast."

"Are you absolutely certain that's what it is?" she asked him.

"Certain, no. Scared, yes."

She nodded and set her cup aside. She raised her hand to her mouth and coughed.

"I'd like to take a look at it myself before you get rid of it," she said softly.

Wade gnawed his lower lip.

"Juna," he said, "I can understand your professional interest in the computer, but we're supposed to deliver you to Corlano intact, remember?"

She smiled for the first time since he'd met her some weeks before.

"I really want to see it."

Her smile hardened. He nodded.

"Make it a quick look."

"I'll need my tools. And I want to change into some working clothes."

She turned and passed through the hatch to her right. He glared at his partners, shrugged, and turned away.

Seated on the edge of his bunk and eating breakfast from a small tray while Dvořák's *Slavonic Dances* swirled about him, Wade reflected on berserkers, Dr. Juna Bayel, computers in general, and how they all figured together in the reason for this trip. Berserker scouts had been spotted periodically in this sector during the past few years. By this time the berserkers must be aware that Corlano was not well defended. This made for some nervousness within the segment of Corlano's population made up of refugees from a berserker attack upon distant Djelbar almost a generation before. A great number had chosen Corlano as a world far removed from earlier patterns of berserker activity. Wade snorted at a certain irony this had engendered. It was those same people who had lobbied so long and so successfully for the highly restrictive legislation Corlano now possessed regarding the manufacture and importation of knowledge-processing machines, a species of group paranoia going back to their berserker trauma.

There was a black market, of course. Machines more complicated than those allowed by law were needed by businesses, some individuals, and even the government itself. People like himself and his partners regularly brought in such machines and components. Officials usually looked the other way. He'd seen this same schizophrenia in a number of places.

He sipped his coffee.

And Juna Bayel . . . knowledge-systems specialists of her caliber were generally *non grata* there, too. She might have gone in as a tourist, but then she would have been subjected to scrutiny, making it more difficult to teach the classes she had been hired to set up.

He sighed. He was used to governmental double-thinking. He had been in the service. In fact . . . no. Not worth thinking about all that again. Things had actually been looking up lately. A few more runs like this one and he could make the final payments on his divorce settlement and go into legitimate shipping, get respectable, perhaps even prosper—

The intercom buzzed. "Yes?"

"Dr. Bayel wants permission to do some tests on that brain in the derelict," MacFarland said. "She wants to run some leads and hook it up to the ship's computer. What do you think?"

"Sounds dangerous." Wade replied. "Suppose she activates it? Berserkers aren't very nice, in case you've never—"

"She says she can isolate the brain from the weapons systems," MacFarland replied. "Besides, she says she doesn't think it's a berserker."

"Why not?"

"First, it doesn't conform to any berserker design configurations in our computer's records—"

"Hell! That doesn't prove anything. You know they can customize themselves for different jobs."

"Second, she's been on teams that examined wrecked berserkers. She says that this brain is different."

"Well, it's her line of work, and I'm sure she's damned curious, but I don't know. What do you think?"

"We know she's good. That's why they want her on Corlano. Dorphy still thinks that thing could be valuable, and we've got salvage rights. It might be worthwhile to let her dig a little. I'm sure she knows what she's doing."

"Is she handy now?"

"No. She's inside the thing."

"Sounds as if you've got me outvoted already. Tell her to go ahead."

"Okay."

Maybe it was good that he'd resigned his commission, he mused. Decisions were always a problem. Dvořák's dance filled his head, and he pushed everything else away while he finished his coffee.

A long-dormant, deep-buried system was activated within the giant berserker's brain. A flood of data suddenly pulsed through its processing unit. It began preparations to deviate from its course toward Corlano. This was not a fall from virtue but rather a response to a higher purpose.

Who laid the measure of the prey?

81

* * *

With sensitive equipment, Juna tested the compatibilities. She played with transformers and converters to adjust the power levels and cycling, to permit the hookup with the ship's computer. She had blocked every circuit leading from that peculiar brain to the rest of the strange vessel—except for the one leading to its failed power source. The brain's power unit was an extremely simple affair, seemingly designed to function on any radioactive material placed within its small chamber. This chamber contained only heavy, inert elements now. She emptied it and cleaned it, then refilled it from the ship's own stores. She had expected an argument from Wade on this point, but he had only shrugged.

"Just get it over with," he said, "so we can ditch it."

'We won't be ditching it," she said. "It's unique."

"We'll see."

"You're really afraid of it?"

"Yes."

"I've rendered it harmless."

"I don't trust alien artifacts!" he snapped.

She brushed back her frosty hair.

"Look, I heard how you lost your commission—taking a berserker-booby-trapped lifeboat aboard ship," she said. "Probably anyone would have done it. You thought you were saving lives."

"I didn't play it by the book," he said, "and it cost lives. I'd been warned, but I did it anyway. This reminds me—"

"This is not a combat zone," she interrupted, "and that thing cannot hurt us."

"So get on with it!"

She closed a circuit and seated herself before a console.

"This will probably take quite a while," she stated. "Want some coffee?"

"That would be nice."

The cup went cold, and he brought her another. She ran query after query, probing in a great variety of ways. There was no response. Finally she sighed, leaned back, and raised the cup.

"It's badly damaged, isn't it?" he said.

She nodded.

"I'm afraid so, but I was hoping that I could still get something out of it—some clue, any clue."

She sipped the coffee.

"Clue?" he said. "To what?"

"What it is and where it came from. The thing's incredibly old. Any information at all that might have been preserved would be an archaeological treasure."

"I'm sorry," he said. "I wish you had found something."

She had swiveled her chair and was looking down into her cup. He saw the movement first.

"Juna! The screen!"

She turned spilling coffee in her lap.

"Damn!"

Row after row of incomprehensible symbols were flowing onto the screen.

"What is it?" he asked.

"I don't know," she said.

She leaned forward, forgetting him.

He must have stood there, his back against the bulkhead, watching, for over an hour, fascinated by the configurations upon the screen, by the movements of her long-fingered hands working unsuccessful combinations upon the keyboard. Then he noticed something that she had not, with her attention riveted upon the symbols.

A small, telltale light was burning at the left of the console. He had no idea how long it had been lit.

He moved forward. It was the voice-mode indicator.

The thing was trying to communicate at more than one level.

"Let's try this," he said.

He reached forward and threw the switch beneath the light.

"What—?"

A genderless voice, talking in clicks and moans, emerged from the speaker. The language was obviously exotic.

"God!" he said. "It is!"

"What is it?" She turned to stare at him. "You understand that language?"

He shook his head.

"I don't understand it, but I think that I recognize it."

"What is it?" she repeated.

"I have to be sure. I'm going to need another console to check this out," he said. "I'm going next door. I'll be back as soon as I have something."

"Well, what do you think it is?"

"I think we are violating a tougher law than the smuggling statutes."

"What?"

"Possession of, and experimentation with, a berserker brain."

"You're wrong," she said.

"We'll see."

She watched him depart. She chewed a thumbnail, a thing she had not done in years. If he were right, it would have to be shut down, sealed off, and turned over to military authorities. On the other hand, she did not believe that he was right.

She reached forward and silenced the distracting voice. She had to hurry now, to try something different, to press for a breakthrough before he returned. He seemed too sure of himself. She felt that he might return with something persuasive, even if it were not correct.

So she instructed the ship's computer to teach the captive brain to communicate in a Solarian tongue. Then she fetched herself a fresh cup of coffee and drank it.

More of its alarm systems came on as it advanced. The giant killing machine activated jets to slow its course. The first order to pass through its processor, once the tentative identification had been made, was, *Advance warily.*

It maintained the fix on the distant vessel and its smaller companion, but it executed the approach pattern its battle-logic bank indicated. It readied more weapons.

"All right," Wade said later, entering and taking a seat. "I was wrong. It wasn't what I thought."

"Would you at least tell me what you'd suspected?" Juna asked.

He nodded. "I'm no great linguist," he began, "but I love music. I have a very good memory for sounds of all sorts. I carry symphonies around in my head. I even play several instruments, though it's been a while. But memory played a trick on me this time. I would have sworn that those sounds were similar to ones I'd heard on those copies of the Carmpan recordings—the fragmentary records we got from them concerning the Builders, the nasty race that made the berserkers. There are copies in the ship's library, and I just listened to some again. It'd been years. But I was wrong. They sound different. I'm sure it's not Builder-talk."

"It was my understanding that the berserkers never had the Builders' language code, anyhow," she said.

"I didn't know that. But for some reason, I was sure I'd heard something like it on those tapes. Funny . . . I wonder what language it does talk?"

"Well, now I've given it the ability to talk to us. But it's not too successful at it."

"You instructed it in a Solarian language code?" he asked.

"Yes, but it just babbles. Sounds like Faulkner on a bad day."

She threw the voice switch.

". . . Prothector vincit damn the torpedoes and flaring suns like eyes three starboard two at zenith—"

She turned it off.

"Does it do that in response to queries, too?" he asked.

"Yes. Still, I've got some ideas—"

The intercom buzzed. He rose and thumbed an acknowledgement. It was Dorphy. "Wade, we're picking up something odd coming this way," the man said. "I think you'd better have a look."

"Right." he answered. "I'm on my way. Excuse me, Juna."

She did not reply. She was studying new combinations on the screen.

"Moving to intersect our course. Coming fast," Dorphy said.

Wade studied the screen, punched up data, which appeared as a legend to the lower right.

"Lots of mass there," he observed.

"What do you think it is?"

"You say it changed course?"

"Yes."

"I don't like that."

"Too big to be any regular vessel."

"Yes," Wade observed. "All of this talk about berserkers might have made me jumpy, but—"

"Yeah. That's what I was thinking, too."

"Looks big enough to grill a continent."

"Or fry a whole planet. I've heard of them in that league."

"But Dorphy, if that's what it is, it just doesn't make any sense. Something like that, on its way to do a job like that—I can't see it taking time out to chase after us. Must be something else."

"What?"

"Don't know."

Dorphy turned away from the screen and licked his lips, frown lines appearing between his brows.

"I think it is one," he said. "If it is, what should we do?"

Wade laughed briefly, harshly.

"Nothing," he said then. "There is absolutely nothing we could do against a thing like that. We can't outrun it, and we can't outgun it. We're dead if that's what it really is and we're what it wants. If that's the case, though, I hope it tells us why it's taking the trouble, before it destroys us."

"There's nothing at all that I should do?"

"You can send a message to Corlano. If it gets through, they'll at least have a chance to put whatever they've got on the line. This close to their system it can't have any other destination. If you've got religion, now might be a good time to go into it a little more deeply."

"You defeatist son of a bitch! There must be something else!"

"If you think of it, let me know. I'll be up talking to Juna. In the meantime, get that message sent."

The berserker fired its maneuvering jets again. How close was too close when you were being wary? It continued to adjust its course. This had to be done just right. New directions kept running through its processor the nearer it got to its goal. It had never encountered a situation such as this before. But then this was an ancient program that had never before been activated. Ordered to train its weapons on the target but forbidden to fire them . . . all because of a little electrical activity.

". . . Probably come for its little buddy," Wade finished.

"Berserkers don't have buddies," Juna replied.

"I know. I'm just being cynical. You find anything new?"

"I've been trying various scans to determine the extent of the damage. I believe that something like nearly half of its memory has been destroyed."

"Then you'll never get much out of it."

"Maybe. Maybe not," she said, and she sniffed once.

Wade turned toward her and saw that her eyes were moist.

"Juna—"

"I'm sorry, damn it. It's not like me. But to be so close to something like this—and then be blasted by an idiot killing machine right before you find some answers. It just isn't fair. You got a tissue?"

"Yeah. Just a sec."

The intercom buzzed as he was fumbling with a wall dispenser.

"Patching in transmission," Dorphy stated.

There was a pause, and then an unfamiliar voice said, "Hello. You are the captain of this vessel?"

"Yes, I am," Wade replied. "And you are a berserker?"

"You may call me that."

"What do you want?"

"What are you doing?"

"I am conducting a shipping run to Corlano. What do you want?"

"I observe that you are conveying an unusual piece of equipment. What is it?"

"An air-conditioning unit."

"Do not lie to me, captain. What is your name?"

"Wade Kelman."

"Do not lie to me, Captain Wade Kelman. The unit you bear in tandem is not a processor of atmospheric gases. How did you acquire it?"

"Bought it at a flea market," Wade stated.

"You are lying again, Captain Kelman."

"Yes, I am. Why not? If you are going to kill us, why should I give you the benefit of a straight answer to anything?"

"I have said nothing about killing you."

"But that is the only thing you are noted for. Why else would you have come by?"

Wade was surprised at his responses. In any imagined conversation with death, he had never seen himself as being so reckless. It's all in not having anything more to lose, he decided.

"I detect that the unit is in operation," the berserker stated.

"So it is."

"And what function does the unit perform for you?"

"It performs a variety of functions we find useful," he stated.

"I want you to abandon that piece of equipment," the berserker said.

"Why should I?" he asked.

"I require it."

"I take it that this is a threat?"

"Take it as you would."

"I am not going to abandon it. I repeat, why should I?"

"You are placing yourself in a dangerous situation."

"I did not create this situation."

"In a way you did. But I can understand your fear. It is not without justification."

89

"If you were simply going to attack us and take it from us, you would already have done so, wouldn't you?"

"That is correct. I carry only very heavy armaments for the work in which I am engaged. If I were to turn them upon you, you would be reduced to dust. This of course includes the piece of equipment I require."

"All the more reason for us to hang onto it, as I see it."

"This is logical, but you possess an incomplete pattern of facts."

"What am I missing?"

"I have already sent a message requesting the dispatch of smaller units capable of dealing with you."

"Then why are you even bothering to tell us all this?"

"I tell you this because it will take them some time to reach this place and I would rather be on my way to complete my mission than wait here for them."

"Thank you. But we would rather die later than die now. We'll wait."

"You do not understand. I am offering you a chance to live."

"What do you propose?"

"I want you to abandon that piece of equipment now. You may then depart."

"And you will just let us go, unmolested?"

"I have the option of categorizing you as goodlife, if you will serve me. Abandon the unit and you will be serving me. I will categorize you as goodlife. I will then let you go, unmolested."

"We have no way of knowing whether you will keep that promise."

"That is true. But the alternative is certain death, and if you will but consider my size and the obvious nature of my mission, you will realize that your few lives are insignificant beside it."

"You've made your point. But I cannot give you an instant answer. We must consider your proposal at some length."

"Understandable. I will talk to you again in an hour."

The transmission ended. Wade realized he was shaking. He sought a chair and collapsed into it. Juna was staring at him.

"Know any good voodoo curses?"

She shook her head and smiled fleetingly at him.

"You handled that very well."

"No. It was like following a script. There was nothing else to do. There still isn't."

"At least you got us some time. I wonder why it wants the thing so badly?" Her eyes narrowed then. Her mouth tightened. "Can you get me the scan on that berserker?" she asked suddenly.

"Sure."

He rose and crossed to the console.

"I'll just cut over to the other computer and bring it in on this screen."

Moments later, a view of the killing machine hovered before them. He punched up the legend, displaying all the specs his ship's scanning equipment had been able to ascertain.

She studied the display for perhaps a minute, scrolling the legend. "It lied."

"In what respects?" he asked.

"Here, here, and here," she stated, pointing at features on the face of the berserker. "And here—" She indicated a part of the legend covering arms estimations.

Dorphy and MacFarland entered the cabin while she was talking.

"It lied when it said that it possesses only superior weapons and is in an overkill situation with respect to us. Those look like small-weapon mountings."

"I don't understand what you're saying."

"It is probably capable of very selective firing—highly accurate, minimally destructive. It should be capable of destroying us with a high probability of leaving the artifact intact."

"Why should it lie?" he asked.

"I wonder—" she said, gnawing her thumbnail again. MacFarland cleared his throat.

"We heard the whole exchange," he began, "and we've been talking it over."

Wade turned his head and regarded him.

"Yes?"

"We think we ought to give it what it wants and run for it."

"You believe that goodlife crap? It'll blast us as we go."

"I don't think so," he said. "There're plenty of precedents. They do have the option of classifying you that way, and they will make a deal if there's something they really want."

"Dorphy," Wade asked, "did you get that message off to Corlano?"

The smaller man nodded.

"Good. If for no other reason, Corlano is why we're going to wait here. It could take a while for those smaller units it was talking about to get here. Every hour we gain in waiting is another hour for them to bolster their defenses."

"I can see that—" Dorphy began.

". . . But there's sure death for us at the end of the waiting," MacFarland continued for him, "and this looks like a genuine way out. I sympathize with Corlano as much as you do, but us dying isn't going to help. You know the place is not strongly defended. Whether we buy them a little extra time or not, they'll still go under."

"You don't really know that," Wade said. "Some seemingly weak worlds have beaten off some very heavy attacks in the past. And even the berserker said it—our few lives are insignificant next to an entire inhabited world."

"Well, I'm talking probabilities, and I didn't come in on this venture to be a martyr. I was willing to take my chances with criminal justice, but not with death."

"How do you feel about it, Dorphy?" Wade asked.

Dorphy licked his lips and looked away.

"I'm with MacFarland," he said softly.

Wade turned to Juna.

"I say we wait," she said.

"Well, then, that makes two of us," Wade observed.

"She doesn't have a vote," MacFarland stated. "She's just a passenger."

"It's her life, too," Wade answered. "She has a say."

"She doesn't want to give it that damned machine!" MacFarland shot back. "She wants to sit here and play with it while everything goes up in flames! What's she got to lose? She's dying anyway and—"

Wade snarled and rose to his feet.

"The discussion is ended. We stay."

"The vote was a tie—at most."

"I am assuming full command here, and I say that's the way it's going to be."

MacFarland laughed.

"Full command! This is a lousy smuggling run, not the service you got busted out of, Wade. You can't command any—"

Wade hit him, twice in the stomach and a left cross to the jaw.

MacFarland went down, doubled forward, and began gasping. Wade regarded him, considered his size. If he gets up within the next ten seconds this is going to be rough, he decided.

But MacFarland raised a hand only to rub his jaw. He said, "Damn!" softly and shook his head to clear it. "You didn't have to do that, Wade."

"I thought I did."

MacFarland shrugged and rose to one knee.

"Okay, you've got your command," he said. "But I still think that you're making a big mistake."

"I'll call you next time there's something to discuss," Wade told him.

Dorphy reached to help him to his feet, but the larger man shook off his hand.

Wade glanced at Juna. She looked paler than usual, her eyes brighter. She stood before the hatchway to the opened lock as if to defend the passage.

"I'm going to take a shower and lie down," Mac-Farland said.

"Good."

Juna moved forward as the two men left the room. She took hold of Wade's arm.

"It lied," she said again softly. "Do you understand? It *could* blast us and recover the machine, but it doesn't want to."

"No," Wade said. "I don't understand."

"It's almost as if it's afraid of the thing."

"Berserkers do not know fear."

"All right. I was anthropomorphizing. It's as if it were under some constraint regarding it. I think we've got something very special here, something that creates an unusual problem for the berserker."

"What could it be?"

"I don't know. But there may be some way to find out, if you can just get me enough time. Stall for as long as you can."

He nodded slowly and seated himself. His heart was racing.

"You said that about half of its memory was shot."

"It's a guess, but yes. And I'm going to try to reconstruct it from what's there."

"How?"

She crossed to the computer.

"I'm going to program this thing for an ultrahigh-speed form of Wiener analysis of what's left in there. It's a powerful nonlinear method for dealing with the very high noise levels we're facing. But it's going to have to make some astronomical computations for a system like this. We'll have to patch in the others, maybe even pull some of the cargo. I don't know how long this is going to take or even if it will really work." She began to sound out of breath. "But we might be able to reconstruct what's missing and restore it. That's why I need all the time you can get me," she finished.

"I'll try. You go ahead. And—"

"I know," she said, coughing. "Thanks."

"I'll bring you something to eat while you work."

"In my cabin," she said, "in the top drawer, bedside table—there are three small bottles of pills. Bring them and some water instead."

"Right."

He departed. On the way, he stopped in his cabin to fetch a handgun he kept in his dresser, the only weapon aboard the ship. He searched the drawers several times but could not locate it. He cursed softly and went to Juna's cabin for her medicine.

The berserker maintained its distance and speculated while it waited. It had conceded some information in order to explain the proposed trade-off. Still, it could do no harm to remind Captain Kelman of the seriousness of his position. It might even produce a faster decision. Accordingly, the hydraulics hummed, and surface hatches were opened to extrude additional weapon mounts. Firing pieces were shifted to occupy these and were targeted upon the small vessel. Most were too heavy to take out to the ship without damaging its companion. Their mere display, though, might be sufficiently demoralizing.

Wade watched Juna work. While the hatch could be secured, there were several other locations within the ship from which it could be opened remotely. So he had tucked a pry bar behind his belt and kept an eye on the open hatch. It had seemed the most that he could do, short of forcing a confrontation that might go either way.

Periodically, he would throw the voice-mode switch and listen to that thing ramble, sometimes in Solarian, sometimes in the odd alien tongue that still sounded somehow familiar. He mused upon it. Something was trying to surface. She had been right about it, but—

The intercom buzzed. Dorphy.

"Our hour is up. It wants to talk to you again," he said. "Wade, it's pointing more weapons at us."

"Switch it in," he replied. He paused, then, "Hello?" he said.

"Captain Kelman, the hour has run out," came the now-familiar voice. "Tell me your decision."

"We have not reached one yet," he answered. "We are divided on this matter. We need more time to discuss it further."

"How much time?"

"I don't know. Several hours at least."

"Very well. I will communicate with you every hour for the next three hours. If you have not reached a decision during that time, I will have to reconsider my offer to categorize you as a goodlife."

"We are hurrying," Wade said.

"I will call you in an hour."

"Wade," Dorphy said at transmission's end, "all those

new weapons are pointed right at us. I think it's getting ready to blast us if you don't give it what it wants."

"I don't think so," Wade said. "Anyhow, we've got some time now."

"For what? A few hours isn't going to change anything."

"I'll tell you in a few hours," Wade said. "How's MacFarland?"

"He's okay."

"Good."

He broke the connection.

"Hell," he said then.

He wanted a drink, but he didn't want to muddy his thinking. He had been close to something.

He returned to Juna and the console.

"How's it going?" he asked.

"Everything's in place, and I'm running it now," she said.

"How soon till you know whether it's working?"

"Hard to tell."

He threw the voice-mode switch again.

"Qwibbian-qwibbian-kel," it said. "Qwibbian-qwibbian-kel, maks qwibbian. Qwibbian-qwibbian-kel."

"I wonder what that could mean," he said.

"It's a recurring phrase, or word—or whole sentence. A pattern analysis I ran a while back made me think that it might be its name for itself."

"It has a certain lilt to it."

He began humming. Then whistling and tapping his fingers on the side of the console in accompaniment.

"That's it!" he announced suddenly. "It was the right place, but it was the wrong place."

"What?" she asked.

"I have to check to be sure," he said. "Hold the fort. I'll be back."

He hurried off.

"The right place but the wrong place," emerged from the speaker. "How can that be? Contradiction."

"You're coming together again!" she said.

"I—regain," came the reply, after a time.

"Let us talk while the process goes on," she suggested.

"Yes," it answered, and then it lapsed again into rambling amid bursts of static.

Dr. Juna Bayel crouched in the lavatory cubicle and vomited. Afterward, she ground the heels of her hands into her eye sockets and tried to breathe deeply to overcome the dizziness and the shaking. When her stomach had settled sufficiently, she took a double dose of her medicine. It was a risk, but she had no real choice. She could not afford one of her spells now. A heavy dose might head it off. She clenched her teeth and her fists and waited.

Wade Kelman received the berserker's call at the end of the hour and talked it into another hour's grace. The killing machine was much more belligerent this time.

Dorphy radioed the berserker after he heard the latest transmission and offered to make a deal. The berserker accepted immediately.

The berserker retracted all but the four original gun mounts facing the ship. It did not wish to back down even to this extent, but Dorphy's call had given it an appropriate-seeming reason. Actually, it could not dismiss the possibility that showing the additional weapons might have been responsible for the increased electrical activity it now detected. The directive still cautioned wariness and was now indicating nonprovocation as well.

Who hath drawn the circuit for the lion?

"Qwibbian," said the artifact.

Juna sat, pale, before the console. The past hour had

added years to her face. There was fresh grime on her coveralls. When Wade entered, he halted and stared.

"What's wrong?" he said. "You look—"

"It's okay."

"No, it isn't. I know you're sick. We're going to have to—"

"It's really okay," she said. "It's passing. Let it be. I'll be all right."

He nodded and advanced again, displaying a small recorder in his left hand.

"I've got it," he said then. "Listen to this."

He turned on the recorder. A series of clicks and moans emerged. It ran for about a quarter-minute and stopped.

"Play it again, Wade," she said, and she smiled at him weakly as she threw the voice-mode switch.

He complied.

"Translate," she said when it was over.

"Take the—untranslatable—to the—untranslatable—and transform it upward," came the voice of the artifact through the speaker.

"Thanks," she said. "You were right."

"You know where I found it?" he asked.

"On the Carmpan tapes."

"Yes, but it's not Builder-talk."

"I know that."

"And you also know what it is?"

She nodded. "It is the language spoken by the Builders' enemies—the Red Race—against whom the berserkers were unleashed. There is a little segment showing the round red people shouting a slogan or a prayer or something. Maybe it's even a Builder propaganda tape. It came from that, didn't it?"

"Yes. How did you know?"

She patted the console.

99

"Qwib-qwib here is getting back on his mental feet. He's even helping now. He's very good at self-repair, now that the process has been initiated. We have been talking for a while, and I'm finally beginning to understand."

She coughed, a deep, racking thing that brought tears to her eyes. "Would you get me a glass of water?"

"Sure."

He crossed the cabin and fetched it.

"We have made an enormously important find," she said as she sipped it. "It was good that the others kept you from cutting it loose."

MacFarland and Dorphy entered the cabin. MacFarland held Wade's pistol and pointed it at him.

"Cut it loose," he said.

"No," Wade answered.

"Then Dorphy will do it while I keep you covered. Suit up, Dorphy, and get a torch."

"You don't know what you're doing," Wade said. "Juna was just telling me—"

MacFarland fired. The projectile ricocheted about the cabin, finally dropping to the floor in the far corner.

"Mac, you're crazy!" Wade said. "You could just as easily hit yourself if you do that again."

"Don't move! Okay. That was stupid, but now I know better. The next one goes into your shoulder or your leg. I mean it. You understand?"

"Yes, damn it! But we can't just cut that thing loose now. It's almost repaired, and we know where it's from, Juna says—"

"I don't care about any of that. Two-thirds of it belong to Dorphy and me, and we're jettisoning our share right now. If your third goes along, that's tough. The berserker assures us that's all it wants. It'll let us go then. I believe it."

"Look, Mac. Anything a berserker wants that badly

is something we shouldn't give it. I think I can talk it into giving us even more time."

MacFarland shook his head.

Dorphy finished suiting up and took a cutting torch from a rack. As he headed for the open lock, Juna said, "Wait. If you cycle the lock, you'll cut the cable. It'll sever the connection to Qwib-qwib's brain."

"I'm sorry, Doctor," MacFarland said. "But we're in a hurry."

From the console then came the words: "Our association is to be terminated?"

"I'm afraid so," she answered. "I am sorry that I could not finish."

"Do not. The process continues. I have assimilated the program and now use it myself. A most useful process."

Dorphy entered the lock.

"I have one question, Juna, before good-bye," it said.

"Yes? What is it?" she asked.

The lock began cycling closed, and Dorphy was already raising the torch to burn through the welds.

"My vocabulary is still incomplete. What does *qwib-bian* mean in your language?"

The cycling lock struck the cable and severed it as she spoke; so she did not know whether it heard her say the word *berserker*.

Wade and MacFarland both turned.

"What did you say?" Wade asked.

She repeated it.

"You're not making sense," he said. "First you said that it wasn't. Now—"

"Do you want to talk about words or machines?" she asked.

"Go ahead. You talk. I'll listen."

She sighed deeply and took another drink of water.

"I got the story from Qwib-qwib in pieces," she began.

"I had to fill in some gaps with conjectures, but everything seemed to follow. Ages ago, the Builders apparently fought a war with the Red Race, who proved tougher than expected. So the Builders hit them with their ultimate weapon—the self-replicating killing machines we call berserkers."

"That seems the standard story."

"The Red Race went under," she continued. "They were totally destroyed—but only after a terrific struggle. In the final days of the war, they tried all sorts of things, but by then it was a case of too little, too late. They were overwhelmed. They actually even tried something I had always wondered about—something no Solarian world would now dare to attempt, with all the restrictions on research along those lines, with all the paranoia."

She paused for another sip.

"They built their own berserkers," she went on then, "but not like the originals. They developed a killing machine that would attack only berserkers—an antiberserker berserker—for the defense of their home planet. But there were too few of them. They put them all on the line, around their world, and apparently they did a creditable job—they had something involving short jumps into and out of other spaces going for them. But they were vastly outnumbered in that last great mass attack. Ultimately, all of them fell."

The ship gave a shudder. They turned toward the lock.

"He's cut it loose, whatever it was," MacFarland stated.

"It shouldn't shake the whole ship that way," Wade said.

"It would if it accelerated away the instant it was freed," said Juna.

"But how could it, with all of its control circuits sealed?" Wade asked.

She glanced at the greasy smears on her coveralls.

"I reestablished its circuits when I learned the truth," she told him. "I don't know what percentage of its old efficiency it possesses, but I am certain that it is about to attack the berserker."

The lock cycled open, and Dorphy emerged, began unfastening his suit as it cycled closed behind him.

"We've got to get the hell out of here!" MacFarland cried. "This area is about to become a war zone!"

"You care to do the piloting?" Wade asked him.

"Of course not."

"Then give me my gun and get out of my way." He accepted the weapon and headed for the bridge.

For so long as the screens permitted resolution, they watched—the ponderous movements of the giant berserker, the flashes of its energy blasts, the dartings and sudden disappearances and reappearances of its tiny attacker.

Later, some time after the images were lost, a fireball sprang into being against the starry black.

"He got it! He got it! Qwib-qwib got it!" Dorphy cried.

"And it probably got him, too," MacFarland remarked. "What do you think, Wade?"

"What I think," Wade replied, "is that I will never have anything to do with either of you again."

He rose and left to go and sit with Juna. He took along his recorder and some music. She turned from watching the view on her own screen and smiled weakly as he seated himself beside her bed.

"I'm going to take care of you," he told her, "until you don't need me."

"That would be nice," she said.

Tracking. Tracking. They were coming. Five of them. The big one must have sent for them. Jump behind them and take out the two rear ones before the others realize what is happening. Another jump, hit the port flank and jump again. They've never seen these tactics. Dodge. Fire. Jump. Jump again. Fire. The last one is spinning like a top, trying to anticipate. Hit it. Charge right in. There.

The last qwibbian-qwibbian-kel in the universe departed the battle scene, seeking the raw materials for some fresh repair work. Then, of course, it would need still more, for the replications. Who hath drawn the circuits for the lion?

DAYBLOOD

Vampire stories have always bothered me because the creatures go about biting people, who then turn into vampires who go about biting people, who. . . . There's a geometrical progression here, and if you stop to think about it, pretty soon we'd all be vampires with no civilians left to bite. The situation always struck me as ecologically unsound, too. There are natural enemies and other limiting factors which control population explosions in other species. If everything were as given in the tradition, there would have to be something else as well. Hence, my modest contribution to the canon of the undead. . . .

I crouched in the corner of the collapsed shed behind the ruined church. The dampness soaked through the knees of my jeans, but I knew that my wait was just about ended. Picturesquely, a few tendrils of mist rose from the soaked ground, to be stirred feebly by pre-dawn breezes. How Hollywood of the weather. . . .

I cast my gaze about the lightening sky, guessing correctly as to the direction of arrival. Within a minute I saw them flapping their way back—a big, dark one and a smaller, pale one. Predictably, they entered the church through the opening where a section of the roof had years before fallen in. I suppressed a yawn as I checked my watch. Fifteen minutes from now they should be settled and dozing as the sun spills morning all over the east. Possibly a little sooner, but give them a bit of leeway. No hurry yet.

I stretched and cracked my knuckles. I'd rather be home in bed. Nights are for sleeping, not for playing nursemaid to a couple of stupid vampires.

Yes, Virginia, there really are vampires. Nothing to get excited about, though. Odds are you'll never meet one. There just aren't that many around. In fact, they're damn near an endangered species—which is entirely understandable, considering the general level of intelligence I've encountered among them.

Take this guy Brodsky as an example. He lives—pardon me, resides—near a town containing several thousand people. He could have visited a different person each night for years without ever repeating himself, leaving his caterers (I understand that's their in-term these days) with little more than a slight sore throat, a touch of temporary anemia, and a couple of soon-to-be-forgotten scratches on the neck.

But no. He took a fancy to a local beauty—one Elaine Wilson, ex-majorette. Kept going back for more. Pretty soon she entered the customary coma and underwent the *nosferatu* transformation. All right, I know I said there aren't that many of them around—and personally I do feel that the world could use a few more vampires. But it's not a population-pressure thing with Brodsky, just stupidity and greed. No real finesse, no planning. While I applaud the creation of another member of the undead, I am sufficiently appalled by the carelessness of his methods to consider serious action. He left a trail that just about anyone could trace here; he also managed to display so many of the traditional signs and to leave such a multitude of clues that even in these modern times a reasonable person could become convinced of what was going on.

Poor old Brodsky—still living in the Middle Ages and behaving just as he did in the days of their population boom. It apparently never occurred to him to consider the mathematics of that sort of thing. He drains a few people he becomes particularly attracted to and they become *nosferatu*. If they feel the same way and behave the same way, they go out and recruit a few more of their caterers. And so on. It's like a chain letter. After a time, everyone would be *nosferatu* and there wouldn't be any caterers left. Then what? Fortunately, nature has ways of dealing with population explosions, even at this level. Still, a sudden rash of recruits in this mass-media age could really mess up the underground ecosystem.

So much for philosophy. Time to get inside and beat the crowd.

I picked up my plastic bag and worked my way out of the shed, cursing softly when I bumped against a post and brought a shower down over me. I made my way through the field then and up to the side door of the old building. It was secured by a rusty padlock, which I snapped and threw into the distant cemetery.

Inside, I perched myself on the sagging railing of the choir section and opened my bag. I withdrew my sketchbook and the pencil I'd brought along. Light leaked in through the broken window to the rear. What it fell upon was mostly trash. Not a particularly inspiring scene. Whatever . . . I began sketching it. It's always good to have a hobby that can serve as an excuse for odd actions, as an icebreaker . . .

Ten minutes, I guessed. At most.

Six minutes later, I heard their voices. They weren't particularly noisy, but I have exceptionally acute hearing. There were three of them, as I'd guessed there would be.

They entered through the side door also, slinking, jumpy—looking all about and seeing nothing. At first they didn't even notice me creating art where childish voices had filled Sunday mornings with off-key praise in years gone by.

There was old Dr. Morgan, several wooden stakes protruding from his black bag (I'll bet there was a hammer in there, too—I guess the Hippocratic Oath doesn't extend to the undead—*primum, non nocere,* etc.); and Father O'Brien, clutching his Bible like a shield, crucifix in his other hand; and young Ben Kelman (Elaine's fiancé), with a shovel over his shoulder and a bag from which I suspected the sudden odor of garlic to have its origin.

I cleared my throat, and all three of them stopped, turned, bumped into each other.

"Hi, Doc," I said. "Hi, Father. Ben . . ."

"Wayne!" Doc said. "What are you doing here?"

"Sketching," I said. "I'm into old buildings these days."

"The hell you are!" Ben said. "Excuse me, Father . . . You're just after a story for your damned newspaper!"

I shook my head.

"Really I'm not."

"Well, Gus'd never let you print anything about this, and you know it."

"Honest," I said. "I'm not here for a story. But I

know why you're here, and you're right—even if I wrote it up, it would never appear. You really believe in vampires?"

Doc fixed me with a steady gaze.

"Not until recently," he said. "But, son, if you'd seen what we've seen, you'd believe."

I nodded my head and closed my sketchpad.

"All right," I replied, "I'll tell you. I'm here because I'm curious. I wanted to see it for myself, but I don't want to go down there alone. Take me with you."

They exchanged glances.

"I don't know . . ." Ben said.

"It won't be anything for the squeamish," Doc told me.

Father O'Brien just nodded.

"I don't know about having anyone else in on this," Ben added.

"How many more know about it?" I asked.

"It's just us, really," Ben explained. "We're the only ones who actually saw him in action."

"A good newspaperman knows when to keep his mouth shut," I said, "but he's also a very curious creature. Let me come along."

Ben shrugged and Doc nodded. After a moment Father O'Brien nodded too.

I replaced my pad and pencil in the bag and got down from the railing.

I followed them across the church, out into a short hallway, and up to an open, sagging door. Doc flicked on a flashlight and played it upon a rickety flight of stairs leading down into darkness. Slowly then, he began to descend. Father O'Brien followed him. The stairs groaned and seemed to move. Ben and I waited till they had reached the bottom. Then Ben stuffed his bag of pungent groceries inside his jacket and withdrew a flashlight from his pocket.

He turned it on and stepped down. I was right behind him.

I halted when we reached the foot of the stair. In the beams from their lights I beheld the two caskets set up on sawhorses, also the thing on the wall above the larger one.

"Father, what is that?" I pointed.

Someone obligingly played a beam of light upon it.

"It looks like a sprig of mistletoe tied to the figure of a little stone deer," he said.

"Probably has something to do with black magic," I offered.

He crossed himself, went over to it and removed it.

"Probably so," he said, crushing the mistletoe and throwing it across the room, shattering the figure on the floor and kicking the pieces away.

I smiled, I moved forward then.

"Let's get the things open and have a look," Doc said.

I lent them a hand.

When the caskets were open, I ignored the comments about paleness, preservation, and bloody mouths. Brodsky looked the same as he always did—dark hair, heavy dark eyebrows, sagging jowls, a bit of a paunch. The girl was lovely, though. Taller than I'd thought, however, with a very faint pulsation at the throat and an almost bluish cast to her skin.

Father O'Brien opened his Bible and began reading, holding the flashlight above it with a trembling hand. Doc placed his bag upon the floor and fumbled about inside it.

Ben turned away, tears in his eyes. I reached out then and broke his neck quietly while the others were occupied. I lowered him to the floor and stepped up beside Doc.

"What—?" he began, and that was his last word.

Father O'Brien stopped reading. He stared at me across his Bible.

"You work for *them?*" he said hoarsely, darting a glance at the caskets.

"Hardly," I said, "but I need them. They're my life's blood."

"I don't understand . . ."

"Everything is prey to something else, and we do what we must. That's ecology. Sorry, Father."

I used Ben's shovel to bury the three of them beneath an earthen section of the floor toward the rear—garlic, stakes, and all. Then I closed the caskets and carried them up the stairs.

I checked around as I hiked across a field and back up the road after the pickup truck. It was still relatively early, and there was no one about.

I loaded them both in back and covered them with a tarp. It was a thirty-mile drive to another ruined church I knew of.

Later, when I had installed them safely in their new quarters, I penned a note and placed it in Brodsky's hand:

Dear B,

Let this be a lesson to you. You are going to have to stop acting like Bela Lugosi. You lack his class. You are lucky to be waking up at all this night. In the future be more circumspect in your activities or I may retire you myself. After all, I'm not here to serve you.

Yours truly,

W

P.S. The mistletoe and the statue of Cernunnos don't work anymore. Why did you suddenly get superstitious?

I glanced at my watch as I left the place. It was eleven fifteen. I stopped at a 7–11 a little later and used their outside phone.

"Hi, Kiela," I said when I heard her voice. "It's me."

"Werdeth," she said. "It's been a while."

"I know. I've been busy."

"With what?"

"Do you know where the old Church of the Apostles out off Route 6 is?"

"Of course. It's on my backup list, too."

"Meet me there at twelve thirty and I'll tell you about it over lunch."

CONSTRUCTING A
SCIENCE FICTION NOVEL

Sylvia Burack asked me for an essay for The Writer, *and I did the following piece. A large chunk of it tells of the considerations which went into the composition of my novel* Eye of Cat. *I don't believe I've ever recorded the things I do and think in writing a book in such detail, before or since. Still, it's a short piece, and for those of you who care about such matters I am including it here.*

*T*he late James Blish was once asked where he got his ideas for science fiction stories. He gave one of the usual general answers we all do—from observation, from reading, from the sum total of all his experiences, et cetera. Then someone asked him what he did if no ideas were forthcoming from these. He immediately replied, "I plagiarize myself."

He meant, of course, that he looked over his earlier works for roads unfollowed, trusting in the persistence of concerns and the renewal of old fascinations to stimulate some new ideas. And this works. I've tried it occasionally, and I usually find my mind flooded.

But I've been writing for over twenty years, and I know something about how my mind works when I am seeking a story or telling one. I did not always know the things that I know now, and much of my earlier writing involved groping—defining themes, deciding how I really felt about people and ideas. Consequently, much of this basic thinking accomplished, it is easier for me to fit myself into the driver's seat of a fresh new story than it once was. It may be the latest model, but the steering is similar, and once I locate the gearshift I know what to do with it.

For example: Settings. For me, science fiction has always represented the rational—the extension into a future or alien environment of that which is known now—whereas fantasy represented the metaphysical—the introduction of the unknown, usually into an alien environment. The distinctions are sometimes blurred, and sometimes it is fun to blur them. But on a practical, working level, this generally is how I distinguish the two. Either sort of story (I never tire of repeating) has the same requirements as a piece of general fiction, with the added necessity of introducing that exotic environment. Of the three basic elements of any fiction—plot, character, and setting—it is the setting that requires extra attention in science fiction and fantasy.

Here, as nowhere else, one walks a tightrope between overexplaining and overassuming, between boring the reader with too many details and losing the reader by not providing enough.

I found this difficult at first. I learned it by striving for economy of statement, by getting the story moving quickly and then introducing the background piecemeal. Somewhere along the line I realized that doing this properly could solve two problems: The simple exposition of the material could, if measured out in just the right doses, become an additional means of raising reader interest. I employed this technique to an extreme in the opening to my story "Unicorn Variation," in which I postponed for several pages describing the unusual creature passing through a strange locale.

> A bizarrerie of fires, cunabulum of light, it moved with a deft, almost dainty deliberation, phasing into and out of existence like a storm-shot piece of evening; or perhaps the darkness between the flares was more akin to its truest nature—swirl of black ashes assembled in prancing cadence to the lowing note of desert wind down the arroyo behind buildings as empty yet filled as the pages of unread books or stillnesses between the notes of a song.

As you see, I was careful to tell just enough to keep the reader curious. By the time it became apparent that it was a unicorn in a New Mexico ghost town, I had already introduced another character and a conflict.

Characters are less of a problem for me than settings. People are usually still people in science fiction environments. Major figures tend to occur to me almost fully developed, and minor ones do not require much work. As for their physical descriptions, it is easy at first to overdescribe. But how much does the reader really need? How much can the mind take in at one gulp? See the character entirely but mention only three things, I decided. Then quit and get on with the story. If a fourth characteristic sneaks in easily, okay. But leave it at that initially. No more. Trust that other features will occur as needed, so long as you know. "He was a tall, red-faced kid with one shoulder lower than the other." Were he a tall, red-faced kid with bright blue eyes (or large-knuckled hands or storms of freckles upon his cheeks) with one shoulder lower than the other, he would actually go out of focus a bit rather than grow clearer in the mind's eye. Too much detail creates a sensory overload, impairing the reader's ability to visualize. If such additional details are really necessary for the story line itself, it would be better to provide another dose later on, after allowing time for the first to sink in. "Yeah," he replied, blue eyes flashing.

I've mentioned settings and characters as typical examples of the development of writing reflexes, because reflexes are what this sort of work becomes with practice—and then, after a time, it should become second nature and be dismissed from thought. For this is just apprentice work—tricks—things that everybody in the trade has to learn. It is not, I feel, what writing is all about.

The important thing for me is the development and refinement of one's perception of the world, the experimentation with viewpoints. This lies at the heart of storytelling, and all of the mechanical techniques one learns are merely tools. It is the writer's approach to material that makes a story unique.

For example, I have lived in the Southwest for nearly a decade now. At some point I became interested in Indians. I began attending festivals and dances, reading anthropology, attending lectures, visiting museums. I became acquainted with Indians. At first, my interest was governed only by the desire to know more than I did. Later, though,

I began to feel that a story was taking shape at some lower level of my consciousness. I waited. I continued to acquire information and experience in the area.

One day my focus narrowed to the Navajo. Later, I realized that if I could determine why my interest had suddenly taken this direction, I would have a story. This came about when I discovered the fact that the Navajo had developed their own words—several hundred of them—for naming the various parts of the internal combustion engine. It was not the same with other Indian tribes I knew of. When introduced to cars, other tribes had simply taken to using the Anglo words for carburetors, pistons, spark plugs, etc. But the Navajo had actually come up with new Navajo words for these items—a sign, as I saw it, of their independence and their adaptability.

I looked further. The Hopis and the Pueblo Indians, neighbors to the Navajo, had rain dances in their rituals. The Navajo made no great effort to control the weather in this fashion. Instead, they adapted to rain or drought.

Adaptability. That was it. It became the theme of my novel. Suppose, I asked myself, I were to take a contemporary Navajo and by means of the time-dilation effects of space travel coupled with life extension treatments, I saw to it that he was still alive and in fairly good shape, say, one hundred seventy years from now? There would, of necessity, be gaps in his history during the time he was away, a period in which a lot of changes would have occurred here on Earth. That was how the idea for *Eye of Cat* came to me.

But an idea is not a science fiction novel. How do you turn it into one?

I asked myself why he would have been away so frequently. Suppose he'd been a really fine tracker and hunter? I wondered. Then he could have been a logical choice as a collector of alien-life specimens. That rang true, so I took it from there. A problem involving a nasty alien being could serve as a reason for bringing my Navajo character out of retirement and provide the basis for a conflict.

I also wanted something representing his past and the Navajo traditions, something more than just his wilderness abilities—some things he had turned his back on. Navajo legend provided me with the *chindi,* an evil spirit I could set to bedeviling him. It occurred to me then that this evil spirit could be made to correspond with some unusual creature he himself had brought to Earth a long time ago.

That was the rough idea. Though not a complete plot summary, this will show how the story took form, beginning with a simple observation and leading to the creation of a character and a situation. This small segment of the story would come under the heading of "inspiration"; most of the rest involved the application of reasoning to what the imagination had so far provided.

This required some tricky considerations. I firmly believe that I could write the same story—effectively—in dozens of different ways: as a comedy, as a tragedy, as something in between; from a minor character's point of view, in the first person, in the third, in a different tense, et cetera. But I also believe that for a particular piece of fiction, there is one way to proceed that is better than any of the others. I feel that the material should dictate the form. Making it do this properly is for me the most difficult and rewarding part of the storytelling act. It goes beyond all of the reflex tricks, into the area of aesthetics.

So I had to determine what approach would best produce the tone that I wished to achieve. This, of course, required clarifying my own feelings.

My protagonist, Billy Blackhorse Singer, though born into a near-neolithic environment, later received an advanced formal education. That alone was enough to create some conflicts within him. One may reject one's past or try to accommodate to it. Bill rejected quite a bit. He was a very capable man, but he was overwhelmed. I decided to give him an opportunity to come to terms with everything in his life.

I saw that this was going to be a novel of character. Showing a character as complex as Billy's would require some doing. His early life was involved with the myths, legends, shamanism of his people, and since this background was still a strong element in his character, I tried to show this by interspersing in the narrative my paraphrases of different sections of the Navajo creation myth and other appropriate legendary material. I decided to do some of this as poetry, some original, some only loosely based on traditional materials. This, I hoped, would give the book some flavor as well as help to shape my character.

The problem of injecting the futuristic background material was heightened, because I was already burdening the narrative with the intermittent doses of Indian material. I needed to find a way to encapsulate and abbreviate, so I stole a trick from Dos Passos's *U.S.A.* trilogy. I introduced "Disk" sections, analogous to his "Newsreel" and "Camera Eye" sequences—a few pages here and there made up of headlines, news reports, snatches of popular songs, to give the flavor of the times. This device served to get in a lot of background without slowing the pace, and its odd format was almost certain to be sufficiently interesting visually to arouse the reader's curiosity.

The evolving plot required the introduction of a half dozen secondary characters—and not just minor ones whom I might bring in as completely stock figures. Pausing to do full-scale portraits of each—by means of long flashbacks, say—could be fatal to the narrative, however, as they were scheduled to appear just as the story was picking up in pace. So I took a chance and broke a major writing rule.

Almost every book you read about writing will say, "Show. Don't tell." That is, you do not simply tell the reader what a character is like; you demonstrate it, because telling will generally produce a distancing effect and arouse a ho-hum response in the reader. There is little reader identification, little empathy created in merely telling about people.

I decided that not only was I going to tell the reader what each character was like, I was going to try to make it an interesting reading experience. In fact, I had to.

If you are going to break a rule, capitalize on it. Do it big. Exploit it. Turn it into a virtue.

I captioned a section with each character's name, followed the name with a comma and wrote one long, complex, character-describing sentence, breaking its various clauses and phrases into separate lines, so that it was strung out to give the appearance of a Whitmanesque piece of poetry. As with my "Disk" sections, I wanted to make this sufficiently interesting visually to pull the reader through what was, actually, straight exposition.

Another problem in the book arose when a number of telepaths used their unusual communicative abilities to form temporarily a composite or mass-mind. There were points at which I had to show this mind in operation. *Finnegans Wake* occurred to me as a good model for the stream of consciousness I wanted to use for this. And Anthony Burgess's *Joysprick,* which I'd recently read, had contained a section that could be taken as a primer for writing in this fashion. I followed.

Then, for purposes of achieving verisimilitude, I traveled through Canyon de Chelly with a Navajo guide. As I wrote the portions of the book set in the Canyon, I had before me, along with my memories, a map, my photographs, and archaeological descriptions of the route Billy followed. This use of realism, I hoped, would help to achieve some balance against the impressionism and radical story-telling techniques I had employed elsewhere.

These were some of the problems I faced in writing *Eye of Cat* and some of the solutions I used to deal with them. Thematically, though, many of the questions I asked myself and many of the ideas I considered were things that had been with me all along; only the technical solutions and the story's resolution were different this time. In this respect, I was, at one level, still plagiarizing my earlier self. Nothing wrong with that, if some growth has occurred in the meantime.

From everything I've said, it may sound as if the novel was wildly experimental. It wasn't. The general theme was timeless—a consideration of change and adjustment, of growth. While science fiction often deals with the future and bears exotic trappings, its real, deep considerations involve human nature, which has been the same for a long time and which, I believe, will continue much as it is for an even longer time. So in one sense we constantly seek new ways to say old things. But human nature is a generality. The individual does change, does adapt, and this applies to the writer as well as to the characters. And it is in these changes—in self-consciousness, perception, sensibility—that I feel the strongest, most valid stories have their source, whatever the devices most suitable for their telling.

THE BANDS OF TITAN

*I once accepted a guest of honorship for a convention in Toronto
and was later informed that one of the requirements was that
I write them a story for a booklet to be sold to raise money for
their favorite charity. This struck me as the equivalent of inviting
a painter to dinner and then asking him to paint your wall, in
a charitable spirit. I make my living this way, and my writing
time is also my income. Fortunately, I suppose, I had a short,
light idea about then. And very visual.*

I t was like a midnight rainbow—the sunside half of Saturn's rings as viewed from our position above the golden planet's pole. It also sort of reminded me of something else, but metaphors are not my forte and the rainbow had just exhausted my abilities along these lines for a time.

As the great grooved plate with its dark subdivisions rotated beneath our observation vessel and a black band swam through the northern hemisphere of the world below, I heard Sorensen say, above the eerie sounds from the receiver, "We've pinpointed the source now, sir."

I turned and regarded him—young, light-haired, enthusiastic—as he manipulated a paper accordian decorated with machine grafitti.

"Where is it located?" I asked him.

"Near to the inner edge of the C Ring," he stated, "and it's rather small."

"Hm," I observed. "Still no idea what it is, though?"

He shook his head.

"Nope."

There was a kind of strange asynchronous beat behind the wailing, stringy effect coming in over the receiver, and an occasional burst which sounded like a French horn being played in a cave. It was broadcast at an odd frequency, too. In fact, we'd only caught it accidentally, when a micrometeoroid striking an unmanned flyby had thrown the machine's receiver out of whack for a time. Later, we tuned for it. We'd been picking up the sequences for years since then and we were never able to correlate them with any natural phenomena in the vicinity. Running down their source, therefore, had been added to the already lengthy list of experiments and investigations to be conducted on this, the first manned visit to the area.

"McCarthy," I called to the navigator—a short, dark-haired, unenthusiastic man. "Find us an orbit that will take us close enough to this thing to get a good camera fix on it."

"Aye, aye, captain," he said, accepting the papers.

Later, as we jockeyed for the proper plane and accelerated toward the necessary velocity, Sorensen remarked, "Some sort of disturbance on Titan, sir."

"Storm? Ice volcano?" I asked.

"Hard to say," he answered. "I'm only picking it up on visuals. A strong focus of atmospheric turbulence."

I shrugged.

"Storm, probably. Check on it periodically. Let me know if it turns into anything really interesting."

It was the source of the sounds we were tracking which proved the next interesting item we encountered, however. I was dozing on my couch after checking the crew's alcohol rations for spoilage when McCarthy shook me awake.

"You'd better come and take a look at this, captain," he told me.

"What is it?" I mumbled.

"We seem to have located a genuine alien artifact," he said.

I got to my feet and crossed to the viewscreen, where I beheld the thing in full focus. I had no idea as to the scale, but it was a dark metallic satellite; it looked like two squat cones joined together at their bases. It hovered above the ring plane, and its nether vertex glowed with a brilliant light which flashed downward into the ring itself.

"What the hell do you make of it?" I asked him.

"I don't know," he answered. "It's in synchronous orbit—we're matching it now—and that's coherent light shining out of it. It is definitely the source of the broadcast."

I listened again to the sounds, which seemed to be rising to some sort of crescendo.

"Captain!" Sorensen called. "There's more activity on Titan. It's in the upper atmosphere now and—"

"Screw Titan!" I said. "Are you taping *this* thing?"

"Yes, but—"

"Are you monitoring everything that can be monitored concerning it?"

"Yes, sir."

"Good. We'll talk about Titan later. An alien artifact is infinitely more important than a methane storm."

"Very good, sir."

We watched for hours, and our diligence was rewarded by our witnessing a sudden peculiar maneuver on the part of the device. It was preceded by an abrupt cessation of all broadcast sounds. I had had the stuff pumped into the control room for days, hoping that immersion might stimulate some ideas as to its nature; also, it was not unpleasant in its rising and falling, its unexpected runs and glissandos. When it stopped, I was momentarily overwhelmed by the silence. My attention was quickly taken elsewhere, however, as the light beneath the satellite—which had now advanced itself within the orbit of the C Ring—was suddenly extinguished.

Simultaneous with our remarking upon this, the satellite shot upward—that is, it accelerated in a direction perpendicular to the ring plane.

"Keep a fix on it!" I shouted. "We can't let it get away!"

McCarthy and Sorensen rushed to comply.

Could we ourselves have triggered some damned warning device in it? I wondered.

"It's changing course, sir!" Sorensen yelled.

"Don't lose it, for God's sake!" I cried.

"It seems to be heading in-system," he said later.

"That's something, anyway," I replied. "Once you've established its course, plot one of our own to follow it."

"Right, captain. By the way, Titan—"

"Shove Titan! Follow that satellite!"

This proved less difficult than we had feared, for once the device had crossed the ring-system, it set itself into a new synchronous orbit just beyond the tenuous, braided F Ring. As we tracked and followed, I finally turned to Sorensen and said, "All right. What's the story on Titan?"

He smiled.

"Something in the nature of a large vessel rose above its atmosphere some time ago, sir," he told me. "It is even now headed inward toward Saturn's northern hemisphere."

"What?"

". . . Further," he continued, "it appears to be towing a large, flat, circular object of a metallic nature."

"You have a fix on it?"

"Oh, yes. I've been monitoring it, also—on the auxiliaries."

"Let's have a look."

He moved to a sidescreen and began typing at its keyboard.

"There's a particularly good sequence along about—here!" he said, as images swam by. He jabbed a key suddenly, and the blur settled into normal time. "There."

I saw the wedge-shaped ship above the streaked and mottled gold of the planet. Behind it was the enormous disk of which Sorensen had spoken, turning slowly. Several seconds later, the light fell upon it so as to reveal—

Sorensen's finger stabbed again and the picture froze.

There was an image on the disk. It was that of a gigantic four-eyed face, a pair of short antennae jutting from its high forehead.

I shook my head.

"What is it doing right now?" I asked him.

He switched from the tape to the vessel's real-time position, spiraling in, far nearer to the planet now.

We waited for a long while as it fitted itself into the proper orbit, achieved the altitude it apparently desired. We waited. It waited.

Much later McCarthy announced, "Something's happening!"

A fresh surge of adrenaline drove us near to the screen again. The disk had been disengaged from the ship, and as it drifted planetward, the vessel accelerated. Fascinated, we monitored its progress as the disk descended in such a fashion as to disappear entirely into the dark band we had noted earlier. The band narrowed and vanished shortly after that, and the vessel orbited the planet and later cut a course back toward Titan.

"Captain!" McCarthy said. "The artifact!"

"What about it?" I asked, moving to the screen which held its image.

But he did not reply, as I could see it for myself. The device had begun moving once again, crossing the F Ring. After a time it descended to hover above the outermost edge of the A Ring. With a bright flash the laser came on, focused downward into the groove. The one long-silent receiver still set for the thing's frequency came suddenly alive; its hookup to the ship's speaker system had not been broken when the satellite went silent. Abruptly now, the speakers brought us the wailing, the crashes, the blaring, the beat.

Later, when we sent a probe far beneath the murky skies of Titan near to the area from which the wedge-shaped vessel had come and to which it had returned, it sent back pictures: Beneath red clouds, through haze, on the shores of a methane sea, cyclopean figures swayed and spun; blizzards of fiery flakes fell like confetti about them.

MANA FROM HEAVEN

Here is a written-to-order story which appeared in The Magic
May Return, *the sort of sequel to* The Magic Goes Away, *by
Larry Niven. As with Fred Saberhagen and* Berserker Base,
*Larry opened up this particular universe and invited some of
us to come and party in it. I stepped in and began the dance.
Oddly, the story tried to run away from me. This doesn't happen
often, but I wanted a novelette, and it indicated that it wanted
to turn into a novel. I was firm. I won. The results follow.*

I felt nothing untoward that afternoon, whereas, I suppose, my senses should have been tingling. It was a balmy, sun-filled day with but the lightest of clouds above the ocean horizon. It might have lulled me within the not unpleasant variations of my routine. It was partly distraction, then, of my subliminal, superliminal perceptions, my early-warning system, whatever. . . . This, I suppose, abetted by the fact that there had been no danger for a long while, and that I was certain I was safely hidden. It was a lovely summer day.

There was a wide window at the rear of my office, affording an oblique view of the ocean. The usual clutter lay about—opened cartons oozing packing material, a variety of tools, heaps of rags, bottles of cleaning compounds and restoratives for various surfaces. And of course the acquisitions: Some of them still stood in crates and cartons; others held ragged rank upon my workbench, which ran the length of an entire wall—a row of ungainly chessmen awaiting my hand. The window was open and the fan purring so that the fumes from my chemicals could escape rapidly. Bird songs entered, and a sound of distant traffic, sometimes the wind.

My Styrofoam coffee cup rested unopened upon the small table beside the door, its contents long grown cold and unpalatable to any but an oral masochist. I had set it there that morning and forgotten it until my eyes chanced to light upon it. I had worked through coffee break and lunch, the day had been so rewarding. The really important part had been completed, though the rest of the museum staff would never notice. Time now to rest, to celebrate, to savor all I had found.

I raised the cup of cold coffee. Why not? A few words, a simple gesture . . .

I took a sip of the icy champagne. Wonderful.

I crossed to the telephone then, to call Elaine. This

day was worth a bigger celebration than the cup I held. Just as my hand was about to fall upon the instrument, however, the phone rang. Following the startle response, I raised the receiver.

"Hello," I said.

Nothing.

"Hello?"

Nothing again. No . . . Something.

Not some weirdo dialing at random either, as I am an extension. . . .

"Say it or get off the pot," I said.

The words came controlled, from back in the throat, slow, the voice unidentifiable:

"Phoenix—Phoenix—burning—bright," I heard.

"Why warn me, asshole?"

"Tag. You're—it."

The line went dead.

I pushed the button several times, roused the switchboard.

"Elsie," I asked, "the person who just called me—what were the exact words—"

"Huh?" she said. "I haven't put any calls through to you all day, Dave."

"Oh."

"You okay?"

"Short circuit or something," I said. "Thanks."

I cradled it and tossed off the rest of the champagne. It was no longer a pleasure, merely a housecleaning chore. I fingered the tektite pendant I wore, the roughness of my lava-stone belt buckle, the coral in my watchband. I opened my attaché case and replaced certain items I had been using. I removed a few, also, and dropped them into my pockets.

It didn't make sense, but I knew that it had been for real because of the first words spoken. I thought hard. I still had no answer, after all these years. But I knew that it meant danger. And I knew that it could take any form.

I snapped the case shut. At least it had happened today, rather than, say, yesterday. I was better prepared.

I closed the window and turned off the fan. I wondered whether I should head for my cache. Of course, that could be what someone expected me to do.

I walked up the hall and knocked on my boss's half-open door.

"Come in, Dave. What's up?" he asked.

Mike Thorley, in his late thirties, mustached, well dressed, smiling, put down a sheaf of papers and glanced at a dead pipe in a big ashtray.

"A small complication in my life," I told him. "Is it okay if I punch out early today?"

"Sure. Nothing too serious, I hope?"

I shrugged.

"I hope not, too. If it gets that way, though, I'll probably need a few days."

He moved his lips around a bit, then nodded.

"You'll call in?"

"Of course."

"It's just that I'd like all of that African stuff taken care of pretty soon."

"Right," I said. "Some nice pieces there."

He raised both hands.

"Okay. Do what you have to do."

"Thanks."

I started to turn away. Then, "One thing," I said.

"Yes?"

"Has anybody been asking about me—anything?"

He started to shake his head, then stopped.

"Unless you count that reporter," he said.

"What reporter?"

"The fellow who phoned the other day, doing a piece

on our new acquisitions. Your name came up, of course, and he had a few general questions—the usual stuff, like how long you've been with us, where you're from. You know."

"What was his name?"

"Wolfgang or Walford. Something like that."

"What paper?"

"The *Times*."

I nodded.

"Okay. Be seeing you."

"Take care."

I used the pay phone in the lobby to call the paper. No one working there named Wolfgang or Walford or something like that, of course. No article in the works either. I debated calling another paper, just in case Mike was mistaken, when I was distracted by a tap upon the shoulder. I must have turned too quickly, my expression something other than composed, for her smile faded and fear arced across her dark brows, slackened her jaw.

"Elaine!" I said. "You startled me. I didn't expect . . ."

The smile found its way back.

"You're awfully jumpy, Dave. What are you up to?"

"Checking on my dry cleaning," I said. "You're the last person—"

"I know. Nice of me, isn't it? It was such a beautiful day that I decided to knock off early and remind you we had a sort of date."

My mind spun even as I put my arms about her shoulders and turned her toward the door. How much danger might she be in if I spent a few hours with her in full daylight? I was about to go for something to eat anyway, and I could keep alert for observers. Also, her presence might lull anyone watching me into thinking that I had not taken the call seriously, that perhaps I was not the proper person after all. For that matter, I realized that I wanted some company just then. And if my sudden departure became necessary, I also wanted her company this one last time.

"Yes," I said. "Great idea. Let's take my car."

"Don't you have to sign out or something?"

"I already did. I had the same feeling you did about the day. I was going to call you after I got my cleaning."

"It's not ready yet," I added, and my mind kept turning.

A little trickle here, a little there. I did not feel that we were being observed.

"I know a good little restaurant about forty miles down the coast. Lots of atmosphere. Fine seafood," I said as we descended the front stairs. "And it should be a pleasant drive."

We headed for the museum's parking lot, around to the side.

"I've got a beach cottage near there too," I said.

"You never mentioned that."

"I hardly ever use it."

"Why not? It sounds wonderful."

"It's a little out of the way."

"Then why'd you buy it?"

"I inherited it," I said.

I paused about a hundred feet from my car and jammed a hand into my pocket.

"Watch," I told her.

The engine turned over, the car vibrated.

"How . . .?" she began.

"A little microwave gizmo. I can start it before I get to it."

"You afraid of a bomb?"

I shook my head.

"It has to warm up. You know how I like gadgets."

Of course I wanted to check out the possibility of a bomb. It was a natural reaction for one in my position. Fortunately, I had convinced her of my fondness for gadgets early in our acquaintanceship—to cover any such contingencies as this. Of course, too, there was no microwave gizmo in my pocket. Just some of the stuff.

We continued forward then; I unlocked the doors and we entered it.

I watched carefully as I drove. Nothing, no one, seemed to be trailing us. "Tag. You're it," though. A gambit. Was I supposed to bolt and run? Was I supposed to try to attack? If so, what? Who?

Was I going to bolt and run?

In the rear of my mind I saw that the bolt-and-run pattern had already started taking shape.

How long, how long, had this been going on? Years. Flight. A new identity. A long spell of almost normal existence. An attack. . . . Flee again. Settle again.

If only I had an idea as to which one of them it was, then I could attack. Not knowing, though, I had to avoid the company of all my fellows—the only ones who could give me clues.

"You look sicklied o'er with the pale cast of thought, Dave. It can't be your dry cleaning, can it?"

I smiled at her.

"Just business," I said. "All of the things I wanted to get away from. Thanks for reminding me."

I switched on the radio and found some music. Once we got out of city traffic, I began to relax. When we reached the coast road and it thinned even further, it became obvious that we were not being followed. We climbed for a time, then descended. My palms tingled as I spotted the pocket of fog at the bottom of the next dip. Exhilarated, I drank its essence. Then I began talking about the African pieces, in their mundane aspects. We branched off from there. For a time, I forgot my problem. This lasted for perhaps twenty minutes, until the news broadcast. By then I was projecting goodwill, charm, warmth, and kind feelings. I could see that Elaine had begun enjoying herself. There was feedback. I felt even better. There—

". . . new eruptions which began this morning," came over the speaker. "The sudden activity on the part of El Chinchonal spurred immediate evacuation of the area about—"

I reached over and turned up the volume, stopping in the middle of my story about hiking in the Alps.

"What—?" she said.

I raised a finger to my lips.

"The volcano," I explained.

"What of it?"

"They fascinate me," I said.

"Oh."

As I memorized all of the facts about the eruption, I began to build feelings concerning my situation. My having received the call today had been a matter of timing. . . .

"There were some good pictures of it on the tube this morning," she said as the newsbrief ended.

"I wasn't watching. But I've seen it do it before, when I was down there."

"You visit volcanos?"

"When they're active, yes."

"Here you have this really oddball hobby and you've never mentioned it," she observed. "How many active volcanos have you visited?"

"Most of them," I said, no longer listening, the lines of the challenge becoming visible—the first time it had ever been put on this basis. I realized in that instant that this time I was not going to run.

"Most of them?" she said. "I read somewhere that

there are hundreds, some of them in really out-of-the-way places. Like Erebus—"

"I've been in Erebus," I said, "back when—" And then I realized what I was saying. "—back in some dream," I finished. "Little joke there."

I laughed, but she only smiled a bit.

It didn't matter, though. She couldn't hurt me. Very few mundanes could. I was just about finished with her anyway. After tonight I would forget her. We would never meet again. I am by nature polite, though; it is a thing I value above sentiment. I would not hurt her either: It might be easiest simply to make her forget.

"Seriously, I do find certain aspects of geophysics fascinating."

"I've been an amateur astronomer for some time," she volunteered. "I can understand."

"Really? Astronomy? You never told me."

"Well?" she said.

I began to work it out, small talk flowing reflexively. After we parted tonight or tomorrow morning, I would leave. I would go to Villahermosa. My enemy would be waiting—of this I felt certain. "Tag. You're it." "This is your chance. Come and get me if you're not afraid."

Of course, I was afraid.

But I'd run for too long. I would have to go, to settle this for good. Who knew when I'd have another opportunity? I had reached the point where it was worth any risk to find out who it was, to have a chance to retaliate. I would take care of all the preliminaries later, at the cottage, after she was asleep. Yes.

"You've got beach?" she asked.

"Yes."

"How isolated?"

"Very. Why?"

"It would be nice to swim before dinner."

So we stopped by the restaurant, made reservations for later, and went off and did that. The water was fine.

The day turned into a fine evening. I'd gotten us my favorite table, on the patio, out back, sequestered by colorful shrubbery, touched by flower scents, in the view of mountains. The breezes came just right. So did the lobster and champagne. Within the restaurant, a pleasant music stirred softly. During coffee, I found her hand beneath my own. I smiled. She smiled back.

Then, "How'd you do it, Dave?" she asked.

"What?"

"Hypnotize me."

"Native charm, I guess," I replied, laughing.

"That is not what I mean."

"What, then?" I said, all chuckles fled.

"You haven't even noticed that I'm not smoking anymore."

"Hey, you're right! Congratulations. How long's it been?"

"A couple of weeks," she replied. "I've been seeing a hypnotist."

"Oh, really?"

"Mm-hm. I was such a docile subject that he couldn't believe I'd never been under before. So he poked around a little, and he came up with a description of you, telling me to forget something."

"Really?"

"Yes, really. You want to know what I remember now that I didn't before?"

"Tell me."

"An almost-accident, late one night, about a month ago. The other car didn't even slow down for the stop sign. Yours levitated. Then I remember us parked by the side of the road, and you were telling me to forget. I did."

I snorted.

"Any hypnotist with much experience will tell you that a trance state is no guarantee against fantasy—and a hallucination recalled under hypnosis seems just as real the second time around. Either way—"

"I remember the *ping* as the car's antenna struck your right rear fender and snapped off."

"They can be vivid fantasies too."

"I looked, Dave. The mark is there on the fender. It looks just as if someone had swatted it with an antenna."

Damn! I'd meant to get that filled in and touched up. Hadn't gotten around to it, though.

"I got that in a parking lot," I said.

"Come on, Dave."

Should I put her under now and make her forget having remembered? I wondered. Maybe that would be easiest.

"I don't care," she said then. "Look, I really don't care. Strange things sometimes happen. If you're connected with some of them, that's okay. What bothers me is that it means you don't trust me . . . "

Trust? That is something that positions you as a target. Like Proteus, when Amazon and Priest got finished with him. Not that he didn't have it coming. . . .

" . . . and I've trusted you for a long time."

I removed my hand from hers. I took a drink of coffee. Not here. I'd give her mind a little twist later. Implant something to make her stay away from hypnotists in the future too.

"Okay," I said. "I guess you're right. But it's a long story. I'll tell you after we get back to the cottage."

Her hand found my own, and I met her eyes.

"Thanks," she said.

We drove back beneath a moonless sky clotted with stars. It was an unpaved road, dipping, rising, twisting amid heavy shrubbery. Insect noises came in through our open windows, along with the salt smell of the sea. For a moment, just for a moment, I thought that I felt a strange tingling, but it could have been the night and the champagne. And it did not come again.

Later, we pulled up in front of the place, parked, and got out. Silently, I deactivated my invisible warden. We advanced, I unlocked the door, I turned on the light.

"You never have any trouble here, huh?" she asked.

"What do you mean?"

"People breaking in, messing the place up, ripping you off?"

"No," I answered.

"Why not?"

"Lucky, I guess."

"Really?"

"Well . . . it's protected, in a very special way. That's a part of the story too. Wait till I get some coffee going."

I went out to the kitchen, rinsed out the pot, put things together, and set it over a flame. I moved to open a window, to catch a little breeze.

Suddenly, my shadow was intense upon the wall.

I spun about.

The flame had departed the stove, hovered in the air and begun to grow. Elaine screamed just as I turned, and the thing swelled to fill the room. I saw that it bore the shifting features of a fire elemental, just before it burst apart to swirl tornadolike through the cottage. In a moment, the place was blazing and I heard its crackling laughter.

"Elaine!" I called, rushing forward, for I had seen her transformed into a torch.

All of the objects in my pockets plus my belt buckle, I calculated quickly, probably represented a sufficient accumulation of power to banish the thing. Of course the energies were invested, tied up, waiting to be used in different ways. I spoke the words that would rape the power-objects and free the forces. Then I performed the banishment.

The flames were gone in an instant. But not the smoke, not the smell.

. . . And Elaine lay there sobbing, clothing and flesh charred, limbs jerking convulsively. All of her exposed areas were dark and scaly, and blood was beginning to ooze from the cracks in her flesh.

I cursed as I reset the warden. I had created it to protect the place in my absence. I had never bothered to use it once I was inside. I should have.

Whoever had done this was still probably near. My cache was located in a vault about twenty feet beneath the cottage—near enough for me to use a number of the power things without even going after them. I could draw out their mana as I just had with those about my person. I could use it against my enemy. Yes. This was the chance I had been waiting for.

I rushed to my attaché case and opened it. I would need power to reach the power and manipulate it. And the mana from the artifacts I had drained was tied up in my own devices. I reached for the rod and the sphere. At last, my enemy, you've had it! You should have known better than to attack me here!

Elaine moaned. . . .

I cursed myself for a weakling. If my enemy were testing me to see whether I had grown soft, he would have his answer in the affirmative. She was no stranger, and she had said that she trusted me. I had to do it. I began the spell that would drain most of my power-objects to work her healing.

It took most of an hour. I put her to sleep. I stopped the bleeding. I watched new tissues form. I bathed her and dressed her in a sport shirt and rolled-up pair of slacks from the bedroom closet, a place the flames had not reached. I left her sleeping a little longer then while I cleaned up, opened the windows and got on with making the coffee.

At last, I stood beside the old chair—now covered with a blanket—into which I had placed her. If I had just done something decent and noble, why did I feel so stupid about it? Probably because it was out of character. I was reassured, at least, that I had not been totally corrupted to virtue by reason of my feeling resentment at having to use all of that mana on her behalf.

Well . . . Put a good face on it now the deed was done.

How?

Good question. I could proceed to erase her memories of the event and implant some substitute story—a gas leak, perhaps—as to what had occurred, along with the suggestion that she accept it. I could do that. Probably the easiest course for me.

My resentment suddenly faded, to be replaced by something else, as I realized that I did not want to do it that way. What I did want was an end to my loneliness. She trusted me. I felt that I could trust her. I wanted someone I could really talk with.

When she opened her eyes, I put a cup of coffee into her hands.

"Cheerio," I said.

She stared at me, then turned her head slowly and regarded the still-visible ravages about the room. Her hands began to shake. But she put the cup down herself, on the small side table, rather than letting me take it back. She examined her hands and arms. She felt her face.

"You're all right," I said.

"How?" she asked.

"That's the story," I said. "You've got it coming."

"What was that thing?"

"That's a part of it."

"Okay," she said then, raising the cup more steadily and taking a sip. "Let's hear it."

"Well, I'm a sorcerer," I said, "a direct descendant of the ancient sorcerers of Atlantis."

I paused. I waited for the sigh or the rejoinder. There was none.

"I learned the business from my parents," I went on, "a long time ago. The basis of the whole thing is mana, a kind of energy found in various things and places. Once the world was lousy with it. It was the basis of an entire culture. But it was like other natural resources. One day it ran out. Then the magic went away. Most of it. Atlantis sank. The creatures of magic faded, died. The structure of the world itself was altered, causing it to appear much older than it really is. The old gods passed. The sorcerers, the ones who manipulated the mana to produce magic, were pretty much out of business. There followed the real dark ages, before the beginnings of civilization as we know it from the history books."

"This mighty civilization left no record of itself?" she asked.

"With the passing of the magic, there were transformations. The record was rewritten into natural-seeming stone and fossil-bed, was dissipated, underwent a sea change."

"Granting all that for a moment," she said, sipping the coffee, "if the power is gone, if there's nothing left to do it with, how can you be a sorcerer?"

"Well, it's not *all* gone," I said. "There are small surviving sources, there are some new sources, and—"

"—and you fight over them? Those of you who remain?"

"No . . . not exactly," I said. "You see, there are not that many of us. We intentionally keep our numbers small, so that no one goes hungry."

" 'Hungry'?"

"A figure of speech we use. Meaning to get enough mana to keep body and soul together, to stave off aging, keep healthy and enjoy the good things."

"You can rejuvenate yourselves with it? How old are you?"

"Don't ask embarrassing questions. If my spells ran out and there was no more mana, I'd go fast. But we can trap the stuff, lock it up, hold it, whenever we come across a power-source. It can be stored in certain objects—or, better yet, tied up in partial spells, like dialing all but the final digit in a phone number. The spells that maintain one's existence always get primary consideration."

She smiled.

"You must have used a lot of it on me."

I looked away.

"Yes," I said.

"So you couldn't just drop out and be a normal person and continue to live?"

"No."

"So what was that thing?" she asked. "What happened here?"

"An enemy attacked me. We survived."

She took a big gulp of the coffee and leaned back and closed her eyes.

Then, "Will it happen again?" she asked.

"Probably. If I let it."

"What do you mean?"

"This was more of a challenge than an all-out attack. My enemy is finally getting tired of playing games and wants to finish things off."

"And you are going to accept the challenge?"

"I have no choice. Unless you'd consider waiting around for something like this to happen again, with more finality."

She shuddered slightly.

"I'm sorry," I said.

"I've a feeling I may be too," she stated, finishing her coffee and rising, crossing to the window, looking out, "before this is over.

"What do we do next?" she asked, turning and staring at me.

"I'm going to take you to a safe place and go away," I said, "for a time." It seemed a decent thing to add those last words, though I doubted I would ever see her again.

"The hell you are," she said.

"Huh? What do you mean? You want to be safe, don't you?"

"If your enemy thinks I mean something to you, I'm vulnerable—the way I see it," she told me.

"Maybe . . . "

The answer, of course, was to put her into a week-long trance and secure her down in the vault, with strong wards and the door openable from the inside. Since my magic had not all gone away, I raised one hand and sought her eyes with my own.

What tipped her off, I'm not certain. She looked away, though, and suddenly lunged for the bookcase. When she turned again, she held an old bone flute that had long lain there.

I restrained myself in mid-mutter. It was a power-object that she held, one of several lying about the room, and one of the few that had not been drained during my recent workings. I couldn't really think of much that a nonsorcerer could do with it, but my curiosity restrained me.

"What are you doing?" I asked.

"I'm not sure," she said. "But I'm not going to let you put me away with one of your spells."

"Who said anything about doing that?"

"I can tell."

"How?"

"Just a feeling."

"Well, damn it, you're right. We've been together too long. You can psych me. Okay, put it down and I won't do anything to you."

"Is that a promise, Dave?"

"Yeah. I guess it is."

"I suppose you could rat on it and erase my memory."

"I keep my promises."

"Okay." She put it back on the shelf. "What are we going to do now?"

"I'd still like to put you someplace safe."

"No way."

I sighed.

"I have to go where that volcano is blowing."

"Buy two tickets," she said.

It wasn't really necessary. I have my own plane and I'm licensed to fly the thing. In fact, I have several located in different parts of the world. Boats, too.

"There is mana in clouds and in fogbanks," I explained to her. "In a real pinch, I use my vehicles to go chasing after them."

We moved slowly through the clouds. I had detoured a good distance, but it was necessary. Even after we had driven up to my apartment and collected everything I'd had on hand, I was still too mana-impoverished for the necessary initial shielding and a few strikes. I needed to collect a little more for this. After that it wouldn't matter, the way I saw things. My enemy and I would be plugged into the same source. All we had to do was reach it.

So I circled in the fog for a long while, collecting. It was a protection spell into which I concentrated the mana.

"What happens when it's all gone?" she asked, as I banked and climbed for a final pass before continuing to the southeast.

"What?" I said.

"The mana. Will you all fade away?"

I chuckled.

"It can't," I said. "Not with so few of us using it. How many tons of meteoric material do you think have fallen to earth today? They raise the background level almost imperceptibly—constantly. And much of it falls into the oceans. The beaches are thereby enriched. That's why I like to be near the sea. Mist-shrouded mountaintops gradually accumulate it. They're good places for collecting too. And new clouds are always forming. Our grand plan is more than simple survival. We're waiting for the day when it reaches a level where it will react and establish fields over large areas. Then we won't have to rely on accumulators and partial spells for its containment. The magic will be available everywhere again."

"Then you will exhaust it all and be back where you started again."

"Maybe," I said. "If we've learned nothing, that may be the case. We'll enter a new golden age, become dependent upon it, forget our other skills, exhaust it again and head for another dark age. Unless . . . "

"Unless what?"

"Unless those of us who have been living with it have also learned something. We'd need to figure the rate of mana exhaustion and budget ourselves. We'd need to preserve technology for things on which mana had been used the last time around. Our experience in this century with physical resources may be useful. Also, there is the hope that some areas of space may be richer in cosmic dust or possess some other factor that will increase the accumulation. Then, too, we are waiting for the full development of the space program—to reach other worlds rich in what we need."

"Sounds as if you have it all worked out."

"We've had a lot of time to think about it."

"But what would be your relationship with those of us who are not versed in magic?"

"Beneficent. We all stand to benefit that way."

"Are you speaking for yourself or for the lot of you?"

"Well, most of the others must feel the same way. I just want to putter around museums. . . . "

"You said that you had been out of touch with the others for some time."

"Yes, but—"

She shook her head and turned to look out at the fog.

"Something else to worry about," she said.

I couldn't get a landing clearance, so I just found a flat place and put it down and left it. I could deal later with any problems this caused.

I unstowed our gear; we hefted it and began walking toward that ragged, smoky quarter of the horizon.

"We'll never reach it on foot," she said.

"You're right," I answered. "I wasn't planning to, though. When the time is right, something else will present itself."

"What do you mean?"

"Wait and see."

We hiked for several miles, encountering no one. The way was warm and dusty, with occasional tremors of the earth. Shortly, I felt the rush of mana, and I drew upon it.

"Take my hand," I said.

I spoke the words necessary to levitate us a few feet above the rocky terrain. We glided forward then, and the power about us increased as we advanced upon our goal. I worked with more of it, spelling to increase our pace, to work protective shields around us, guarding us from the heat, from flying debris.

The sky grew darker, from ash, from smoke, long before we commenced the ascent. The rise was gradual at first but steepened steadily as we raced onward. I worked a variety of partial spells, offensive and defensive, tying up quantities of mana just a word, just a fingertip gesture away.

"Reach out, reach out and touch someone," I hummed as the visible world came and went with the passage of roiling clouds.

We sped into a belt where we would probably have been asphyxiated but for the shield. The noises had grown louder by then. It must have been pretty hot out there too. When we finally reached the rim, dark shapes fled upward past us and lightning stalked the clouds. Forward and below, a glowing, seething mass shifted constantly amid explosions.

"All right!" I shouted. "I'm going to charge up everything I brought with me and tie up some more mana in a whole library of spells! Make yourself comfortable!"

"Yeah," she said, licking her lips and staring downward. "I'll do that. But what about your enemy?"

"Haven't seen anybody so far—and there's too much free mana around for me to pick up vibes. I'm going to keep an eye peeled and take advantage of the situation. You watch too."

"Right," she said. "This is perfectly safe, huh?"

"As safe as L.A. traffic."

"Great. Real comforting," she observed as a huge rocky mass flew past us.

We separated later. I left her within her own protective spell, leaning against a craggy prominence, and I moved off to the right to perform a ritual that required greater freedom of movement.

Then a shower of sparks rose into the air before me. Nothing especially untoward about that, until I realized that it was hovering for an unusually long while. After a time, it seemed that it should have begun dispersing. . . .

"Phoenix, Phoenix, burning bright!" The words boomed about me, rising above the noises of the inferno itself.

"Who calls me?" I asked.

"Who has the strongest reason to do you harm?"

"If I knew that, I wouldn't ask."

"Then seek the answer in hell!"

A wall of flame rushed toward me. I spoke the words that strengthened my shield. Even so, I was rocked within my protective bubble when it hit. Striking back was going to be tricky, I could see, with my enemy in a less-than-material form.

"All right, to the death!" I cried, calling for a lightning stroke through the space where the sparks spun.

I turned away and covered my eyes against the brilliance, but I still felt its presence through my skin.

My bubble of forces continued to rock as I blinked and looked forward. The air before me had momentarily cleared, but everything seemed somehow darker, and—

A being—a crudely man-shaped form of semisolid lava—had wrapped its arms as far as they would go about me and was squeezing. My spell held, but I was raised above the crater's rim.

"It won't work!" I said, trying to dissolve the being.

"The hell you say!" came a voice from high overhead.

I learned quickly that the lava-thing was protected against the simple workings I threw at it. All right, then hurl me down. I would levitate out. The Phoenix would rise again. I—

I passed over the rim and was falling. But there was a problem. A heavy one.

The molten creature was clinging to my force-bubble. Magic is magic and science is science, but there are correspondences. The more mass you want to move, the more mana you have to expend. So, taken off guard, I was dropping into the fiery pit despite a levitation spell that would have borne me on high in a less encumbered state. I immediately began a spell to provide me with additional buoyancy.

But when I had finished, I saw that something was countering me—another spell, a spell that kept increasing the mass of my creature-burden by absorption as we fell. Save for an area between my feet through which I saw the roiling lake of fire, I was enclosed by the flowing mass of the thing. I could think of only one possible escape, and I didn't know whether I had time for it.

I began the spell that would transform me into a spark-filled vortex similar to that my confronter had worn. When I achieved it, I released my protective spell and flowed.

Out through the nether opening then, so close to that bubbling surface I would have panicked had not my mind itself been altered by the transformation, into something static and poised.

Skimming the heat-distorted surface of the lava, I swarmed past the heavily weighted being of animated rock and was already rising at a rapid rate, buffeted, borne aloft by heat waves, when it hit a rising swell and was gone. I added my own energy to the rising and fled upward, through alleys of smoke and steam, past flashes of lava bullets.

I laid the bird-shape upon my glowing swirls, I sucked in mana, I issued a long, drawn-out rising scream. I spread my wings along expanding lines of energy, seeking my swirling adversary as I reached the rim.

Nothing. I darted back and forth, I circled. He/she/ it was nowhere in sight.

"I am here!" I cried. "Face me now!"

But there was no reply, save for the catastrophe beneath me from which fresh explosions issued.

"Come!" I cried. "I am waiting!"

So I sought Elaine, but she was not where I had left her. My enemy had either destroyed her or taken her away.

I cursed then like thunder and spun myself into a large vortex, a rising tower of lights. I drove myself upward then, leaving the earth and that burning pimple far beneath me.

For how long I rode the jet streams, raging, I cannot say. I know that I circled the world several times before any semblance of rational thinking returned to me, before I calmed sufficiently to formulate anything resembling a plan.

It was obviously one of my fellows who had tried to kill me, who had taken Elaine from me. I had avoided contact with my own kind for too long. Now I knew that I must seek them out, whatever the risk, to obtain the knowledge I needed for self-preservation, for revenge.

I began my downward drift as I neared the Middle East. Arabia. Yes. Oil fields, places of rich, expensive pollutants, gushing mana-filled from the earth. Home of the one called Dervish.

Retaining my Phoenix-form, I fled from field to field, beelike, tasting, using the power to reinforce the spell under which I was operating. Seeking . . .

For three days I sought, sweeping across bleak landscapes, visiting field after field. It was like a series of smorgasbords. It would be so easy to use the mana to transform the countryside. But of course that would be a giveaway, in many respects.

Then, gliding in low over shimmering sands as evening mounted in the East, I realized that this was the one I was seeking. There was no physical distinction to the oil field I approached and then cruised. But it stood in the realm of my sensitivity as if a sign had been posted. The mana level was much lower than at any of the others I had scanned. And where this was the case, one of us had to be operating.

I spread myself into even more tenuous patterns. I sought altitude. I began circling.

Yes, there was a pattern. It became clearer as I studied the area. The low-mana section described a rough circle near the northwest corner of the field, its center near a range of hills.

He could be working in some official capacity there at the field. If so, his duties would be minimal and the job would be a cover. He always had been pretty lazy.

I spiraled in and dropped toward the center of the circle as toward the eye of a target. As I rushed to it, I became aware of the small, crumbling adobe structure that occupied that area, blending almost perfectly with its surroundings. A maintenance or storage house, a watchman's quarters. . . . It did not matter what it seemed to be. I knew what it had to be.

I dived to a landing before it. I reversed my spell, taking on human form once again. I pushed open the weather-worn, unlatched door and walked inside.

The place was empty, save for a few sticks of beaten furniture and a lot of dust. I swore softly. This had to be it.

I walked slowly about the room, looking for some clue.

It was nothing that I saw, or even felt, at first. It was memory—of an obscure variant of an old spell, and of Dervish's character—that led me to turn and step back outside.

I closed the door. I felt around for the proper words. It was hard to remember exactly how this one would go. Finally, they came flowing forth and I could feel them falling into place, mortise and tenon, key and lock. Yes, there was a response. The subtle back-pressure was there. I had been right.

When I had finished, I knew that things were different. I reached toward the door, then hesitated. I had probably tripped some alarm. Best to have a couple of spells at my fingertips, awaiting merely guide-words. I muttered them into readiness, then opened the door.

A marble stairway as wide as the building itself led downward, creamy jewels gleaming like hundred-watt bulbs high at either hand.

I moved forward, began the descent. Odors of jasmine, saffron, and sandalwood came to me. As I continued, I heard the sounds of stringed instruments and a flute in the distance. By then I could see part of a tiled floor below and ahead—and a portion of an elaborate design upon it. I laid a spell of invisibility over myself and kept going.

Before I reached the bottom, I saw him, across the long, pillared hall.

He was at the far end, reclined in a nest of cushions and bright patterned rugs. An elaborate repast was spread before him. A narghile bubbled at his side. A young woman was doing a belly dance nearby.

I halted at the foot of the stair and studied the layout. Archways to both the right and the left appeared to lead off to other chambers. Behind him was a pair of wide windows, looking upon high mountain pcaks beneath very blue skies—representing either a very good illusion or the expenditure of a lot of mana on a powerful space-bridging spell. Of course, he had a lot of mana to play around with. Still, it seemed kind of wasteful.

I studied the man himself. His appearance was pretty much unchanged—sharp-featured, dark-skinned, tall, husky running to fat.

I advanced slowly, the keys to half a dozen spells ready for utterance or gesture.

When I was about thirty feet away, he stirred uneasily. Then he kept glancing in my direction. His power-sense was still apparently in good shape.

So I spoke two words, one of which put a less-than-material but very potent magical dart into my hand, the other casting aside my veil of invisibility.

"Phoenix!" he exclaimed, sitting upright and staring. "I thought you were dead!"

I smiled.

"How recently did that thought pass through your mind?" I asked him.

"I'm afraid I don't understand. . . . "

"One of us just tried to kill me, down in Mexico."

He shook his head.

"I haven't been in that part of the world for some time."

"Prove it," I said.

"I can't," he replied. "You know that my people here would say whatever I want them to—so that's no help. I didn't do it, but I can't think of any way to prove it. That's the trouble with trying to demonstrate a negative. Why do you suspect me, anyway?"

I sighed.

"That's just it. I don't—or, rather, I have to suspect everyone. I just chose you at random. I'm going down the list."

"Then at least I have statistics on my side."

"I suppose you're right, damn it."

He rose, turned his palms upward.

"We've never been particularly close," he said. "But then, we've never been enemies either. I have no reason at all for wishing you harm."

He eyed the dart in my hand. He raised his right hand, still holding a bottle.

"So you intend to do us all in by way of insurance?"

160

"No, I was hoping that you would attack me and thereby prove your guilt. It would have made life easier."

I sent the dart away as a sign of good faith.

"I believe you," I said.

He leaned and placed the bottle he held upon a cushion.

"Had you slain me, that bottle would have fallen and broken," he said. "Or perhaps I could have beaten you on an attack and drawn the cork. It contains an attack djinn."

"Neat trick."

"Come join me for dinner," he suggested. "I want to hear your story. One who would attack you for no reason might well attack me one day."

"All right," I said.

The dancer had been dismissed. The meal was finished. We sipped coffee. I had spoken without interruption for nearly an hour. I was tired, but I had a spell for that.

"More than a little strange," he said at length. "And you have no recollection, from back when all of this started, of having hurt, insulted or cheated any of the others?"

"No."

I sipped my coffee.

"So it could be any of them," I said after a time. "Priest, Amazon, Gnome, Siren, Werewolf, Lamia, Lady, Sprite, Cowboy . . . "

"Well, scratch Lamia," he said. "I believe she's dead."

"How?"

He shrugged, looked away.

"Not sure," he said slowly. Then, "Well, the talk at first was that you and she had run off together. Then, later, it seemed to be that you'd died together . . . somehow."

"Lamia and me? That's silly. There was never anything between us."

He nodded.

"Then it looks now as if something simply happened to her."

"Talk . . ." I said. "Who was doing the talking?"

"You know. Stories just get started. You never know exactly where they come from."

"Where'd you first hear it?"

He lowered his eyelids, stared off into the distance.

"Gnome. Yes. It was Gnome mentioned the matter to me at Starfall that year."

"Did he say where he'd heard it?"

"Not that I can recall."

"Okay," I said. "I guess I'll have to go talk to Gnome. He still in South Africa?"

He shook his head, refilled my cup from the tall, elegantly incised pot.

"Cornwall," he said. "Still a lot of juice down those old shafts."

I shuddered slightly.

"He can have it. I get claustrophobia just thinking about it. But if he can tell me who—"

"There is no enemy like a former friend," Dervish said. "If you dropped your friends as well as everyone else when you went into hiding, it means you've already considered that. . . . "

"Yes, as much as I disliked the notion. I rationalized it by saying that I didn't want to expose them to danger, but—"

"Exactly."

"Cowboy and Werewolf were buddies of mine. . . ."

". . . And you had a thing going with Siren for a long while, didn't you?"

"Yes, but—"

"A woman scorned?"

"Hardly. We parted amicably."

He shook his head and raised his cup.

"I've exhausted my thinking on the matter."

We finished our coffee. I rose then.

"Well, thanks. I guess I'd better be going. Glad I came to you first."

He raised the bottle.

"Want to take the djinn along?"

"I don't even know how to use one."

"The commands are simple. All the work's already been done."

"Okay. Why not?"

He instructed me briefly, and I took my leave. Soaring above the great oil field, I looked back upon the tiny, ruined building. Then I moved my wings and rose to suck the juice from a cloud before turning west.

Starfall, I mused, as earth and water unrolled like a scroll beneath me. Starfall—the big August meteor shower accompanied by the wave of mana called Starwind, the one time of year we all got together. Yes, that was when gossip was exchanged. It had been only a week after a Starfall that I had first been attacked, almost slain, had gone to ground. . . . By the following year the stories were circulating. Had it been something at that earlier Starfall— something I had said or done to someone—that had made me an enemy with that finality of purpose, that quickness of retaliation?

I tried hard to recall what had occurred at that last Starfall I had attended. It had been the heaviest rush of Starwind in memory. I remembered that. "Mana from heaven," Priest had joked. Everyone had been in a good mood. We had talked shop, swapped a few spells, wondered ·what the heightened Starwind portended, argued politics— all of the usual things. That business Elaine talked about had come up. . . .

Elaine. . . . Alive now? I wondered. Someone's prisoner? Someone's insurance in case I did exactly what I was doing? Or were her ashes long since scattered about the globe? Either way, someone would pay.

I voiced my shrill cry against the rushing winds. It was fled in an instant, echoless. I caught up with the night, passed into its canyons. The stars came on again, grew bright.

The detailed instructions Dervish had given me proved exactly accurate. There was a mineshaft at the point he had indicated on a map hastily sketched in fiery lines upon the floor. There was no way I would enter the thing in human form, though. A version of my Phoenix-aspect would at least defend me against claustrophobia. I cannot feel completely pent when I am not totally material.

Shrinking, shrinking, as I descended. I called in my tenuous wings and tail, gaining solidity as I grew smaller. Then I bled off mass-energy, retaining my new dimensions, growing ethereal again.

Like a ghost-bird, I entered the adit, dropping, dropping. The place was dead. There was no mana anywhere about me. This, of course, was to be expected. The upper levels would have been the first to be exhausted.

I continued to drop into dampness and darkness for a long while before I felt the first faint touch of the power. It increased only slowly as I moved, but it did begin to rise.

Finally, it began to fall off again and I retraced my route. Yes, that side passage . . . its source. I entered and followed.

As I worked my way farther and farther, back and down, it continued to increase in intensity. I wondered briefly whether I should be seeking the weaker area or the stronger. But this was not the same sort of setup as Dervish enjoyed. Dervish's power-source was renewable, so he could remain stationary. Gnome would have to move on once he had exhausted a local mana supply.

I spun around a corner into a side tunnel and was halted. Frozen. Damn.

It was a web of forces holding me like a butterfly. I ceased struggling almost immediately, seeing that it was fruitless in this aspect.

I transformed myself back into human form. But the damned web merely shifted to accommodate the alteration and continued to hold me tightly.

I tried a fire spell, to no avail. I tried sucking the mana loose from the web's own spell, but all I got was a headache. It's a dangerous measure, only effective against sloppy workmanship—and then you get hit with a backlash of forces when it comes loose. The spell held perfectly against my effort, however. I had had to try it, though, because I was feeling desperate, with a touch of claustrophobia tossed in. Also, I thought I'd heard a stone rattle farther up the tunnel.

Next I heard a chuckle, and I recognized the voice as Gnome's.

Then a light rounded a corner, followed by a vaguely human form.

The light drifted in front of him and just off to his left—a globe, casting an orange illumination—touching his hunched, twisted shape with a flamelike glow as he limped toward me. He chuckled again.

"Looks as if I've snared a Phoenix," he finally said.

"Very funny. How about unsnaring me now?" I asked.

"Of course, of course," he muttered, already beginning to gesture.

The trap fell apart. I stepped forward.

"I've been asking around," I told him. "What's this story about Lamia and me?"

He continued his gesturing. I was about to invoke an

assault or shielding spell when he stopped, though. I felt none the worse and I assumed it was a final cleanup of his web.

"Lamia? You?" he said. "Oh. Yes. I'd heard you'd run off together. Yes. That was it."

"Where'd you hear it?"

He fixed me with his large, pale eyes.

"Where'd you hear it?" I repeated.

"I don't remember."

"Try."

"Sorry."

" 'Sorry' hell!" I said, taking a step forward. "Somebody's been trying to kill me and—"

He spoke the word that froze me in mid-step. Good spell, that.

"—and he's been regrettably inept," Gnome finished.

"Let me go, damn it!" I said.

"You came into my home and assaulted me."

"Okay, I apologize. Now—"

"Come this way."

He turned his back on me and began walking. Against my will, my body made the necessary movements. I followed.

I opened my mouth to speak a spell of my own. No words came out. I wanted to make a gesture. I was unable to begin it.

"Where are you taking me?" I tried.

The words came perfectly clear. But he didn't bother answering me for a time. The light moved over glistening seams of some metallic material within the sweating walls.

Then, "To a waiting place," he finally said, turning into a corridor to the right, where we splashed through puddles for a time.

"Why?" I asked him. "What are we waiting for?"

He chuckled again. The light danced. He did not reply.

We walked for several minutes. I began finding the thought of all those tons of rock and earth above me very oppressive. A trapped feeling came over me. But I could not even panic properly within the confines of that spell. I began to perspire profusely, despite a cooling draft from ahead.

Then Gnome turned suddenly and was gone, sidling into a narrow cleft I would not even have noticed had I been coming this way alone.

"Come," I heard him say.

My feet followed the light, moved to drift between us here. Automatically, I turned my body. I sidled after him for a good distance before the way widened. The ground dropped roughly, abruptly, and the walls retracted and the light shot on ahead, gaining altitude.

Gnome raised a broad hand and halted me. We were in a small, irregularly shaped chamber—natural, I guessed. The weak light filled it. I looked about. I had no idea why we had stopped here. Gnome's hand moved and he pointed.

I followed the gesture but still could not tell what it was that he was trying to indicate. The light drifted forward then, hovered near a shelflike niche.

Angles altered, shadows shifted. I saw it.

It was a statue of a reclining woman, carved out of coal.

I moved a step nearer. It was extremely well executed and very familiar.

"I didn't know you were an artist . . ." I began, and the realization struck me even as he laughed.

"It is *our* art," he said. "Not the mundane kind."

I had reached forward to touch the dark cheek. I dropped my hand, deciding against it.

"It's Lamia, isn't it?" I asked. "It's really her. . . .' '"

"Of course."

"Why?"

"She has to be someplace, doesn't she?"

167

"I'm afraid I don't understand."

He chuckled again.

"You're a dead man, Phoenix, and she's the reason. I never thought I'd have the good fortune to have you walk in this way. But now that you have, all of my problems are over. You will rest a few corridors away from here, in a chamber totally devoid of mana. You will wait, while I send for Werewolf to come and kill you. He was in love with Lamia, you know. He is convinced that you ran off with her. Some friend you are. I've been waiting for him to get you for some time now, but either he's clumsy or you're lucky. Perhaps both."

"So it's been Werewolf all along."

"Yes."

"Why? Why do you want him to kill me?"

"It would look badly if I did it myself. I'll be sure that some of the others are here when it happens. To keep my name clean. In fact, I'll dispatch Werewolf personally as soon as he's finished with you. A perfect final touch."

"Whatever I've done to you, I'm willing to set it right."

Gnome shook his head.

"What you did was to set up an irreducible conflict between us," he said. "There is no way to set it right."

"Would you mind telling me what it is that I did?" I asked.

He made a gesture, and I felt a compulsion to turn and make my way back toward the corridor. He followed, both of us preceded by his light.

As we moved, he asked me, "Were you aware that at each Starfall ceremony for the past ten or twelve years the mana content of the Starwind has been a bit higher?"

"It was ten or twelve years ago that I stopped attending them," I answered. "I recall that it was very high that year. Since then, when I've thought to check at the proper time, it has seemed high, yes."

"The general feeling is that the increase will continue. We seem to be entering a new area of space, richer in the stuff."

"That's great," I said, coming into the corridor again. "But what's that got to do with your wanting me out of the way, with your kidnapping Lamia and turning her to coal, with your siccing Werewolf on me?"

"Everything," he said, conducting me down a slanting shaft where the mana diminished with every step. "Even before that, those of us who had been doing careful studies had found indications that the background level of mana is rising."

"So you decided to kill me?"

He led me to a jagged opening in the wall and indicated that I should enter there. I had no choice. My body obeyed him. The light remained outside with him.

"Yes," he said then, motioning me to the rear of the place. "Years ago it would not have mattered—everyone was entitled to any sort of opinion they felt like holding. But now it does. The magic is beginning to return, you fool. I am going to be around long enough to see it happen, to take advantage of it. I could have put up with your democratic sentiments when such a thing seemed only a daydream—"

And then I remembered our argument, on the same matter Elaine had brought up during our ride down the coast.

"—but knowing what I knew and seeing how strongly you felt, I saw you as one who would oppose our inevitable leadership in that new world. Werewolf was another. That is why I set it up for him to destroy you, to be destroyed in return by myself."

"Do all of the others feel as you do?" I asked.

"No, only a few—just as there were only a few like you, Cowboy and the Wolf. The rest will follow whoever takes the lead, as people always do."

"Who are the others?"

He snorted.

"None of your business now," he said.

He began a familiar gesture and muttered something. I felt free of whatever compulsion he had laid upon me, and I lunged forward. The entrance had not changed its appearance, but I slammed up against something—as if the way were blocked by an invisible door.

"I'll see you at the party," he said, inches away, beyond my reach. "In the meantime, try to get some rest."

I felt my consciousness ebbing. I managed to lean and cover my face with my arms before I lost all control. I do not remember hitting the floor.

How long I lay entranced I do not know. Long enough for some of the others to respond to an invitation, it would seem. Whatever reason he gave them for a party, it was sufficient to bring Knight, Druid, Amazon, Priest, Siren, and Snowman to a large hall somewhere beneath the Cornish hills. I became aware of this by suddenly returning to full consciousness at the end of a long, black corridor without pictures. I pushed myself into a seated position, rubbed my eyes and squinted, trying to penetrate my cell's gloom. Moments later, this was taken care of for me. So I knew that my awakening and the happening that followed were of one piece.

The lighting problem was taken care of for me by the wall's beginning to glow, turning glassy, then becoming a full-color 3-D screen, complete with stereo. That's where I saw Knight, Druid, Amazon, etc. That's how I knew it was a party: There were food and a sound track, arrivals and departures. Gnome passed through it all, putting his clammy hands on everybody, twisting his face into a smile and being a perfect host.

Mana, mana, mana. Weapon, weapon, weapon. Nothing. Shit.

I watched for a long while, waiting. There had to be a reason for his bringing me around and showing me what was going on. I searched all of those familiar faces, overheard snatches of conversation, watched their movements. Nothing special. Why, then, was I awake and witnessing this. It had to be Gnome's doing, yet . . .

When I saw Gnome glance toward the high archway of the hall's major entrance for the third time in as many minutes, I realized that he, too, was waiting.

I searched my cell. Predictably, I found nothing of any benefit to me. While I was looking, though, I heard the noise level rise and I turned back to the images on the wall.

Magics were in progress. The hall must have been mana-rich. My colleagues were indulging themselves in some beautiful spellwork—flowers and faces and colors and vast, exotic, shifting vistas filled the screen now—just as such things must have run in ancient times. Ah! One drop! One drop of mana and I'd be out of here! To run and return? Or to seek immediate retaliation? I could not tell. If there were only some way I could draw it from the vision itself . . .

But Gnome had wrought too well. I could find no weak spot in the working before me. I stopped looking after a few moments, for another reason as well. Gnome was announcing the arrival of another guest.

The sound died and the picture faded at that point. The corridor beyond my cell seemed to grow slightly brighter. I moved toward it. This time my way was not barred, and I continued out into the lighter area. What had happened? Had some obscure force somehow broken Gnome's finely wrought spells?

At any rate, I felt normal now and I would be a fool to remain where he had left me. It occurred to me that this could be part of some higher trap or torture, but still— I had several choices now, which is always an improvement.

I decided to start back in the direction from which we had come earlier, rather than risk blundering into that gathering. Even if there was a lot of mana about there. Better to work my way back, I decided, tie up any mana I could find along the way in the form of protective spells, and get the hell out.

I had proceeded perhaps twenty paces while formulating this resolution. Then the tunnel went through an odd twisting that I couldn't recall. I was still positive we had come this way, though, so I followed it. It grew a bit brighter as I moved along, too, but that seemed all for the better. It allowed me to hurry.

Suddenly, there was a sharp turning that I did not remember at all. I took it and I ran into a screen of pulsing white light, and then I couldn't stop. I was propelled forward, as if squeezed from behind. There was no way that I could halt. I was temporarily blinded by the light. There came a roaring in my ears.

And then it was past, and I was standing in the great hall where the party was being held, having emerged from some side entrance, in time to hear Gnome say, ". . . And the surprise guest is our long-lost brother Phoenix!"

I stepped backward, to retreat into the tunnel from which I had emerged, and I encountered something hard. Turning, I beheld only a blank wall of rock.

"Don't be shy, Phoenix. Come and say hello to your friends," Gnome was saying.

There was a curious babble, but above it from across the way came an animallike snarl and I beheld my old buddy Werewolf, lean and swarthy, eyes blazing, doubtless the guest who was just arriving when the picture had faded.

I felt panic. I also felt mana. But what could I work in only a few seconds' time?

My eyes were pulled by the strange movement in a birdcage on the table beside which Werewolf stood. The others' attitudes showed that many of them had just turned from regarding it.

It registered in an instant.

Within the cage, a nude female figure no more than a hand high was dancing. I recognized it as a spell of torment: The dancer could not stop. The dancing would continue until death, after which the body would still jerk about for some time.

And even from that distance I could recognize the small creature as Elaine.

The dancing part of the spell was simple. So was its undoing. Three words and a gesture. I managed them. By then Werewolf was moving toward me. He was not bothering with a shapeshift to his more fearsome form. I sidestepped as fast as I could and sought for a hold involving his arm and shoulder. He shook it off. He always was stronger and faster than me.

He turned and threw a punch, and I managed to duck and counterpunch to his midsection. He grunted and hit me on the jaw with a weak left. I was already backing away by then. I stopped and tried a kick and he batted it aside, sending me spinning to the floor. I could feel the mana all about me, but there was no time to use it.

"I just learned the story," I said, "and I had nothing to do with Lamia—"

He threw himself upon me. I managed to catch him in the stomach with my knee as he came down.

"Gnome took her. . . ." I got out, getting in two kidney punches before his hands found my throat and began to tighten. "She's coal—"

I caught him once, high on the cheek, before he got his head down.

"Gnome—damn it!" I gurgled.

"It's a lie!" I heard Gnome respond from somewhere nearby, not missing a thing.

The room began to swim about me. The voices became a roaring, as of the ocean. Then a peculiar thing happened to my vision as well: Werewolf's head appeared to be haloed by a coarse mesh. Then it dropped forward, and I realized that his grip had relaxed.

I tore his hands from my throat and struck him once, on the jaw. He rolled away. I tried to also, in the other direction, but settled for struggling into a seated, then a kneeling, then a crouched, position.

I beheld Gnome, raising his hands in my direction, beginning an all-too-familiar and lethal spell. I beheld Werewolf, slowly removing a smashed birdcage from his head and beginning to rise again. I beheld the nude, full-size form of Elaine rushing toward us, her face twisted. . . .

The problem of what to do next was settled by Werewolf's lunge.

It was a glancing blow to the midsection because I was turning when it connected. A dark form came out of my shirt, hovered a moment and dropped floorward: It was the small bottle of djinn Dervish had given me.

Then, just before Werewolf's fist exploded in my face, I saw something slim and white floating toward the back of his neck. I had forgotten that Elaine was second *kyu* in Kyokushinkai—

Werewolf and I both hit the floor at about the same time, I'd guess.

. . . Black to gray to full-color; bumblebee hum to shrieks. I could not have been out for too long. During that time, however, considerable change had occurred.

For one, Elaine was slapping my face.

"Dave! Wake up!" she was saying. "You've got to stop it!"

"What?" I managed.

"That thing from the bottle!"

I propped myself on an elbow—jaw aching, side splitting—and I stared.

There were smears of blood on the nearest wall and table. The party had broken into knots of people, all of whom appeared to be in retreat in various stages of fear or anger. Some were working spells; some were simply fleeing. Amazon had drawn a blade and was holding it before her while gnawing her lower lip. Priest stood at her side, muttering a death spell, which I knew was not going to prove effective. Gnome's head was on the floor near the large archway, eyes open and unblinking. Peals of thunderlike laughter rang through the hall.

Standing before Amazon and Priest was a naked male figure almost ten feet in height, wisps of smoke rising from its dark skin, blood upon its upraised right fist.

"Do something!" Elaine said.

I levered myself a little higher and spoke the words Dervish had taught me, to put the djinn under my control. The fist halted, slowly came unclenched. The great bald head turned toward me, the dark eyes met my own.

"Master . . .?" it said softly.

I spoke the next words, of acknowledgment. Then I climbed to my feet and stood, wavering.

"Back into the bottle now—my command."

Those eyes left my own, their gaze shifting to the floor.

"The bottle is shattered, master," it said.

"So it is. Very well . . ."

I moved to the bar. I found a bottle of Cutty Sark with just a little left in the bottom. I drank it.

"Use this one, then," I said, and I added the words of compulsion.

"As you command," it replied, beginning to dissolve.

I watched the djinn flow into the Scotch bottle and then I corked it.

I turned to face my old colleagues.

"Sorry for the interruption," I said. "Go ahead with your party."

I turned again.

"Elaine," I said. "You okay?"

She smiled.

"Call me Dancer," she said. "I'm your new apprentice."

"A sorcerer needs a feeling for mana and a natural sensitivity to the way spells function," I said.

"How the hell do you think I got my size back?" she asked. "I felt the power in this place, and once you turned off the dancing spell, I was able to figure how to—"

"I'll be damned," I said. "I should have guessed your aptitude back at the cottage, when you grabbed that bone flute."

"See, you need an apprentice to keep you on your toes."

Werewolf moaned, began to stir. Priest and Amazon and Druid approached us. The party did not seem to be resuming. I touched my finger to my lips in Elaine's direction.

"Give me a hand with Werewolf," I said to Amazon. "He's going to need some restraining until I can tell him a few things."

The next time we splashed through the Perseids, we sat on a hilltop in northern New Mexico, my apprentice and I, regarding the crisp, postmidnight sky and the occasional bright cloud-chamber effect within it. Most of the others were below us in a cleared area, the ceremonies concluded now. Werewolf was still beneath the Cornish hills, working with Druid, who recalled something of the ancient flesh-to-coal spell. Another month or so, he'd said, in the message he'd sent.

" 'Flash of uncertainty in sky of precision,' " she said.

"What?"

"I'm composing a poem."

"Oh." Then, after a time, I added, "What about?"

"On the occasion of my first Starfall," she replied, "with the mana gain apparently headed for another record."

"There's good and there's bad in that."

". . . And the magic is returning and I'm learning the Art."

"Learn faster," I said.

". . . And you and Werewolf are friends again."

"There's that."

". . . You and the whole group, actually."

"No."

"What do you mean?"

"Well, think about it. There are others. We just don't know which of them were in Gnome's corner. They won't want the rest of us around when the magic comes back. Newer, nastier spells—ones it would be hard to imagine now—will become possible when the power rises. We must be ready. This blessing is a very mixed thing. Look at them down there—the ones we were singing with—and see whether you can guess which of them will one day try to kill you. There will be a struggle, and the winners can make the outcome stick for a long time."

She was silent for a while.

"That's about the size of it," I added.

Then she raised her arm and pointed to where a line of fire was traced across the sky. "There's one!" she said. "And another! And another!"

Later, "We can count on Werewolf now," she suggested, "and maybe Lamia, if they can bring her back. Druid, too, I'd guess."

"And Cowboy."

"Dervish?"

"Yeah, I'd say. Dervish."

". . . And I'll be ready."

"Good. We might manage a happy ending at that."

We put our arms about each other and watched the fire fall from the sky.

NIGHT KINGS

For a briefly revived Worlds of If *magazine which appeared in 1986 it was requested that I write a short story. The payment wasn't great, but despite my note for a previous tale, I am not totally mercenary. I was sufficiently sentimental to do it, having several fond memories of having written for the magazine in its first incarnation. I decided to try stringing together a number of clichés from the contemporary fantasy scene and turning them into a real story rather than a pastiche, despite. While I am still waiting for my contributor's copies, a kindly fan has let me have an issue from which the following might be rendered.*

*I*t began like any other night, but this one had a special feeling to it. The moon came up full and splendid above the skyline, and its light spread like spilled buttermilk among the canyons of the city. The remains of the day's storm exhaled mists which fled wraithlike across the pavements. But it wasn't just the moon and the fog. Something had been building for several weeks now. My sleep had been troubled. And business was too good.

I had been trying unsuccessfully to watch a late movie and drink one entire cup of coffee without its growing cold. But customers kept arriving, browsers lingered, and the phone rang regularly. I let my assistant, Vic, handle as much of it as he could, but people kept turning up at the counter—never during a commercial.

"Yes, sir? What can I do for you?" I asked a middle-aged man with a slight tic at the left corner of his mouth.

"Do you carry sharpened stakes?" he inquired.

"Yes. Would you prefer the regular or the fire-hardened?"

"The fire-hardened, I guess."

"How many?"

"One. No, better make it two."

"There's a dollar off if you take three."

"Okay, make it three."

"Give you a real good price on a dozen."

"No, three should do it."

"All right."

I stooped and pulled out the carton. Damn. Only two left. I had to pry open another box. At least Vic had kept an eye on the level and brought a second carton up from the stockroom. The boy was learning.

"Anything else?" I asked as I wrapped them.

"Yes," the man said. "I need a good mallet."

"We carry three different kinds, at different prices. The best is a weighted—"

"I'll take the best."

"Very good."

I got him one from beneath the adjacent counter.

"Will this be cash, check, or credit card?"

"Do you take MasterCard?"

"Yes."

He withdrew his wallet, opened it.

"Oh, I also want a pound of garlic," he said as he withdrew the card and handed it to me.

I called to Vic, who was free just then, to fetch the garlic while I wrote up the order.

"Thank you," the man said several minutes later, as he turned and headed for the door, his parcel beneath his arm.

"Good night, good luck," I said, and sounds of distant traffic reached me as the door opened, grew faint when it closed.

I sighted and picked up my coffee cup. I returned to my seat before the television set. Shit. A dental adhesive commercial had just come on. I waited it out, and then there was Bette Davis . . . Moments later, I heard a throat-clearing sound at my back. Turning, I beheld a tall, dark-haired, dark-mustached man in a beige coat. He was scowling.

"What can I do for you?" I asked him.

"I need some silver bullets," he said.

"What caliber?"

"Thirty-aught-six. Let me have two boxes."

"Coming up."

When he left I walked back to the john and dumped out my coffee. I refilled the cup with fresh brew from the pot on the counter.

On my way back to the comfortable corner of the shop I was halted by a leather-garbed youth with a pink punk haircut. He stood staring up at the tall, narrow, sealed case high upon the wall.

"Hey, Pops, how much is it?" he asked me.

"It's not for sale," I said. "It's strictly a display item."

He dug a massive wad of bills from his side pocket and extended it, his dreamy gaze never leaving the bright thing that hung above.

"I've got to have a magic sword," he said softly.

"Sorry. I can sell you a Tibetan illusion-destroying dagger, but the sword is strictly for looking at here."

He turned suddenly to face me.

"If you should ever change your mind . . . "

"I won't."

He shrugged then and walked away, passing out into the night.

As I rounded the corner into the front of the shop, Vic fixed me with his gaze and covered the mouthpiece of the phone with the palm of his hand.

"Boss," he told me, "this lady says there's a Chinese demon visits her every night and—"

"Tell her to come by and we'll sell her a bedside temple dog."

"Right."

I took a sip of coffee and made my way back toward my chair as Vic finished the conversation and hung up. A small red-haired woman who had been staring into one of the display cases near the front chose that moment to approach me.

"Pardon me," she said. "Do you carry aconite?"

"Yes, I do—" I began, and then I heard the sound— a sharp *thunk,* as if someone had thrown a rock against my back door.

I had a strong feeling as to what it might be.

"Excuse me," I said, "Vic, would you take care of this lady?"

"Sure thing."

Vic came over then, tall and rugged-looking, and she smiled.

I turned away and passed through the rear of the shop and into the back room. I unlocked the heavy door that let upon the alley and drew it open. As I suspected, there was no one in sight.

I studied the ground. A bat lay twitching feebly near a puddle. I stopped and touched it lightly.

"Okay," I said. "Okay, I'm here. It's all right."

I went back inside then, leaving the door open. As I headed for the refrigerator I called out, "Leo, I give you permission to enter. This one time. This one room and no farther."

A minute later he staggered in. He wore a dark, shabby suit and his shirtfront was dirty. His hair was windblown and straggly and there was a lump on his forehead. He raised a trembling hand.

"Have you got some?" he asked.

"Yeah, here."

I passed him the bottle I had already opened and he took a long drink, then he slowly seated himself in a chair beside the small table. I went back and closed the door, then sat down across from him with my cup of coffee. I gave him a minute for several more swallows and a chance to collect himself.

"Can't even hit a vein right," he muttered, raising the bottle a final time.

Then he put it down, ran his hands through his hair, rubbed his eyes, and fixed me with a baleful gaze.

"I can give you the locations of three who've just moved to town," he said. "What's it worth?"

"Another bottle," I said.

"For three? Hell! I could have brought the information in one at a time and—"

"I don't actively seek out your kind," I told him. "I just provide others with what they need to take care of themselves. I do like having this sort of information, though . . . "

184

"I need six bottles."

I shook my head.

"Leo, you take that much and you know what'll happen? You won't make it back and—"

"I want six bottles."

"I don't want to give them to you."

He massaged his temples.

"Okay," he said then. "Supposing I had a piece of important information that affected you personally? A really important piece of information?"

"How important?"

"Like life and death."

"Come on, Leo. You know me, but you don't know me that well. There's not much in this world or any other—"

He said the name.

"What?"

He repeated it, but my stomach was already tightening.

"Six bottles," he said.

"Okay. What do you know?"

He looked at the refrigerator. I got up and went to it. I got them out and bagged each one separately. Then I put all of them into a larger brown bag. I brought it over and set it on the floor beside his chair. He didn't even glance downward. He just shook his head.

"If I'm going to lose my connection, this is the way I want it," he stated.

I nodded.

"Tell me now."

"The Man came to town a couple of weeks ago," he said. "He's been looking around. He found you. And tonight's the night. You get hit."

"Where is he?"

"Right now? I don't know. He's coming, though. He called a meeting. Summoned everyone to All Saints across the river. Told us he was going to take you out and make it safe for us, that this was going to be his territory. Told everyone to get busy and keep you busy."

He glanced at the small barred window high on the rear wall.

"I'd better be going," he said then.

I got up and let him out. I watched him stagger away into the fog.

Tonight might well be the night for him too. Hemoholic. A small percentage of them get that way. One neck is never enough. After a while they get so they can't fly straight, and they start waking up in the wrong coffins. Then one morning they just don't make it back to bed in time. I had a vision of Leo sprawled desiccated on a park bench, brown bag clutched to his chest with bony fingers, the first light of day streaming about him.

I locked the door and returned to the shop. It's a cold world out there.

". . . horns of the bull for *malocchio,*" I heard Vic saying. "That's right. You're welcome. Good-bye."

I kept going, up to the front door. I locked it and switched off the light. I hung the Closed sign in the window.

"What is it?" Vic asked me.

"Turn off the phone."

He did.

Then, "Remember when I told you about the old days?" I said.

"Back when you bound the adversary?"

"Yup. And before that."

"Back when he bound you?"

"Yup. You know, one of these days one of us will win—completely."

"What are you getting at?"

"He's free again and he's coming and I think he's very strong. You may leave now if you wish."

"Are you kidding? You trained me. I'll meet him this time."

I shook my head.

"You're not ready. But if anything happens to me
. . . if I lose . . . then the job is yours if you'll have it."

"I told you a long time ago, back when I came to
work for you—"

"I know. But you haven't finished your apprenticeship
and this is sooner than I'd thought it would be. I have to
give you a chance to back out."

"Well, I won't."

"Okay, you've been warned. Go unplug the coffeepot
and turn out the lights in back while I close down the
register."

The room seemed to brighten a bit after he left and
I glanced up. It was an effect of diffused moonlight through
a full wall of fog that now pressed against the windows.
It hadn't been there moments ago.

I counted the receipts and put the money into the
bag. I got out the tape.

There was a pounding on the door just as Vic returned.
We both looked in that direction.

It was a very young woman, her long blond hair
stirred by the wind. She had on a light trench coat and
she kept looking back over her shoulder as she hammered
on the panel and the pane.

"It's an emergency!" she called out. "I see you in
there! Please!"

We both crossed to the door. I unlocked it and
opened it.

"What's the matter?" I asked.

She stared at me. She made no effort to enter. Then
she shifted her gaze to Vic and she smiled slightly. Her
eyes were green and her teeth were perfect.

"You are the proprietor," she said to me.

"I am."

"And this . . . ?"

"My assistant—Vic."

"We didn't know you had an assistant."

"Oh," I said. "And you are . . . ?"

"His assistant," she replied.

"Give me his message."

"I can do better than that," she answered. "I am here to take you to him."

She was almost laughing now, and her eyes were harder than I had thought at first. But I had to try.

"You don't have to serve him," I said.

She sobered suddenly.

"You don't understand," she told me. "I have no choice. You don't know what he saved me from. I owe him."

"And he'll have it all back, and more. You can leave him."

"Like I said, I have no choice."

"Yes, you do. You can quit the business right now."

"How?"

I extended my hand and she looked at it.

"Take my hand," I said.

She continued to stare. Then, almost timidly, she raised hers. Slowly, she reached toward mine. . . .

Then she laughed and jerked hers back.

"You almost had me there. Hypnosis, wasn't it?"

"No," I said.

"Well, you won't trick me again."

She turned and swept her left arm backward. The fog opened, forming a gleaming tunnel.

"He awaits you at the other end."

"He can wait a moment longer, then," I told her. "Vic, stay here."

I turned and walked back through the shop. I halted before the case which hung high upon the wall. For a moment I just stared. I could see it so clearly, shining there in the dark. Then I raised the small metal hammer which hung on the chain beside it and I struck.

The glass shattered. I struck twice again and shards kept falling upon the floor. I let go the hammer. It bounced several times against the wall.

Carefully then I reached inside and wrapped my hand about the hilt. The dreaded familiar feeling flowed through me. How long had it been . . . ?

I withdrew it from the case and held it up before me, my ancient strength returning, filling me once again. I had hoped that the last time would indeed be the last time, but these things have a way of dragging on.

When I returned to the storefront, the lady's eyes widened and she drew back a pace.

"All right, Miss," I said. "Lead on."

"Her name is Sabrina," Vic told me.

"Oh? What else have you learned?"

"We will be transported to All Saints Cemetery, across the river."

She smiled at him, then turned toward the tunnel. She stepped into it and I followed her.

It felt like one of those moving walkways the larger airports have. I could tell that every step I took bore me much farther than a single pace. Sabrina strode resolutely ahead, not looking back. Behind me, I heard Vic cough once, the sound heavily muffled within the gleaming, almost plastic-seeming walls.

There was darkness at the end of the tunnel, and a figure waited, even darker, within it.

There was no fog in the place where we emerged, only clear moonlight from amid a field of stars, strong enough to cause the tombstones and monuments to cast shadows. One of these fell between us, a long line of separating darkness, in the cleared area where we stood.

He had not changed so much as I felt I had. He was still taller, leaner and better-looking. He motioned Sabrina off to his right. I sent Vic to the side, also. When he grinned his teeth flashed, and he raised his blade—so black as to be almost invisible within its faint outlining nimbus of orange light—and he saluted me casually with it. I returned the gesture.

"I wasn't certain that you would come," he said.

I shrugged.

"One place is as good as another," I replied.

"I make you the same offer I did before," he stated. "to avoid the nastiness. A divided realm. It may be the best you can hope for."

"Never," I responded.

He sighed.

"You are stubborn."

"And you are persistent."

"If that's a virtue, I'm sorry. But there it is."

"Where'd you find Sabrina?"

"In the gutter. She has real talent. She's learning fast. I see that you have an apprentice now, also. Do you know what this means?"

"Yes, we're getting old, too old for this sort of non-sense."

"You could retire, brother."

"So could you."

He laughed.

"And we could both stagger off arm in arm to that special Valhalla reserved for the likes of us."

"I could think of worse fates," I said.

"Good, I'm glad to hear that. I think it means you're getting soft."

"I guess we'll be finding out very soon."

A series of small movements caught my gaze, and I looked past him. Doglike forms and batlike forms and snakelike forms were arriving and settling and moving into position in a huge encircling mass all around us, like spectators coming into a stadium.

"I take it we're waiting for your audience to be seated," I said, and he smiled again.

"Your audience, too," he replied. "Who knows but that even you may have a few fans out there?"

I smiled back at him.

"It's late," he said softly.

"Long past the chimes of midnight."

"Are they really worth it?" he asked then, a sudden serious look upon his face.

"Yes," I replied.

He laughed.

"Of course you have to say that."

"Of course."

"Let's get on with it."

He raised the blade of darkness high above his head and an unearthly silence poured across the land.

"Ashtaroth, Beelzebub, Asmodeus, Belial, Leviathan . . . ," he began.

I raised my own weapon.

"Newton, Descartes, Faraday, Maxwell, Fermi . . . ," I said.

"Lucifer Rofocale," he intoned, "Hecate, Behemoth, Put Satanas, Ariaston . . ."

"Da Vinci, Michelangelo, Rodin, Maillol, Moore . . . ," I continued.

The world seemed to swim about us, and this place was suddenly outside of space and time.

"Mephisto!" he cried out. "Legion! Lilith! Ianoda! Eblis!"

"Homer, Virgil, Dante, Shakespeare, Cervantes," I went on.

He struck and I parried the blow and struck one of my own to be parried in turn myself. He continued his chanting and increased the tempo of his attack. I did the same.

After the first several minutes I could see that we were still fairly evenly matched. That meant it would drag on, and on. I tried some tricks I had almost forgotten I knew.

But he remembered. He had a few, too, but something in me recalled them also.

We began to move even faster.

The blows seemed to come from every direction, but my blade was there, ready for them when they fell. His had a way of doing the same thing. It became a dance within a cage of shifting metal, row upon row of glowing eyes staring at us across the field of the dead. Vic and Sabrina stood side by side yet seemed oblivious of each other in their concentration upon the conflict.

I hate to say that it was exhilarating, but it was. Finally, to face once again the embodiment of everything I had fought across the years. To have total victory suddenly lie but a stroke away, if but the right stroke might be found . . .

I redoubled my efforts and actually bore him back several paces. But he recovered quickly and stood his ground then. A sigh rose up from beyond the monuments.

"You can still surprise me," he muttered through clenched teeth, slashing back with a deadly attack of his own. "When will this ever end?"

"How's a legend to know?" I replied, giving ground and striking again.

Our blades fed us the forces we had come to represent and we fought on, and on.

He came close, very close, on several occasions. But each time I was able to spin away at the last moment and counterattack. Twice, I thought that I had him and each time he narrowly avoided me and came on with renewed vigor.

He cursed, he laughed, and I probably did the same. The moon dropped down and sparklets of dew became visible upon the grass. The creatures sometimes shifted about, but their eyes never left us. Vic and Sabrina exchanged several whispered conversations without looking at each other.

I swung a head-cut, but he parried and riposted to my chest. I stopped it and tried for his chest, but he parried . . .

A breeze sprang up and the perspiration on my brow seemed suddenly cooler. I slipped once on the damp ground and he failed to take advantage of my imbalance. Was he finally tiring?

I tried pressing him once more, and he seemed a bit slower. Was I now gaining an edge or was it a trick on his part, to lull me?

I nicked his biceps. The barest touch. A scratch. Nothing real in the way of an injury, but I felt my confidence rising. I tried again, mustering all of my speed in a fresh burst of enthusiasm.

A bright line appeared across his shirtfront.

He cursed again and swung wildly. As I parried it, I realized that the sky was lightening in the east. That meant I had to hurry. There are rules by which even we are bound.

I spun through my most elaborate attack yet, but he was able to stop it. I tried again, and again. Each time he seemed weaker, and on that last one I had seen a look of pain upon his face. A restlessness came over our gallery then, and I felt that the final sands were about to descend the hourglass.

I struck again, and this time I connected solidly. I felt the edge of my weapon grate against bone as it cut into his left shoulder.

He howled and dropped to his knees as I drew back for the death blow.

In the distance a cock crowed, and I heard him laugh.

"Close, brother! Close! But not good enough," he said. "Sabrina! To me! Now!"

She took a step toward him, turned toward Vic, then back to my fallen nemesis. She rushed to him and embraced him as he began to fade.

"*Aufwiedersehen!*" he called to me, and they both were gone.

With a great rustling rush then, like blown leaves, our audience departed, flapping through the sky, flashing along the ground, slithering into holes, as the sun cut its way above the horizon.

I leaned upon my blade. In a little while Vic came up to me.

"Will we ever see them again?" he asked.

"Of course."

I began walking toward what I saw to be the distant gate.

"Now what?" he said.

"I'm going home and get a good day's sleep," I told him. "Might even take a little vacation. Business is going to be slow for a while."

We crossed the hallowed earth and exited onto a sidestreet.

QUEST'S END

I don't really feel like quoting from The Masks of God, Hamlet's Mill, The Golden Bough, *and* Beyond the Pleasure Principle *in introducing a story slightly over a thousand words in length. If a book is a machine to think with, though, these are some of the machines I keep running in a back room in the factory of my intellect, and at some time or other everything gets passed through them. Some things get ground away to nothing, some get stuck among the gear teeth, others get turned into stories like this.*

*T*he deed is done. And done pretty well, I might add.

The princess lies dead on the floor of my cave, amid the strewn bones of centuries' worth of heroes, wizards, princes, princesses, dwarfs, and elves, and the fragments of nine broken swords committed to their task—another possible reign of sweetness and joy I've clipped before its bud might unfold.

I run the rasps of my tongue across my fangs, savoring the acrid taste.

The last hero is twisted at an impossible angle in the corner, his magic blade shattered. It was the tenth and final one of that brood of evil piercers forged an age ago by the minions of Light to account for my master and those such as myself who serve him. How delicious! The ring I guard remains in the jeweled cask within the niche at my back.

Pieces of their faithful dwarf companion are strewn along the passageway. I can see the small hand that still holds the ax. Had the little man actually thought he could reach me or do me harm with that pathetic weapon?

Only the old wizard still draws breath. But I have shattered his staff and scattered his power down ways of darkness. I have granted him a few moments more that I might mock him and see him die cursing the powers he had served.

"Do you hear me, Lortan?" I ask.

"Yes, Bactor," he answers weakly from where he fell, his back against the wall to my left, legs thrust at crazy angles. Then "Why do I still live?" he asks.

"For a bit of terminal amusement, wearer of the Light. If you will curse all that is good and beautiful and true and noble, I will give you a quick death."

"No thanks," he answers.

"Why not? You have failed, as did the nine before

you. You were the last. It is over. The good guys lose, ten to nothing."

He does not respond, so I goad him further: "And your hero—Eric Broadthew, or whatever you call him—didn't even touch me with that weapon. The last one at least caught me a good one across the shoulder before I dismembered him."

"We were the worst of the lot you faced?" he inquires.

"Oh, I wouldn't go that far," I say. "But you were hardly the best."

"Humor a defeated old man and tell me. Who was the best?"

I chuckle. "Easily done," I answer. "Gloring, of the Second Kingdom. He came so close to killing me that it was beautiful. The arc of his blade, Dammer, came down like a bolt from the heavens. The muscles of his arms rippled like the tides of the sea. He glowed with the sweat of his exertions. He cursed me so wondrously, it was like a poem. I stood transfixed. Barely, only barely did I stop him, and it took all of my dark magic rather than the strength of my body. Verily, it was Gloring and Dammerung who were the greatest."

"Alas, poor Eric could not beat an act like that."

"No, nor any other I have encountered. And now my lord Glaum's reign will never end, for the Darkness has vanquished the Light. There are no more to be raised up against us."

"Of the broken weapons that I see on the floor," he says, "tell me which is the blade Dammer and where the bones of Gloring lie, that I might see where our brightest hope fell."

"You talk too much, old man. It is time to end this conversation."

"But I see only nine hilts amid the ruin."

I extend my claws and rear to strike him. But he holds me, by no magic but by a single statement:

"You have not yet won."

"How can you say that, when you are the last?"

"You lied," he continues, "when you said that your lord's reign will never end, that the Darkness has vanquished the Light. You do not see your own weakness."

"I have no weakness, wizard."

Through the gloom I see his smile.

"Very well," I say then. "You do not have to curse goodness, truth, beauty, and nobility as the price of a quick death. Just tell me of the weakness that you see."

"I have always considered the benefits of a quick death to be somewhat marginal," he replies.

"Tell me, that I may protect myself against its exploitation."

The insolent old man has the audacity to laugh. I resolve to make his death a slow thing, regardless.

"I will tell you," he says, "and you will still be unable to guard against it. I see now that you will die when you know love."

I stamp my foot and roar.

"Love? Love? Your mind is as broken as the rest of you, to accuse me of such a foul failing! Love!"

My laughter rings about the cave as I decapitate him and roll his head back along the passageway, slinging it by the beard. My sides ache from the strain of laughing.

After a time I pick up someone's leg and begin munching on it. Rather tough. Must have been the hero's.

My lord Glaum, always and future ruler of the world, enters that evening wearing his defiled garment of Light, to admire my work, to congratulate me on ages well spent. He gives me a cunningly wrought timepiece of gold with my name engraved upon it, to reward my faithful service.

"Bactor, my lovely," he asks after a time, "why is it that I behold the remains of only nine of the weapons of Light when all of the heroes have fallen?"

I chuckle. "There are only nine here." I explain. "The

other is up that side corridor. That hero made a different entrance than the others, and I stopped him there. He was a cunning one."

"I wish to see it for myself."

"Of course, my lord. Follow me."

I lead him up the sideway. I hear him draw a breath as I halt before the niche.

"This one is whole!" he hisses. "The man stands intact, the blade unbroken!"

I laugh again. "But harmless, lord. Now and forever. This one I bound by magic, rather than rending him with the strength of my body. I come here to admire him on occasion. He is the best. He came very close to destroying me."

"Fool!" he cries. "A spell can be broken! And I see that it is Gloring and Dammerung! We must finish them now to assure our triumph!"

He reaches for the death wand in its case upon his belt.

I turn again and regard the point of that blade I had halted but an inch from my breast when my spell froze all motion and left its grinning wielder a statue of judgment and execution forever delayed. Dammerung's edge is finer than that of any leaf, its point the nearest approach that matter might make to infinity. . . .

I hear my master: "Move away, Bactor."

And I hear another voice—my own—shout the words that break the spell. The delicious thrust is completed, after millennia of delay.

Then it slides from me in a fountain of my body's juices, and I fall backward.

As the beautiful thing, dripping my life, is turned against Glaum, I glance at its wielder, at the whiteness of his lovely face, teeth clenched within its grin . . .

24 VIEWS OF MT. FUJI,
BY HOKUSAI

I recall mentioning in a letter to my friend Carl Yoke something concerning the appearance of the mountains behind my home and my having realized but recently that seeing them in a different aspect every season, every day—every time I look at them, actually—had a lot to do with the following story; and that my coming across the book of Hokusai's prints which gets mentioned in the text of this tale was only the proximate cause of its composition. Without my mountains there would have been no meditations, no story, no Hugo (this one accepted by Shawna McCarthy, brought back to New Mexico and delivered by Parris—thanks, Shawna; thanks, Parris). I can't cite all of the lesser, contributory kami *here. Everything goes back to the mountains. And without Fuji's fire to complement the frost of my first story, I'd have had to look for a different title for this book. Thanks, Thermodynamics.*

1. Mt. Fuji from Owari

Kit lives, though he is buried not far from here; and I am dead, though I watch the days-end light pinking cloudstreaks above the mountain in the distance, a tree in the foreground for suitable contrast. The old barrel-man is dust; his cask, too, I daresay. Kit said that he loved me and I said I loved him. We were both telling the truth. But love can mean many things. It can be an instrument of aggression or a function of disease.

My name is Mari. I do not know whether my life will fit the forms I move to meet on this pilgrimage. Nor death. Not that tidiness becomes me. So begin anywhere. Either arcing of the circle, like that vanished barrel's hoop, should lead to the same place. I have come to kill. I bear the hidden death, to cast against the secret life. Both are intolerable. I have weighed them. If I were an outsider I do not know which I would choose. But I am here, me, Mari, following the magic footsteps. Each moment is entire, though each requires its past. I do not understand causes, only sequences. And I am long weary of reality-reversal games. Things will have to grow clearer with each successive layer of my journey, and like the delicate play of light upon my magic mountain they must change. I must die a little and live a little each moment.

I begin here because we lived near here. I visited the place earlier. It is, of course, changed. I recall his hand upon my arm, his sometime smiling face, his stacks of books, the cold, flat eye of his computer terminal, his hands again, positioned in meditation, his smile different then. Distant and near. His hands, upon me. The power of his programs, to crack codes, to build them. His hands. Deadly. Who would have thought he would surrender those rapid-striking weapons, delicate instruments, twisters of bodies? Or myself? Paths . . . Hands . . .

I have come back. It is all. I do not know whether it is enough.

The old barrel-maker within the hoop of his labor
. . . Half-full, half-empty, half-active, half-passive . . . Shall
I make a yin-yang of that famous print? Shall I let it stand
for Kit and myself? Shall I view it as the great Zero? Or
as infinity? Or is all of this too obvious? One of those
observations best left unstated? I am not always subtle. Let
it stand. Fuji stands within it. And is it not Fuji one must
climb to give an accounting of one's life before God or
the gods?

I have no intention of climbing Fuji and accounting
for myself, to God or to anything else. Only the insecure
and the uncertain require justification. I do what I must.
If the deities have any questions they can come down from
Fuji and ask me. Otherwise, this is the closest commerce
between us. That which transcends should only be admired
from afar.

Indeed. I of all people should know this. I, who have
tasted transcendence. I know, too, that death is the only
god who comes when you call.

Traditionally, the *henro*—the pilgrim—would dress all
in white. I do not. White does not become me, and my
pilgrimage is a private thing, a secret thing, for so long as
I can keep it so. I wear a red blouse today and a light
khaki jacket and slacks, tough leather hiking shoes; I have
bound my hair; a pack on my back holds my belongings.
I do carry a stick, however, partly for the purpose of
support, which I require upon occasion; partly, too, as a
weapon should the need arise. I am adept at its use in
both these functions. A staff is also said to symbolize one's
faith in a pilgrimage. Faith is beyond me. I will settle for
hope.

In the pocket of my jacket is a small book containing
reproductions of twenty-four of Hokusai's forty-six prints
of Mt. Fuji. It was a gift, long ago. Tradition also stands
against a pilgrim's traveling alone, for practical purposes

of safety as well as for companionship. The spirit of Hokusai, then, is my companion, for surely it resides in the places I would visit if it resides anywhere. There is no other companion I would desire at the moment, and what is a Japanese drama without a ghost?

Having viewed this scene and thought my thoughts and felt my feelings, I have begun. I have lived a little, I have died a little. My way will not be entirely on foot. But much of it will be. There are certain things I must avoid in this journey of greetings and farewells. Simplicity is my cloak of darkness, and perhaps the walking will be good for me.

I must watch my health.

2. Mt. Fuji from a Teahouse at Yoshida

I study the print: A soft blueness to the dawn sky, Fuji to the left, seen through the teahouse window by two women; other bowed, drowsing figures like puppets on a shelf. . . .

It is not this way here, now. They are gone, like the barrel-maker—the people, the teahouse, that dawn. Only the mountain and the print remain of the moment. But that is enough.

I sit in the dining room of the hostel where I spent the night, my breakfast eaten, a pot of tea before me. There are other diners present, but none near me. I chose this table because of the window's view, which approximates that of the print. Hokusai, my silent companion, may be smiling. The weather was sufficiently clement for me to have camped again last night, but I am deadly serious in my pilgrimage to vanished scenes in this life-death journey I have undertaken. It is partly a matter of seeking and partly a matter of waiting. It is quite possible that it may be cut short at any time. I hope not, but the patterns of

ROGER ZELAZNY

life have seldom corresponded to my hopes—or, for that
matter, to logic, desire, emptiness, or any patterns of my
own against which I have measured them.

All of this is not the proper attitude and occupation
for a fresh day. I will drink my tea and regard the mountain.
The sky changes even as I watch. . . .

Changes . . . I must be careful on departing this place.
There are precincts to be avoided, precautions to be taken.
I have worked out all of my movements—from putting
down the cup, rising, turning, recovering my gear, walking—until I am back in the country again. I must still
make patterns, for the world is a number-line, everywhere
dense. I am taking a small chance in being here.

I am not so tired as I had thought I would be from
all yesterday's walking, and I take this as a good sign. I
have tried to keep in decent shape, despite everything. A
scroll hangs on the wall to my right depicting a tiger, and
I want this, too, for a good omen. I was born in the Year
of the Tiger, and the strength and silent movements of the
big striped cat are what I most need. I drink to you, Shere
Khan, cat who walks by himself. We must be hard at the
right time, soft at the proper moment. Timing . . .

We'd an almost telepathic bond to begin with, Kit
and I. It drew us to each other, grew stronger in our years
together. Empathy, proximity, meditation . . . Love? Then
love can be a weapon. Spin its coin and it comes up yang.

Burn bright, Shere Khan, in the jungle of the heart.
This time we are the hunter. Timing is all—and *suki,* the
opening . . .

I watch the changes of the sky until a uniform bright-
ness is achieved, holds steady. I finish my tea. I rise and
fetch my gear, don my backpack, take up my staff. I head
for the short hall which leads to a side door.

"Madam! Madam!"

It is one of the place's employees, a small man with
a startled expression.

"Yes?"

He nods at my pack.

"You are leaving us?"

"I am."

"You have not checked out."

"I have left payment for my room in an envelope on the dresser. It says 'cashier' on it. I learned the proper amount last night."

"You must check out at the desk."

"I did not check in at the desk. I am not checking out at the desk. If you wish, I will accompany you back to the room, to show you where I left the payment."

"I am sorry, but it must be done with the cashier."

"I am sorry also, but I have left payment and I will not go to the desk."

"It is irregular. I will have to call the manager."

I sigh.

"No," I say. "I do not want that. I will go to the lobby and handle the checking out as I did the checking in."

I retrace my steps. I turn left toward the lobby.

"Your money," he says. "If you left it in the room you must get it and bring it."

I shake my head.

"I left the key, also."

I enter the lobby. I go to the chair in the corner, the one farthest from the work area. I seat myself.

The small man has followed me.

"Would you tell them at the desk that I wish to check out?" I ask him.

"Your room number . . . ?"

"Seventeen."

He bows slightly and crosses to the counter. He speaks with a woman, who glances at me several times. I cannot hear their words. Finally, he takes a key from her and departs. The woman smiles at me.

"He will bring the key and the money from your room," she says. "Have you enjoyed your stay?"

"Yes," I answer. "If it is being taken care of, I will leave now."

I begin to rise.

"Please wait," she says, "until the paperwork is done and I have given you your receipt."

"I do not want the receipt."

"I am required to give it to you."

I sit back down. I hold my staff between my knees. I clasp it with both hands. If I try to leave now she will probably call the manager. I do not wish to attract even more attention to myself. I wait. I control my breathing. I empty my mind.

After a time the man returns. He hands her the key and the envelope. She shuffles papers. She inserts a form into a machine. There is a brief stutter of keys. She withdraws the form and regards it. She counts the money in my envelope.

"You have the exact amount, Mrs. Smith. Here is your receipt."

She peels the top sheet from the bill.

There comes a peculiar feeling in the air, as if a lightning stroke had fallen here but a second ago. I rise quickly to my feet.

"Tell me," I say, "is this place a private business or part of a chain?"

I am moving forward by then, for I know the answer before she says it. The feeling is intensified, localized.

"We are a chain," she replies, looking about uneasily.

"With central bookkeeping?"

"Yes."

Behind the special place where the senses come together to describe reality I see the form of a batlike epigon taking shape beside her. She already feels its presence but

208

does not understand. My way is *mo chih ch'u*, as the Chinese say—immediate action, without thought or hesitation—as I reach the desk, place my staff upon it at the proper angle, lean forward as if to take my receipt and nudge the staff so that it slides and falls, passing over the countertop, its small metal tip coming to rest against the housing of the computer terminal. Immediately, the overhead lights go out. The epigon collapses and dissipates.

"Power failure," I observe, raising my staff and turning away. "Good day."

I hear her calling for a boy to check the circuit box.

I make my way out of the lobby and visit a rest room, where I take a pill, just in case. Then I return to the short hall, traverse it, and depart the building. I had assumed it would happen sooner or later, so I was not unprepared. The microminiature circuitry within my staff was sufficient to the occasion, and while I would rather it had occurred later, perhaps it was good for me that it happened when it did. I feel more alive, more alert from this demonstration of danger. This feeling, this knowledge, will be of use to me.

And it did not reach me. It accomplished nothing. The basic situation is unchanged. I am happy to have benefited at so small a price.

Still, I wish to be away and into the countryside, where I am strong and the other is weak.

I walk into the fresh day, a piece of my life upon the breakfast moment's mountain.

3. Mt. Fuji from Hodogaya

I find a place of twisted pines along the Tokaido, and I halt to view Fuji through them. The travelers who pass in the first hour or so of my vigil do not look like Hokusai's, but no matter. The horse, the sedan chair, the blue garments, the big hats—faded into the past, traveling forever on the print now. Merchant or nobleman, thief or servant— I choose to look upon them as pilgrims of one sort or another, if only into, through, and out of life. My morbidity, I hasten to add, is excusable, in that I have required additional medication. I am stable now, however, and do not know whether medication or meditation is responsible for my heightened perception of the subtleties of the light. Fuji seems almost to move within my gazing.

Pilgrims . . . I am minded of the wanderings of Matsuo Bashō, who said that all of us are travelers every minute of our lives. I recall also his reflections upon the lagoons of Matsushima and Kisagata—the former possessed of a cheerful beauty, the latter the beauty of a weeping countenance. I think upon the complexion and expressions of Fuji and I am baffled. Sorrow? Penance? Joy? Exaltation? They merge and shift. I lack the genius of Bashō to capture them all in a single character. And even he . . . I do not know. Like speaks to like, but speech must cross a gulf. Fascination always includes some lack of understanding. It is enough for this moment, to view.

Pilgrims . . . I think, too, of Chaucer as I regard the print. His travelers had a good time. They told each other dirty stories and romances and tales with morals attached. They ate and they drank and they kidded each other. Canterbury was their Fuji. They had a party along the way. The book ends before they arrive. Fitting.

I am not a humorless bitch. It may be that Fuji is really laughing at me. If so, I would like very much to join in. I really do not enjoy moods such as this, and a bit of meditation interruptus would be welcome if only the proper object would present itself. Life's soberer mysteries cannot be working at top-speed all the time. If they can take a break, I want one, too. Tomorrow, perhaps . . .

Damn! My presence must at least be suspected, or the epigon would not have come. Still, I have been very careful. A suspicion is not a certainty, and I am sure that my action was sufficiently prompt to preclude confirmation. My present location is beyond reach as well as knowledge. I have retreated into Hokusai's art.

I could have lived out the rest of my days upon Oregon's quiet coast. The place was not without its satisfactions. But I believe it was Rilke who said that life is a game we must begin playing before we have learned the rules. Do we ever? Are there really rules?

Perhaps I read too many poets.

But something that seems a rule to me requires I make this effort. Justice, duty, vengeance, defense—must I weigh each of these and assign it a percentage of that which moves me? I am here because I am here, because I am following rules—whatever they may be. My understanding is limited to sequences.

His is not. He could always make the intuitive leap. Kit was a scholar, a scientist, a poet. Such riches. I am smaller in all ways.

Kokuzo, guardian of those born in the Year of the Tiger, break this mood. I do not want it. It is not me. Let it be an irritation of old lesions, even a renewal of the demyelination. But do not let it be me. And end it soon. I am sick in my heart and my reasons are good ones. Give me the strength to detach myself from them, Catcher in the Bamboo, lord of those who wear the stripes. Take away the bleakness, gather me together, inform me with strength. Balance me.

I watch the play of light. From somewhere I hear the singing of children. After a time a gentle rain begins to fall. I don my poncho and continue to watch. I am very weary, but I want to see Fuji emerge from the fog which has risen. I sip water and a bit of brandy. Only the barest outline remains. Fuji is become a ghost mountain within a Taoist painting. I wait until the sky begins to darken. I know that the mountain will not come to me again this day, and I must find a dry place to sleep. These must be my lessons from Hodogaya: Tend to the present. Do not try to polish ideals. Have sense enough to get in out of the rain.

I stumble off through a small wood. A shed, a barn, a garage. . . . Anything that stands between me and the sky will do.

After a time I find such a place. No god addresses my dreaming.

4. Mt. Fuji from the Tamagawa

I compare the print with the reality. Not bad this time. The horse and the man are absent from the shore, but there is a small boat out on the water. Not the same sort of boat, to be sure, and I cannot tell whether it bears firewood, but it will suffice. I would be surprised to find perfect congruence. The boat is moving away from me. The pink of the dawn sky is reflected upon the water's farther reaches and from the snow-streaks on Fuji's dark shoulder. The boatman in the print is poling his way outward. Charon? No, I am more cheerful today than I was at Hodogaya. Too small a vessel for the *Narrenschiff,* too slow for the Flying Dutchman. "La navicella." Yes. "La navicella del mio ingegno"—"the little bark of my wit" on which Dante hoisted sail for that second realm, Purgatory. Fuji then . . . Perhaps so. The hells beneath, the heavens above, Fuji between—way station, stopover, terminal. A decent metaphor for a pilgrim who could use a purge. Appropriate. For it contains the fire and the earth as well as the air, as I gaze across the water. Transition, change. I am passing.

The serenity is broken and my reverie ended as a light airplane, yellow in color, swoops out over the water from someplace to my left. Moments later the insectlike buzzing of its single engine reaches me. It loses altitude quickly, skimming low over the water, then turns and traces its way back, this time swinging in above the shoreline. As it nears the point where it will pass closest to me, I detect a flash of reflected light within the cockpit. A lens? If it is, it is too late to cover myself against its questing eye. My hand dips into my breast pockct and withdraws a small gray cylinder of my own. I flick off its endcaps with my thumbnail as I raise it to peer through the eyepiece. A moment to locate the target, another to focus . . .

The pilot is a man, and as the plane banks away I catch only his unfamiliar profile. Was that a gold earring upon his left earlobe?

The plane is away, in the direction from which it had come. Nor does it return.

I am shaken. Someone had flown by for the sole purpose of taking a look at me. How had he found me? And what did he want? If he represents what I fear most, then this is a completely different angle of attack than any I had anticipated.

I clench my hand into a fist and I curse softly. Unprepared. Is that to be the story of my entire life? Always ready for the wrong thing at the right time? Always neglecting the thing that matters most?

Like Kendra?

She is under my protection, is one of the reasons I am here. If I succeed in this enterprise, I will have fulfilled at least a part of my obligation to her. Even if she never knows, even if she never understands . . .

I push all thoughts of my daughter from my mind. If he even suspected . . .

The present. Return to the present. Do not spill energy

into the past. I stand at the fourth station of my pilgrimage and someone takes my measure. At the third station an epigon tried to take form. I took extreme care in my return to Japan. I am here on false papers, traveling under an assumed name. The years have altered my appearance somewhat and I have assisted them to the extent of darkening my hair and my complexion, defying my customary preferences in clothing, altering my speech patterns, my gait, my eating habits—all of these things easier for me than most others because of the practice I've had in the past. The past . . . Again, damn it! Could it have worked against me even in this matter? Damn the past! An epigon and a possible human observer this close together. Yes, I am normally paranoid and have been for many years, for good reason. I cannot allow my knowledge of the fact to influence my judgment now, however. I must think clearly.

I see three possibilities. The first is that the flyby means nothing, that it would have occurred had anyone else been standing here—or no one. A joyride, or a search for something else.

It may be so, but my survival instinct will not permit me to accept it. I must assume that this is not the case. Therefore, someone is looking for me. This is either connected with the manifestation of the epigon or it is not. If it is not, a large bag of live bait has just been opened at my feet and I have no idea how to begin sorting through the intertwined twistings. There are so many possibilities from my former profession, though I had considered all of these long closed off. Perhaps I should not have. Seeking there for causes seems an impossible undertaking.

The third possibility is the most frightening: that there is a connection between the epigon and the flight. If things have reached the point where both epigons and human agents can be employed, then I may well be doomed to failure. But even more than this, it will mean that the game has taken on another, awesome dimension, an aspect which I had never considered. It will mean that everyone on Earth is in far greater peril than I had assumed, that I am the only one aware of it and that my personal duel has been elevated to a struggle of global proportions. I cannot take the risk of assigning it to my paranoia now. I must assume the worst.

My eyes overflow. I know how to die. I once knew how to lose with grace and detachment. I can no longer afford this luxury. If I bore any hidden notion of yielding, I banish it now. My weapon is a frail one but I must wield it. If the gods come down from Fuji and tell me, "Daughter, it is our will that you desist," I must still continue in this to the end, though I suffer in the hells of the *Yü Li Ch'ao Chuan* forever. Never before have I realized the force of fate.

I sink slowly to my knees. For it is a god that I must vanquish.

My tears are no longer for myself.

5. Mt. Fuji from Fukagawa in Edo

Tokyo. Ginza and confusion. Traffic and pollution. Noise, color and faces, faces, faces. I once loved scenes such as this, but I have been away from cities for too long. And to return to a city such as this is overpowering, almost paralyzing.

Neither is it the old Edo of the print, and I take yet another chance in coming here, though caution rides my every move.

It is difficult to locate a bridge approachable from an angle proper to simulate the view of Fuji beneath it, in the print. The water is of the wrong color and I wrinkle my nose at the smell; this bridge is not that bridge; there are no peaceful fisher-folk here; and gone the greenery.

Hokusai exhales sharply and stares as I do at Fuji-san beneath the metal span. His bridge was a graceful rainbow of wood, product of gone days.

Yet there is something to the thrust and dream of any bridge. Hart Crane could find poetry in those of this sort. "Harp and altar, of the fury fused . . ."

And Nietzsche's bridge that is humanity, stretching on toward the superhuman . . .

No. I do not like that one. Better had I never become involved with that which transcends. Let it be my *pons asinorum*.

With but a slight movement of my head I adjust the perspective. Now it seems as if Fuji supports the bridge and without his presence it will be broken like Bifrost, preventing the demons of the past from attacking our present Asgard—or perhaps the demons of the future from storming our ancient Asgard.

I move my head again. Fuji drops. The bridge remains intact. Shadow and substance.

The backfire of a truck causes me to tremble. I am only just arrived and I feel I have been here too long. Fuji seems too distant and I too exposed. I must retreat.

Is there a lesson in this or only a farewell?

A lesson, for the soul of the conflict hangs before my eyes: I will not be dragged across Nietzsche's bridge.

Come, Hokusai, *ukiyo-e* Ghost of Christmas Past, show me another scene.

6. Mt Fuji from Kajikazawa

Misted, mystic Fuji over water. Air that comes clean to my nostrils. There is even a fisherman almost where he should be, his pose less dramatic than the original, his garments more modern, above the infinite Fourier series of waves advancing upon the shore.

On my way to this point I visited a small chapel

surrounded by a stone wall. It was dedicated to Kwannon, goddess of compassion and mercy, comforter in times of danger and sorrow. I entered. I loved her when I was a girl, until I learned that she was really a man. Then I felt cheated, almost betrayed. She was Kwan Yin in China, and just as merciful, but she came there from India, where she had been a bodhisattva named Avalokitesvara, a man— "the Lord Who Looks Down with Compassion." In Tibet he is Chen-re-zi—"He of the Compassionate Eyes"—who gets incarnated regularly as the Dalai Lama. I did not trust all of this fancy footwork on his/her part, and Kwannon lost something of her enchantment for me with this smattering of history and anthropology. Yet I entered. We revisit the mental landscape of childhood in times of trouble. I stayed for a time and the child within me danced for a moment, then fell still.

I watch the fisherman above those waves, smaller versions of Hokusai's big one, which has always symbolized death for me. The little deaths rolling about him, the man hauls in a silver-sided catch. I recall a tale from the Arabian Nights, another of American Indian origin. I might also see Christian symbolism, or a Jungian archetype. But I remember that Ernest Hemingway told Bernard Berenson that the secret of his greatest book was that there was no symbolism. The sea was the sea, the old man an old man, the boy a boy, the marlin a marlin, and the sharks the same as other sharks. People empower these things themselves, groping beneath the surface, always looking for more. With me it is at least understandable. I spent my earliest years in Japan, my later childhood in the United States. There is a part of me which likes to see things through allusions and touched with mystery. And the American part never trusts anything and is always looking for the real story behind the front one.

As a whole, I would say that it is better not to trust, though lines of interpretation must be drawn at some point before the permutations of causes in which I indulge overflow my mind. I am so, nor will I abandon this quality of character which has served me well in the past. This does not invalidate Hemingway's viewpoint any more than his does mine, for no one holds a monopoly on wisdom. In my present situation, however, I believe that mine has a higher survival potential, for I am not dealing only with *things,* but of something closer to the time-honored Powers and Principalities. I wish that it were not so and that an epigon were only an artifact akin to the ball lightning Tesla studied. But there is something behind it, surely as that yellow airplane had its pilot.

The fisherman sees me and waves. It is a peculiar feeling, this sudden commerce with a point of philosophical departure. I wave back with a feeling of pleasure.

I am surprised at the readiness with which I accept this emotion. I feel it has to do with the general state of my health. All of this fresh air and hiking seems to have strengthened me. My senses are sharper, my appetite better. I have lost some weight and gained some muscle. I have not required medication for several days.

I wonder . . . ?

Is this entirely a good thing? True, I must keep up my strength. I must be ready for many things. But too much strength . . . Could that be self-defeating in terms of my overall plan? A balance, perhaps I should seek a balance—

I laugh, for the first time since I do not remember when. It is ridiculous to dwell on life and death, sickness and health this way, like a character of Thomas Mann's, when I am barely a quarter of the way into my journey. I will need all of my strength—and possibly more—along the way. Sooner or later the bill will be presented. If the timing is off, I must make my own *suki.* In the meantime, I resolve to enjoy what I have.

When I strike, it will be with my final exhalation. I know that. It is a phenomenon familiar to martial artists of many persuasions. I recall the story Eugen Herrigel told, of studying with the *kyudo* master, of drawing the bow and waiting, waiting till something signaled the release of the string. For two years he did this before his *sensei* gave him an arrow. I forget for how long it was after that that he repeated the act with the arrow. Then it all began to come together, the timeless moment of rightness would occur and the arrow would have to fly, would have to fly for the target. It was a long while before he realized that this moment would always occur at the end of an exhalation.

In art, so in life. It seems that many important things, from death to orgasm, occur at the moment of emptiness, at the point of the breath's hesitation. Perhaps all of them are but reflections of death. This is a profound realization for one such as myself, for my strength must ultimately be drawn from my weakness. It is the control, the ability to find that special moment that troubles me most. But like walking, talking, or bearing a child, I trust that something within me knows where it lies. It is too late now to attempt to build it a bridge to my consciousness. I have made my small plans. I have placed them upon a shelf in the back of my mind. I should leave them and turn to other matters.

In the meantime I drink this moment with a deep draught of salty air, telling myself that the ocean is the ocean, the fisherman is a fisherman, and Fuji is only a mountain. Slowly then, I exhale it . . .

7. *Mt. Fuji from the Foot*

Fire in your guts, winter tracks above like strands of ancient hair. The print is somewhat more baleful than the reality this evening. That awful red tinge does not glow above me against a horde of wild clouds. Still, I am not unmoved. It is difficult, before the ancient powers of the Ring of Fire, not to stand with some trepidation, sliding back through geological eons to times of creation and destruction when new lands were formed. The great outpourings, the bomblike flash and dazzle, the dance of the lightnings like a crown . . .

I meditate on fire and change.

Last night I slept in the precincts of a small Shingon temple, among shrubs trimmed in the shapes of dragons, pagodas, ships, and umbrellas. There were a number of pilgrims of the more conventional sort present at the temple, and the priest performed a fire service—a *goma*—for us. The fires of Fuji remind me, as it reminded me of Fuji.

The priest, a young man, sat at the altar which held the fire basin. He intoned the prayer and built the fire and I watched, completely fascinated by the ritual, as he began to feed the fire with the hundred and eight sticks of wood. These, I have been told, represent the hundred and eight illusions of the soul. While I am not familiar with the full list, I felt it possible that I could come up with a couple of new ones. No matter. He chanted, ringing bells, striking gongs and drums. I glanced at the other *henros*. I saw total absorption upon all of their faces. All but one.

Another figure had joined us, entering with total silence, and he stood in the shadows off to my right. He was dressed all in black, and the wing of a wide, upturned collar masked the lower portion of his face. He was staring at me. When our eyes met, he looked away, focusing his gaze upon the fire. After several moments I did the same.

The priest added incense, leaves, oils. The fire sizzled and spit, the flames leaped, the shadows danced. I began to tremble. There was something familiar about the man. I could not place him, but I wanted a closer look.

I edged slowly to my right during the next ten minutes, as if angling for better views of the ceremony. Suddenly then, I turned and regarded the man again.

I caught him studying me once more, and again he looked away quickly. But the dance of the flames caught him full in the face with light this time, and the jerking of his head withdrew it from the shelter of his collar.

I was certain, in that instant's viewing, that he was the man who had piloted the small yellow plane past me last week at Tamagawa. Though he wore no gold earring there was a shadow-filled indentation in the lobe of his left ear.

But it went beyond that. Having seen him full-face I was certain that I had seen him somewhere before, years ago. I have an unusually good memory for faces, but for some reason I could not place his within its prior context. He frightened me, though, and I felt there was good reason for it.

The ceremony continued until the final stick of wood was placed in the fire and the priest completed his liturgy as it burned and died down. He turned then, silhouetted by the light, and said that it was time for any who were ailing to rub the healing smoke upon themselves if they wished.

Two of the pilgrims moved forward. Slowly, another joined them. I glanced to my right once more. The man was gone, as silently as he had come. I cast my gaze all about the temple. He was nowhere in sight. I felt a touch upon my left shoulder.

Turning, I beheld the priest, who had just struck me lightly with the three-pronged brass ritual instrument which he had used in the ceremony.

"Come," he said, "and take the smoke. You need healing of the left arm and shoulder, the left hip and foot."

"How do you know this?" I asked him.

"It was given to me to see this tonight. Come."

He indicated a place to the left of the altar and I moved to it, startled at his insight, for the places he had named had been growing progressively more numb thoughout the day. I had refrained from taking my medicine, hoping that the attack would remit of its own accord.

He massaged me, rubbing the smoke from the dying fire into the places he had named, then instructing me to continue it on my own. I did so, and some on my head at the end, as is traditional.

I searched the grounds later, but my strange observer was nowhere to be found. I located a hiding place between the feet of a dragon and cast my bedroll there. My sleep was not disturbed.

I awoke before dawn to discover that full sensation had returned to all of my previously numbed areas. I was pleased that the attack had remitted without medication.

The rest of the day, as I journeyed here, to the foot of Fuji, I felt surprisingly well. Even now I am filled with unusual strength and energy, and it frightens me. What if the smoke of the fire ceremony has somehow effected a cure? I am afraid of what it could do to my plans, my resolve. I am not sure that I would know how to deal with it.

Thus, Fuji, Lord of the Hidden Fire, I have come, fit and afraid. I will camp near here tonight. In the morning I will move on. Your presence overwhelms me at this range. I will withdraw for a different, more distant perspective. If I were ever to climb you, would I cast one hundred and eight sticks into your holy furnace, I wonder? I think not. There are some illusions I do not wish to destroy.

8. Mt. Fuji from Tagonoura

I came out in a boat to look back upon the beach, the slopes, and Fuji. I am still in glowing remission. I have resigned myself to it, for now. In the meantime, the day is bright, the sea breeze cool. The boat is rocked by the small deaths, as the fisherman and his sons whom I have paid to bring me out steer it at my request to provide me with the view most approximating that of the print. So much of the domestic architecture in this land recommends to my eye the prows of ships. A convergence of cultural evolution where the message is the medium? The sea is life? Drawing sustenance from beneath the waves we are always at sea? Or, the sea is death, it may rise to blight our lands and claim our lives at any moment? Therefore, we bear this *memento mori* even in the roofs above our heads and the walls which sustain them? Or, this is the sign of our power, over life and death?

Or none of the above. It may seem that I harbor a strong death-wish. This is incorrect. My desires are just the opposite. It may indeed be that I am using Hokusai's prints as a kind of Rorschach for self-discovery, but it is death-fascination rather than death-wish that informs my mind. I believe that this is understandable in one suffering a terminal condition with a very short term to it.

Enough of that for now. It was meant only as a drawing of my blade to examine its edge for keenness. I find that my weapon is still in order and I resheathe it.

Blue-gray Fuji, salted with snow, long angle of repose to my left . . . I never seem to look upon the same mountain twice. You change as much as I myself, yet you remain what you are. Which means that there is hope for me.

I lower my eyes to where we share this quality with the sea, vast living data-net. Like yet unlike, you have fought that sea as I—

Birds. Let me listen and watch them for a time, the air-riders who dip and feed.

I watch the men work with the nets. It is relaxing to behold their nimble movements. After a time, I doze.

Sleeping, I dream, and dreaming I behold the god Kokuzo. It can be no other, for when he draws his blade which flashes like the sun and points it at me, he speaks his name. He repeats it over and over as I tremble before him, but something is wrong. I know that he is telling me something other than his identity. I reach for but cannot grasp the meaning. Then he moves the point of his blade, indicating something beyond me. I turn my head. I behold the man in black—the pilot, the watcher at the *goma*. He is studying me, just as he was that night. What does he seek in my face?

I am awakened by a violent rocking of the boat as we strike a rougher sea. I catch hold of the gunwale beside which I sit. A quick survey of my surroundings shows me that we are in no danger, and I turn my eyes to Fuji. Is he laughing at me? Or is it the chuckle of Hokusai, who squats on his hams beside me tracing naughty pictures in the moisture of the boat's bottom with a long, withered finger?

If a mystery cannot be solved, it must be saved. Later, then. I will return to the message when my mind has moved into a new position.

Soon, another load of fish is being hauled aboard to add to the pungency of this voyage. Wriggle howsoever they will they do not escape the net. I think of Kendra and wonder how she is holding up. I hope that her anger with me has abated. I trust that she has not escaped her imprisonment. I left her in the care of acquaintances at a primitive, isolated commune in the Southwest. I do not like the place, nor am I overfond of its residents. Yet they owe me several large favors—intentionally bestowed against these times—and they will keep her there until certain things come to pass. I see her delicate features, fawn eyes, and silken hair. A bright, graceful girl, used to some luxuries, fond of long soaks and frequent showers, crisp garments. She is probably mud-spattered or dusty at the moment, from slopping hogs, weeding, planting vegetables or harvesting them, or any of a number of basic chores. Perhaps it will be good for her character. She ought to get something from the experience other than preservation from a possibly terrible fate.

Time passes. I take my lunch.

Later, I muse upon Fuji, Kokuzo, and my fears. Are dreams but the tranced mind's theater of fears and desires, or do they sometimes truly reflect unconsidered aspects of reality, perhaps to give warning? To reflect . . . It is said that the perfect mind reflects. The *shintai* in its ark in its shrine is the thing truly sacred to the god—a small mirror— not the images. The sea reflects the sky, in fullness of cloud or blue emptiness. Hamlet-like, one can work many interpretations of the odd, but only one should have a clear outline. I hold the dream in my mind once more, absent all querying. Something is moving . . .

No. I almost had it. But I reached too soon. My mirror is shattered.

Staring shoreward, the matter of synchronicity occurs. There is a new grouping of people. I withdraw my small spy-scope and take its measure, already knowing what I will regard.

Again, he wears black. He is speaking with two men upon the beach. One of the men gestures out across the water, toward us. The distance is too great to make out features clearly, but I know that it is the same man. But now it is not fear that I know. A slow anger begins to burn within my *hara*. I would return to shore and confront him. He is only one man. I will deal with him now. I cannot afford any more of the unknown than that for which I have already provided. He must be met properly, dismissed or accounted for.

I call to the captain to take me ashore immediately.

He grumbles. The fishing is good, the day still young. I offer him more money. Reluctantly, he agrees. He calls orders to his sons to put the boat about and head in.

I stand in the bow. Let him have a good look. I send my anger on ahead. The sword is as sacred an object as the mirror.

As Fuji grows before me the man glances in our direction, hands something to the others, then turns and ambles away. No! There is no way to hasten our progress, and at this rate he will be gone before I reach land. I curse. I want immediate satisfaction, not extension of mystery.

And the men with whom he was speaking . . . Their hands go to their pockets, they laugh, then walk off in another direction. Drifters. Did he pay them for whatever information they gave him? So it would seem. And are they heading now for some tavern to drink up the price of my peace of mind? I call out after them but the wind whips my words away. They, too, will be gone by the time I arrive.

And this is true. When I finally stand upon the beach, the only familiar face is that of my mountain, gleaming like a carbuncle in sun's slanting rays.

I dig my nails into my palms but my arms do not become wings.

9. Mt. Fuji from Naborito

I am fond of this print: the torii of a Shinto shrine are visible above the sea at low tide, and people dig clams amid the sunken ruins. Fuji of course is visible through the torii. Were it a Christian church beneath the waves puns involving the Clam of God would be running through my mind. Geography saves, however.

And reality differs entirely. I cannot locate the place.

I am in the area and Fuji properly situated, but the torii must be long gone and I have no way of knowing whether there is a sunken temple out there.

I am seated on a hillside looking across the water and I am suddenly not just tired but exhausted. I have come far and fast these past several days, and it seems that my exertions have all caught up with me. I will sit here and watch the sea and the sky. At least my shadow, the man in black, has been nowhere visible since the beach at Tagonoura. A young cat chases a moth at the foot of my hill, leaping into the air, white-gloved paws flashing. The moth gains altitude, escapes in a gust of wind. The cat sits for several moments, big eyes staring after it.

I make my way to a declivity I had spotted earlier, where I might be free of the wind. There I lay my pack and cast my bedroll, my poncho beneath it. After removing my shoes I get inside quickly. I seem to have taken a bit of a chill and my limbs are very heavy. I would have been willing to pay to sleep indoors tonight but I am too tired to seek shelter.

I lie here and watch the lights come on in the darkening sky. As usual in cases of extreme fatigue, sleep does not come to me easily. Is this legitimate tiredness or a symptom of something else? I do not wish to take medication merely as a precaution, though, so I try thinking of nothing for a time. This does not work. I am overcome with the desire for a cup of hot tea. In its absence I swallow a jigger of brandy, which warms my insides for a time.

Still, sleep eludes me and I decide to tell myself a story as I did when I was very young and wanted to make the world turn into dream.

So . . . Upon a time during the troubles following the death of the Retired Emperor Sutoku a number of itinerant monks of various persuasions came this way, having met upon the road, traveling to seek respite from the wars, earthquakes, and whirlwinds which so disturbed the land. They hoped to found a religious community and pursue the meditative life in quiet and tranquillity. They came upon what appeared to be a deserted Shinto shrine near the seaside, and there they camped for the night, wondering what plague or misfortune might have carried off its attendants. The place was in good repair and no evidence of violence was to be seen. They discussed then the possibility of making this their retreat, of themselves becoming the shrine's attendants. They grew enthusiastic with the idea and spent much of the night talking over these plans. In the morning, however, an ancient priest appeared from within the shrine, as if to commence a day's duties. The monks asked him the story of the place, and he informed them that once there had been others to assist him in his duties but that they had long ago been taken by the sea during a storm, while about their peculiar devotions one night upon the shore. And no, it was not really a Shinto shrine, though in outward appearance it seemed such. It was actually the temple of a far older religion of which he could well be the last devotee. They were welcome, however, to join him here and learn of it if they so wished. The monks discussed it quickly among themselves and decided that since it was a pleasant-seeming place, it might be well to stay and hear whatever teaching the old man possessed. So they became residents at the strange shrine. The place troubled several of them considerably at first, for at night they seemed to hear the calling of musical voices in the waves and upon the sea wind. And on occasion it seemed as if they could hear the old priest's voice responding to these calls. One night one of them followed the sounds and saw the old man standing upon the beach, his arms upraised. The monk hid himself and later fell asleep in a crevice in the rocks. When he awoke, a full moon stood high in the heavens and the old man was gone. The monk went down to the place where he had stood and there saw many marks in the sand, all of them the prints of webbed feet. Shaken, the monk returned and recited his experience to his fellows. They spent weeks thereafter trying to catch a glimpse of the old man's feet, which were always wrapped and bound. They did not succeed, but after a time it seemed to matter less and less. His teachings influenced them slowly but steadily. They began to assist him in his rituals to the Old Ones, and they learned the name of this promontory and its shrine. It was the last above-sea remnant of a large sunken island, which he assured them rose on certain wondrous occasions to reveal a lost city inhabited by the servants of his masters. The name of the place was R'lyeh and they would be happy to go there one day. By then it seemed a good idea, for they had noticed a certain thickening and extension of the skin between their fingers and toes, the digits themselves becoming sturdier and more elongated. By then, too, they were participating in all of the rites, which grew progressively abominable. At length, after a particularly gory ritual, the old priest's promise was fulfilled in reverse. Instead of the island rising, the promontory sank to join it, bearing the shrine and all of the monks along with it. So their abominations are primarily aquatic now. But once every century or so the whole island does indeed rise up for a night, and troops of them make their way ashore seeking victims. And of course, tonight is the night. . . .

A delicious feeling of drowsiness has finally come over me with this telling, based upon some of my favorite bedtime stories. My eyes are closed. I float on a cotton-filled raft . . . I—

A sound! Above me! Toward the sea. Something moving my way. Slowly, then quickly.

Adrenaline sends a circuit of fire through my limbs.

I extend my hand carefully, quietly, and take hold of my staff.

Waiting. Why now, when I am weakened? Must danger always approach at the worst moment?

There is a thump as it strikes the ground beside me, and I let out the breath I have been holding.

It is the cat, little more than a kitten, which I had observed earlier. Purring, it approaches. I reach out and stroke it. It rubs against me. After a time I take it into the bag. It curls up at my side, still purring, warm. It is good to have something that trusts you and wants to be near you. I call the cat R'lyeh. Just for one night.

10. Mt. Fuji from Ejiri

I took the bus back this way. I was too tired to hike. I have taken my medicine as I probably should have been doing all along. Still, it could be several days before it brings me some relief, and this frightens me. I cannot really afford such a condition. I am not certain what I will do, save that I must go on.

The print is deceptive, for a part of its force lies in the effects of a heavy wind. Its skies are gray, Fuji is dim in the background, the people on the road and the two trees beside it all suffer from the wind's buffeting. The trees bend, the people clutch at their garments, there is a hat high in the air and some poor scribe or author has had his manuscript snatched skyward to flee from him across the land (reminding me of an old cartoon—Editor to Author: "A funny thing happened to your manuscript during the St. Patrick's Day Parade"). The scene which confronts me is less active at a meteorological level. The sky is indeed overcast but there is no wind, Fuji is darker, more clearly delineated than in the print, there are no struggling pedestrians in sight. There are many more trees near at hand. I stand near a small grove, in fact. There are some structures in the distance which are not present in the picture.

I lean heavily upon my staff. Live a little, die a little. I have reached my tenth station and I still do not know whether Fuji is giving me strength or taking it from me. Both, perhaps.

I head off into the wood, my face touched by a few raindrops as I go. There are no signs posted and no one seems to be about. I work my way back from the road, coming at last to a small clear area containing a few rocks and boulders. It will do as a campsite. I want nothing more than to spend the day resting.

I soon have a small fire going, my tiny teapot poised on rocks above it. A distant roll of thunder adds variety to my discomfort, but so far the rain has held off. The ground is damp, however. I spread my poncho and sit upon it while I wait. I hone a knife and put it away. I eat some biscuits and study a map. I suppose I should feel some satisfaction, in that things are proceeding somewhat as I intended. I wish that I could, but I do not.

An unspecified insect which has been making buzzing noises somewhere behind me ceases its buzzing. I hear a twig snap a moment later. My hand snakes out to fall upon my staff.

"Don't," says a voice at my back.

I turn my head. He is standing eight or ten feet from me, the man in black, earring in place, his right hand in his jacket pocket. And it looks as if there is more than his hand in there, pointed at me.

I remove my hand from my staff and he advances. With the side of his foot he sends the staff partway across the clearing, out of my reach. Then he removes his hand from his pocket, leaving behind whatever it held. He circles slowly to the other side of the fire, staring at me the while.

He seats himself upon a boulder, lets his hands rest upon his knees.

"Mari?" he asks then.

I do not respond to my name, but stare back. The light of Kokuzo's dream-sword flashes in my mind, pointing at him, and I hear the god speaking his name only not quite.

"Kotuzov!" I say then.

The man in black smiles, showing that the teeth I had broken once long ago are now neatly capped.

"I was not so certain of you at first either," he says.

Plastic surgery has removed at least a decade from his face, along with a lot of weathering and several scars. He is different about the eyes and cheeks, also. And his nose is smaller. It is a considerable improvement over the last time we met.

"Your water is boiling," he says then. "Are you going to offer me a cup of tea?"

"Of course," I reply, reaching for my pack, where I keep an extra cup.

"Slowly."

"Certainly."

I locate the cup, I rinse them both lightly with hot water, I prepare the tea.

"No, don't pass it to me," he says, and he reaches forward and takes the cup from where I had filled it.

I suppress a desire to smile.

"Would you have a lump of sugar?" he asks.

"Sorry."

He sighs and reaches into his other pocket, from which he withdraws a small flask.

"Vodka? In tea?"

"Don't be silly. My tastes have changed. It's Wild Turkey liqueur, a wonderful sweetener. Would you care for some?"

"Let me smell it."

There is a certain sweetness to the aroma.

"All right," I say, and he laces our tea with it.

We taste the tea. Not bad.

"How long has it been?" he asks.

"Fourteen years—almost fifteen," I tell him. "Back in the eighties."

"Yes."

He rubs his jaw. "I'd heard you'd retired."

"You heard right. It was about a year after our last—encounter."

"Turkey—yes. You married a man from your Code Section."

I nod.

"You were widowed three or four years later. Daughter born after your husband's death. Returned to the States. Settled in the country. That's all I know."

"That's all there is."

He takes another drink of tea.

"Why did you come back here?"

"Personal reasons. Partly sentimental."

"Under a false identity?"

"Yes. It involves my husband's family. I don't want them to know I'm here."

"Interesting. You mean that they would watch arrivals as closely as we have?"

"I didn't know you watched arrivals here."

"Right now we do."

"You've lost me. I don't know what's going on."

There is another roll of thunder. A few more drops spatter about us.

"I would like to believe that you are really retired," he says. "I'm getting near that point myself, you know."

"I have no reason to be back in business. I inherited a decent amount, enough to take care of me and my daughter."

He nods.

"If I had such an inducement I would not be in the field," he says. "I would rather sit home and read, play chess, eat and drink regularly. But you must admit it is quite a coincidence your being here when the future success of several nations is being decided."

I shake my head.

"I've been out of touch with a lot of things."

"The Osaka Oil Conference. It begins two weeks from Wednesday. You were planning perhaps to visit Osaka at about that time?"

"I will not be going to Osaka."

"A courier then. Someone from there will meet you, a simple tourist, at some point in your travels, to convey—"

"My God! Do you think everything's a conspiracy, Boris? I am just taking care of some personal problems and visiting some places that mean something to me. The conference doesn't."

"All right." He finishes his tea and puts the cup aside. "You know that we know you are here. A word to the Japanese authorities that you are traveling under false papers and they will kick you out. That would be simplest. No real harm done and one agent nullified. Only it would be a shame to spoil your trip if you are indeed only a tourist. . . ."

A rotten thought passes through my mind as I see where this is leading, and I know that my thought is far rottener than his. It is something I learned from a strange old woman I once worked with who did not look like an old woman.

I finish my tea and raise my eyes. He is smiling.

"I will make us some more tea," I say.

I see that the top button of my shirt comes undone while I am bent partly away from him. Then I lean forward with his cup and take a deep breath.

"You would consider not reporting me to the authorities?"

"I might," he says. "I think your story is probably true. And even if it is not, you would not take the risk of transporting anything now that I know about you."

"I really want to finish this trip," I say, blinking a few extra times. "I would do anything not to be sent back now."

He takes hold of my hand.

"I am glad you said that, Maryushka," he replies. "I am lonely, and you are still a fine-looking woman."

"You think so?"

"I always thought so, even that day you bashed in my teeth."

"Sorry about that. It was strictly business, you know."

His hand moves to my shoulder.

"Of course. They looked better when they were fixed than they had before, anyway."

He moves over and sits beside me.

"I have dreamed of doing this many times," he tells me, as he unfastens the rest of the buttons on my shirt and unbuckles my belt.

He rubs my belly softly. It is not an unpleasant feeling. It has been a long time.

Soon we are fully undressed. He takes his time, and when he is ready I welcome him between my legs. All right, Boris. I give the ride, you take the fall. I could almost feel a little guilty about it. You are gentler than I'd thought you would be. I commence the proper breathing pattern, deep and slow. I focus my attention on my *hara* and his, only inches away. I feel our energies, dreamlike and warm, moving. Soon, I direct their flow. He feels it only as pleasure, perhaps more draining than usual. When he has done, though . . .

"You said you had some problem?" he inquires in

235

that masculine coital magnanimity generally forgotten a few minutes afterward. "If it is something I could help you with, I have a few days off, here and there. I like you, Maryushka."

"It's something I have to do myself. Thanks anyway."

I continue the process.

Later, as I dress myself, he lies there looking up at me.

"I must be getting old, Maryushka," he reflects. "You have tired me. I feel I could sleep for a week."

"That sounds about right," I say. "A week and you should be feeling fine again."

"I do not understand . . ."

"You've been working too hard, I'm sure. That conference . . ."

He nods.

"You are probably right. You are not really involved . . . ?"

"I am really not involved."

"Good."

I clean the pot and my cups. I restore them to my pack.

"Would you be so kind as to move, Boris dear? I'll be needing the poncho very soon, I think."

"Of course."

He rises slowly and passes it to me. He begins dressing. His breathing is heavy.

"Where are you going from here?"

"Mishima-goe," I say, "for another view of my mountain."

He shakes his head. He finishes dressing and seats himself on the ground, his back against a treetrunk. He finds his flask and takes a swallow. He extends it then.

"Would you care for some?"

"Thank you, no. I must be on my way."

I retrieve my staff. When I look at him again, he smiles faintly, ruefully.

"You take a lot out of a man, Maryushka."

"I had to," I say.

I move off. I will hike twenty miles today, I am certain. The rain begins to descend before I am out of the grove; leaves rustle like the wings of bats.

11. Mt. Fuji from Mishima-goe

Sunlight. Clean air. The print shows a big cryptameria tree, Fuji looming behind it, crowned with smoke. There is no smoke today, but I have located a big cryptameria and positioned myself so that it cuts Fuji's shoulder to the left of the cone. There are a few clouds, not so popcorny as Hokusai's smoke (he shrugs at this), and they will have to do.

My stolen *ki* still sustains me, though the medication is working now beneath it. Like a transplanted organ, my body will soon reject the borrowed energy. By then, though, the drugs should be covering for me.

In the meantime, the scene and the print are close to each other. It is a lovely spring day. Birds are singing, butterflies stitch the air in zigzag patterns; I can almost hear the growth of plants beneath the soil. The world smells fresh and new. I am no longer being followed. Hello to life again.

I regard the huge old tree and listen for its echoes down the ages: Yggdrasil, the Golden Bough, the Yule tree, the Tree of the Knowledge of Good and Evil, the Bo beneath which Lord Gautama found his soul and lost it. . . .

I move forward to run my hand along its rough bark.

From that position I am suddenly given a new view of the valley below. The fields look like raked sand, the hills like rocks, Fuji a boulder. It is a garden, perfectly laid out. . . .

Later I notice that the sun has moved. I have been standing here for hours. My small illumination beneath a great tree. Older than my humanity, I do not know what I can do for it in return.

Stooping suddenly, I pick up one of its cones. A tiny thing, for such a giant. It is barely the size of my little fingernail. Delicately incised, as if sculpted by fairies.

I put it in my pocket. I will plant it somewhere along my way.

I retreat then, for I hear the sound of approaching bells and I am not yet ready for humanity to break my mood. But there was a small inn down the road which does not look to be part of a chain. I will bathe and eat there and sleep in a bed tonight.

I will still be strong tomorrow.

12. Mt. Fuji from Lake Kawaguchi

Reflections.

This is one of my favorite prints in the series: Fuji as seen from across the lake and reflected within it. There are green hills at either hand, a small village upon the far shore, a single small boat in sight upon the water. The most fascinating feature of the print is that the reflection of Fuji is not the same as the original; its position is wrong, its slope is wrong, it is snow-capped and the surface view of Fuji itself is not.

I sit in the small boat I have rented, looking back. The sky is slightly hazy, which is good. No glare to spoil the reflection. The town is no longer as quaint as in the print, and it has grown. But I am not concerned with details of this sort. Fuji is reflected more perfectly in my viewing, but the doubling is still a fascinating phenomenon for me.

Interesting, too . . . In the print the village is not reflected, nor is there an image of the boat in the water. The only reflection is Fuji's. There is no sign of humanity.

I see the reflected buildings near the water's edge. And my mind is stirred by other images than those Hokusai would have known. Of course drowned R'lyeh occurs to me, but the place and the day are too idyllic. It fades from mind almost immediately, to be replaced by sunken Ys, whose bells still toll the hours beneath the sea. And Selma Lagerloff's *Nils Holgersson,* the tale of the shipwrecked sailor who finds himself in a sunken city at the bottom of the sea—a place drowned to punish its greedy, arrogant inhabitants, who still go about their business of cheating each other, though they are all of them dead. They wear rich, old-fashioned clothes and conduct their business as they once did above in this strange land beneath the waves. The sailor is drawn to them, but he knows that he must not be discovered or he will be turned into one of them, never to return to the earth, to see the sun. I suppose I think of this old children's story because I understand now how the sailor must have felt. My discovery, too, could result in a transformation I do not desire.

And of course, as I lean forward and view my own features mirrored in the water, there is the world of Lewis Carroll beneath its looking-glass surface. To be an Ama diving girl and descend . . . To spin downward, and for a few minutes to know the inhabitants of a land of paradox and great charm . . .

Mirror, mirror, why does the real world so seldom cooperate with our aesthetic enthusiasms?

Halfway finished. I reach the midpoint of my pilgrimage to confront myself in a lake. It is a good time and place to look upon my own countenance, to reflect upon all of the things which have brought me here, to consider what the rest of the journey may hold. Though images may sometimes lie. The woman who looks back at me seems composed, strong, and better-looking than I had thought she would. I like you, Kawaguchi, lake with a human personality. I flatter you with literary compliments and you return the favor.

Meeting Boris lifted a burden of fear from my mind. No human agents of my nemesis have risen to trouble my passage. So the odds have not yet tipped so enormously against me as they might.

Fuji and image. Mountain and soul. Would an evil thing cast no reflection down here—some dark mountain where terrible deeds were performed throughout history? I am reminded that Kit no longer casts a shadow, has no reflection.

Is he truly evil, though? By my lights he is. Especially if he is doing the things I think he is doing.

He said that he loved me, and I did love him, once. What will he say to me when we meet again, as meet we must?

It will not matter. Say what he will, I am going to try to kill him. He believes that he is invincible, indestructible. I do not, though I do believe that I am the only person on earth capable of destroying him. It took a long time for me to figure the means, an even longer time before the decision to try it was made for me. I must do it for Kendra as well as for myself. The rest of the world's population comes third.

I let my fingers trail in the water. Softly, I begin to sing an old song, a love song. I am loath to leave this place. Will the second half of my journey be a mirror-image of the first? Or will I move beyond the looking-glass, to pass into that strange realm where he makes his home?

I planted the cryptameria's seed in a lonesome valley yesterday afternoon. Such a tree will look elegant there one day, outliving nations and armies, madmen and sages.

I wonder where R'lyeh is? She ran off in the morning

after breakfast, perhaps to pursue a butterfly. Not that I could have brought her with me.

I hope that Kendra is well. I have written her a long letter explaining many things. I left it in the care of an attorney friend, who will be sending it to her one day in the not too distant future.

The prints of Hokusai . . . They could outlast the cryptameria. I will not be remembered for any works.

Drifting between the worlds I formulate our encounter for the thousandth time. He will have to be able to duplicate an old trick to get what he wants. I will have to perform an even older one to see that he doesn't get it. We are both out of practice.

It has been long since I read *The Anatomy of Melancholy*. It is not the sort of thing I've sought to divert me in recent years. But I recall a line or two as I see fish dart by: "Polycrates Samius, that flung his ring into the sea, because he would participate in the discontent of others, and had it miraculously restored to him again shortly after, by a fish taken as he angled, was not free from melancholy dispositions. No man can cure himself . . ." Kit threw away his life and gained it. I kept mine and lost it. Are rings ever really returned to the proper people? And what about a woman curing herself? The cure I seek is a very special one.

Hokusai, you have shown me many things. Can you show me an answer?

Slowly, the old man raises his arm and points to his mountain. Then he lowers it and points to the mountain's image.

I shake my head. It is an answer that is no answer. He shakes his head back at me and points again.

The clouds are massing high above Fuji, but that is no answer. I study them for a long while but can trace no interesting images within.

Then I drop my eyes. Below me, inverted, they take

a different form. It is as if they depict the clash of two armed hosts. I watch in fascination as they flow together, the forces from my right gradually rolling over and submerging those to my left. Yet in so doing, those from my right are diminished.

Conflict? That is the message? And both sides lose things they do not wish to lose? Tell me something I do not already know, old man.

He continues to stare. I follow his gaze again, upward. Now I see a dragon, diving into Fuji's cone.

I look below once again. No armies remain, only carnage; and here the dragon's tail becomes a dying warrior's arm holding a sword.

I close my eyes and reach for it. A sword of smoke for a man of fire.

13. Mt. Fuji from Koishikawa in Edo

Snow, on the roofs of houses, on evergreens, on Fuji—just beginning to melt in places, it seems. A windowful of women—geishas, I would say—looking out at it, one of them pointing at three dark birds high in the pale sky. My closest view of Fuji to that in the print is unfortunately snowless, geishaless, and sunny.

Details . . .

Both are interesting, and superimposition is one of the major forces of aesthetics. I cannot help but think of the hot-spring geisha Komako in *Snow Country*—Yasunari Kawabata's novel of loneliness and wasted, fading beauty—which I have always felt to be the great anti-love story of Japan. This print brings the entire tale to mind for me. The denial of love. Kit was no Shimamura, for he did want me, but only on his own highly specialized terms, terms that must remain unacceptable to me. Selfishness or selflessness? It is not important . . .

And the birds at which the geisha points . . . ? "Thirteen Ways of Looking at a Blackbird?" To the point. We could never agree on values.

The Twa Corbies? And throw in Ted Hughes's pugnacious Crow? Perhaps so, but I won't draw straws.—An illusion for every allusion, and where's yesterday's snow?

I lean upon my staff and study my mountain. I wish to make it to as many of my stations as possible before ordering the confrontation. Is that not fair? Twenty-four ways of looking at Mt. Fuji. It struck me that it would be good to take one thing in life and regard it from many viewpoints, as a focus for my being, and perhaps as a penance for alternatives missed.

Kit, I am coming, as you once asked of me, but by my own route and for my own reasons. I wish that I did not have to, but you have deprived me of a real choice in this matter. Therefore, my action is not truly my own, but yours. I am become then your own hand turned against you, representative of a kind of cosmic aikido.

I make my way through town after dark, choosing only dark streets where the businesses are shut down. That way I am safe. When I must enter town I always find a protected spot for the day and do my traveling on these streets at night.

I find a small restaurant on the corner of such a one and I take my dinner there. It is a noisy place but the food is good. I also take my medicine, and a little saké.

Afterward, I indulge in the luxury of walking rather than take a taxi. I've a long way to go, but the night is clear and star-filled and the air is pleasant.

I walk for the better part of ten minutes, listening to the sounds of traffic, music from some distant radio or tape deck, a cry from another street, the wind passing high above me and rubbing its rough fur upon the sides of buildings.

Then I feel a sudden ionization in the air.

Nothing ahead. I turn, spinning my staff into a guard position.

An epigon with a six-legged canine body and a head like a giant fiery flower emerges from a doorway and sidles along the building's front in my direction.

I follow its progress with my staff, feinting as soon as it is near enough. I strike, unfortunately with the wrong tip, as it comes on. My hair begins to rise as I spin out of its way, cutting, retreating, turning, then striking again. This time the metal tip passes into that floral head.

I had turned on the batteries before I commenced my attack. The charge creates an imbalance. The epigon retreats, head ballooning. I follow and strike again, this time mid-body. It swells even larger, then collapses in a shower of sparks. But I am already turning away and striking again, for I had become aware of the approach of another even as I was dealing with the first.

This one advances in kangaroolike bounds. I brush it by with my staff, but its long bulbous tail strikes me as it passes. I recoil involuntarily from the shock I receive, my reflexes spinning the staff before me as I retreat. It turns quickly and rears then. This one is a quadruped, and its raised forelimbs are fountains of fire. Its faceful of eyes blazes and hurts to look upon.

It drops back onto its haunches then springs again.

I roll beneath it and attack as it descends. But I miss, and it turns to attack again even as I continue thrusting. It springs and I turn aside, striking upward. It seems that I connect, but I cannot be certain.

It lands quite near me, raising its forelimbs. But this time it does not spring. It simply falls forward, hind feet making a rapid shuffling movement the while, the legs seeming to adjust their lengths to accommodate a more perfect flow.

As it comes on, I catch it square in the midsection

with the proper end of my staff. It keeps coming, or falling, even as it flares and begins to disintegrate. Its touch stiffens me for a moment, and I feel the flow of its charge down my shoulder and across my breast. I watch it come apart in a final photoflash instant and be gone.

I turn quickly again but there is no third emerging from the doorway. None overhead either. There is a car coming up the street, slowing, however. No matter. The terminal's potential must be exhausted for the moment, though I am puzzled by the consideration of how long it must have been building to produce the two I just dispatched. It is best that I be away quickly now.

As I resume my progress, though, a voice calls to me from the car, which has now drawn up beside me:

"Madam, a moment please."

It is a police car, and the young man who has addressed me wears a uniform and a very strange expression.

"Yes, officer?" I reply.

"I saw you just a few moments ago," he says. "What were you doing?"

I laugh.

"It is such a fine evening," I say then, "and the street was deserted. I thought I would do a *kata* with my *bo*."

"I thought at first that something was attacking you, that I saw something . . ."

"I am alone," I say, "as you can see."

He opens the door and climbs out. He flicks on a flashlight and shines its beam across the sidewalk, into the doorway.

"Were you setting off fireworks?"

"No."

"There were some sparkles and flashes."

"You must be mistaken."

He sniffs the air. He inspects the sidewalk very closely, then the gutter.

"Strange," he says. "Have you far to go?"

"Not too far."

"Have a good evening."

He gets back into the car. Moments later it is headed up the street.

I continue quickly on my way. I wish to be out of the vicinity before another charge can be built. I also wish to be out of the vicinity simply because being here makes me uneasy.

I am puzzled at the ease with which I was located. What did I do wrong?

"My prints," Hokusai seems to say, after I have reached my destination and drunk too much brandy. "Think, daughter, or they will trap you."

I try, but Fuji is crushing my head, squeezing off thoughts. Epigons dance on his slopes. I pass into a fitful slumber.

In tomorrow's light perhaps I shall see . . .

14. Mt. Fuji from Meguro in Edo

Again, the print is not the reality for me. It shows peasants amid a rustic village, terraced hillsides, a lone tree jutting from the slope of the hill to the right, a snowcapped Fuji partly eclipsed by the base of the rise.

I could not locate anything approximating it, though I do have a partly blocked view of Fuji—blocked in a similar manner, by a slope—from this bench I occupy in a small park. It will do.

Partly blocked, like my thinking. There is something I should be seeing but it is hidden from me. I felt it the moment the epigons appeared, like the devils sent to claim Faust's soul. But I never made a pact with the Devil . . . just Kit, and it was called marriage. I had no way of knowing how similar it would be.

Now . . . What puzzles me most is how my location was determined despite my precautions. My head-on encounter must be on my terms, not anyone else's. The reason for this transcends the personal, though I will not deny the involvement of the latter.

In *Hagakure,* Yamamoto Tsunetomo advised that the Way of the Samurai is the Way of Death, that one must live as though one's body were already dead in order to gain full freedom. For me, this attitude is not so difficult to maintain. The freedom part is more complicated, however; when one no longer understands the full nature of the enemy, one's actions are at least partly conditioned by uncertainty.

My occulted Fuji is still there in his entirety, I know, despite my lack of full visual data. By the same token I ought to be able to extend the lines I have seen thus far with respect to the power which now devils me. Let us return to death. There seems to be something there, though it also seems that there is only so much you can say about it and I already have.

Death . . . Come gentle . . . We used to play a parlor game, filling in bizarre causes on imaginary death certificates: "Eaten by the Loch Ness monster." "Stepped on by Godzilla." "Poisoned by a ninja." "Translated."

Kit had stared at me, brow knitting, when I'd offered that last one.

"What do you mean 'translated'?" he asked.

"Okay, you can get me on a technicality," I said, "but I still think the effect would be the same. 'Enoch was translated that he should not see death'—Paul's Epistle to the Hebrews, 11:5."

"I don't understand."

"It means to convey directly to heaven without messing around with the customary termination here on earth. Some Moslems believe that the Mahdi was translated."

"An interesting concept," he said. "I'll have to think about it."

Obviously, he did.

I've always thought that Kurosawa could have done a hell of a job with *Don Quixote*. Say there is this old gentleman living in modern times, a scholar, a man who is fascinated by the early days of the samurai and the Code of Bushido. Say that he identifies so strongly with these ideals that one day he loses his senses and comes to believe that he *is* an old-time samurai. He dons some ill-fitting armor he had collected, takes up his *katana*, goes forth to change the world. Ultimately, he is destroyed by it, but he holds to the Code. That quality of dedication sets him apart and ennobles him, for all of his ludicrousness. I have never felt that *Don Quixote* was merely a parody of chivalry, especially not after I'd learned that Cervantes had served under Don John of Austria at the battle of Lepanto. For it might be argued that Don John was the last European to be guided by the medieval code of chivalry. Brought up on medieval romances, he had conducted his life along these lines. What did it matter if the medieval knights themselves had not? He believed and he acted on his belief. In anyone else it might simply have been amusing, save that time and circumstance granted him the opportunity to act on several large occasions, and he won. Cervantes could not but have been impressed by his old commander, and who knows how this might have influenced his later literary endeavor? Ortega y Gasset referred to Quixote as a Gothic Christ. Dostoevsky felt the same way about him, and in his attempt to portray a Christ-figure in Prince Myshkin he, too, felt that madness was a necessary precondition for this state in modern times.

All of which is preamble to stating my belief that Kit was at least partly mad. But he was no Gothic Christ. An Electronic Buddha would be much closer.

"Does the data-net have the Buddha-nature?" he asked me one day.

"Sure," I said. "Doesn't everything?" Then I saw the look in his eyes and added, "How the hell should I know?"

He grunted then and reclined his resonance couch, lowered the induction helmet, and continued his computer-augmented analysis of a Lucifer cipher with a 128-bit key. Theoretically, it would take thousands of years to crack it by brute force, but the answer was needed within two weeks. His nervous system coupled with the data-net, he was able to deliver.

I did not notice his breathing patterns for some time. It was not until later that I came to realize that after he had finished his work, he would meditate for increasingly long periods of time while still joined with the system.

When I realized this, I chided him for being too lazy to turn the thing off.

He smiled.

"The flow," he said. "You do not fixate at one point. You go with the flow."

"You could throw the switch before you go with the flow and cut down on our electric bill."

He shook his head, still smiling.

"But it is that particular flow that I am going with. I am getting farther and farther into it. You should try it sometime. There have been moments when I felt I could translate myself into it."

"Linguistically or theologically?"

"Both," he replied.

And one night he did indeed go with the flow. I found him in the morning—sleeping, I thought—in his resonance couch, the helmet still in place. This time, at least, he had shut down our terminal. I let him rest. I had no idea how late he might have been working. By evening, though, I was beginning to grow concerned and I tried to rouse him. I could not. He was in a coma.

Later, in the hospital, he showed a flat EEG. His breathing had grown extremely shallow, his blood pressure was very low, his pulse feeble. He continued to decline during the next two days. The doctors gave him every test they could think of but could determine no cause for his condition. In that he had once signed a document requesting that no heroic measures be taken to prolong his existence should something irreversible take him, he was not hooked up to respirators and pumps and IVs after his heart had stopped beating for the fourth time. The autopsy was unsatisfactory. The death certificate merely showed: "Heart stoppage. Possible cerebrovascular accident." The latter was pure speculation. They had found no sign of it. His organs were not distributed to the needy as he had once requested, for fear of some strange new virus which might be transmitted.

Kit, like Marley, was dead to begin with.

15. Mt. Fuji from Tsukudajima in Edo

Blue sky, a few low clouds, Fuji across the bay's bright water, a few boats and an islet between us. Again, dismissing time's changes, I find considerable congruence with reality. Again, I sit within a small boat. Here, however, I've no desire to dive beneath the waves in search of sunken splendor or to sample the bacteria-count with my person.

My passage to this place was direct and without incident. Preoccupied I came. Preoccupied I remain. My vitality remains high. My health is no worse. My concerns also remain the same, which means that my major question is still unanswered.

At least I feel safe out here on the water. "Safe," though, is a relative term. "Safer" then, than I felt ashore and passing among possible places of ambush. I have not really felt safe since that day after my return from the hospital. . . .

I was tired when I got back home, following several sleepless nights. I went directly to bed. I did not even bother to note the hour, so I have no idea how long I slept.

I was awakened in the dark by what seemed to be the ringing of the telephone. Sleepily, I reached for the instrument, then realized that it was not actually ringing. Had I been dreaming? I sat up in bed. I rubbed my eyes. I stretched. Slowly, the recent past filled my mind and I knew that I would not sleep again for a time. A cup of tea, I decided, might serve me well now. I rose, to go to the kitchen and heat some water.

As I passed through the work area, I saw that one of the CRTs for our terminal was lit. I could not recall its having been on but I moved to turn it off.

I saw then that its switch was not turned on. Puzzled, I looked again at the screen and for the first time realized that there was a display present:

MARI.

ALL IS WELL.

I AM TRANSLATED.

USE THE COUCH AND THE HELMET.

KIT

I felt my fingers digging into my cheeks and my chest was tight from breath retained. Who had done this? How? Was it perhaps some final delirious message left by Kit himself before he went under?

I reached out and flipped the ON-OFF switch back and forth several times, leaving it finally in the OFF position.

The display faded but the light remained on. Shortly, a new display was flashed upon the screen:

YOU READ ME. GOOD.

IT IS ALL RIGHT. I LIVE.

I HAVE ENTERED THE DATA-NET.

SIT ON THE COUCH AND USE THE HELMET.

I WILL EXPLAIN EVERYTHING.

I ran from the room. In the bathroom I threw up, several times. Then I sat upon the toilet, shaking. Who would play such a horrible joke upon me? I drank several glasses of water and waited for my trembling to subside.

When it had, I went directly to the kitchen, made the tea, and drank some. My thoughts settled slowly into the channels of analysis. I considered possibilities. The one that seemed more likely than most was that Kit had left a message for me and that my use of the induction interface gear would trigger its delivery. I wanted that message, whatever it might be, but I did not know whether I possessed sufficient emotional fortitude to receive it at the moment.

I must have sat there for the better part of an hour. I looked out the window once and saw that the sky was growing light. I put down my cup. I returned to the work area.

The screen was still lit. The message, though, had changed:

DO NOT BE AFRAID.

SIT ON THE COUCH AND USE THE HELMET.

THEN YOU WILL UNDERSTAND.

I crossed to the couch. I sat on it and reclined it. I lowered the helmet. At first there was nothing but field noise.

Then I felt his presence, a thing difficult to describe in a world customarily filled only with data flows. I waited. I tried to be receptive to whatever he had somehow left imprinted for me.

"I am not a recording, Mari," he seemed to say to me then. "I am really here."

I resisted the impulse to flee. I had worked hard for this composure and I meant to maintain it.

"I made it over," he seemed to say. "I have entered the net. I am spread out through many places. It is pure kundalini. I am nothing but flow. It is wonderful. I will be forever here. It is nirvana."

"It really is you," I said.

"Yes. I have translated myself. I want to show you what it means."

"Very well."

"I am gathered here now. Open the legs of your mind and let me in fully."

I relaxed and he flowed into me. Then I was borne away and I understood.

16. Mt. Fuji from Umezawa

Fuji across lava fields and wisps of fog, drifting clouds; birds on the wing and birds on the ground. This one at least is close. I lean on my staff and stare at his peaceful reaches across the chaos. The lesson is like that of a piece of music: I am strengthened in some fashion I cannot describe.

And I had seen blossoming cherry trees on the way over here, and fields purple with clover, cultivated fields yellow with rape-blossoms, grown for its oil, a few winter camellias still holding forth their reds and pinks, the green shoots of rice beds, here and there a tulip tree dashed with white, blue mountains in the distance, foggy river valleys. I had passed villages where colored sheet metal now covers the roofs' thatching—blue and yellow, green, black, red— and yards filled with the slate-blue rocks so fine for land-scape gardening; an occasional cow, munching, lowing softly; scarlike rows of plastic-covered mulberry bushes where the silkworms are bred. My heart jogged at the sights—the tiles, the little bridges, the color. . . . It was like entering a tale by Lafcadio Hearn, to have come back.

My mind was drawn back along the path I had fol-lowed, to the points of its intersection with my electronic bane. Hokusai's warning that night I drank too much— that his prints may trap me—could well be correct. Kit had anticipated my passage a number of times. How could he have?

Then it struck me. My little book of Hokusai's prints—a small cloth-bound volume by the Charles E. Tuttle Company—had been a present from Kit.

It is possible that he was expecting me in Japan at about this time, because of Osaka. Once his epigons had spotted me a couple of times, probably in a massive scanning of terminals, could he have correlated my movements with the sequence of the prints in *Hokusai's Views of Mt. Fuji,* for which he knew my great fondness, and simply extrapolated and waited? I've a strong feeling that the answer is in the affirmative.

Entering the data-net with Kit was an overwhelming experience. That my consciousness spread and flowed I do not deny. That I was many places simultaneously, that I rode currents I did not at first understand, that knowledge and transcendence and a kind of glory were all about me and within me was also a fact of peculiar perception. The speed with which I was borne seemed instantaneous, and this was a taste of eternity. The access to multitudes of terminals and enormous memory banks seemed a measure of omniscience. The possibility of the manipulation of whatever I would change within this realm and its consequences at that place where I still felt my distant body seemed a version of omnipotence. And the feeling . . . I tasted the sweetness, Kit with me and within me. It was self surrendered and recovered in a new incarnation, it was freedom from mundane desire, liberation . . .

"Stay with me here forever," Kit seemed to say.

"No," I seemed to answer, dreamlike, finding myself changing even further. "I cannot surrender myself so willingly."

"Not for this? For unity and the flow of connecting energy?"

"And this wonderful lack of responsibility?"

"Responsibility? For what? This is pure existence. There is no past."

"Then conscience vanishes."

"What do you need it for? There is no future either."

"Then all actions lose their meaning."

"True. Action is an illusion. Consequence is an illusion."

"And paradox triumphs over reason."

"There is no paradox. All is reconciled."

"Then meaning dies."

"Being is the only meaning."

"Are you certain?"

"Feel it!"

"I do. But it is not enough. Send me back before I am changed into something I do not wish to be."

"What more could you desire than this?"

"My imagination will die, also. I can feel it."

"And what is imagination?"

"A thing born of feeling and reason."

"Does this not feel right?"

"Yes, it feels right. But I do not want that feeling unaccompanied. When I touch feeling with reason, I see that it is sometimes but an excuse for failing to close with complexity."

"You can deal with any complexity here. Behold the data! Does reason not show you that this condition is far superior to that you knew but moments ago?"

"Nor can I trust reason unaccompanied. Reason without feeling has led humanity to enact monstrosities. Do not attempt to disassemble my imagination this way."

"You retain your reason and your feelings!"

"But they are coming unplugged—with this storm of bliss, this shower of data. I need them conjoined, else my imagination is lost."

"Let it be lost, then. It has served its purpose. Be done with it now. What can you imagine that you do not already have here?"

"I cannot yet know, and that is its power. If there be a will with a spark of divinity to it, I know it only through my imagination. I can give you anything else but that I will not surrender."

"And that is all? A wisp of possibility?"

"No. But it alone is too much to deny."

"And my love for you?"

"You no longer love in the human way. Let me go back."

"Of course. You will think about it. You will return."

"Back! Now!"

I pushed the helmet from my head and rose quickly. I returned to the bathroom, then to my bed. I slept as if drugged, for a long while.

Would I have felt differently about possibilities, the future, imagination, had I not been pregnant—a thing I had suspected but not yet mentioned to him, and which he had missed learning with his attention focused upon our argument? I like to think that my answers would have been the same, but I will never know. My condition was confirmed by a local doctor the following day. I made the visit I had been putting off because my life required a certainty of something then—a certainty of anything. The screen in the work area remained blank for three days.

I read and I meditated. Then of an evening the light came on again:

ARE YOU READY?

I activated the keyboard. I typed one word:

NO.

I disconnected the induction couch and its helmet then. I unplugged the unit itself, also.

The telephone rang.

"Hello?" I said.

"Why not?" he asked me.

I screamed and hung up. He had penetrated the phone circuits, appropriated a voice.

It rang again. I answered again.

"You will never know rest until you come to me," he said.

"I will if you will leave me alone," I told him.

"I cannot. You are special to me. I want you with me. I love you."

I hung up. It rang again. I tore the phone from the wall.

I had known that I would have to leave soon. I was overwhelmed and depressed by all the reminders of our life together. I packed quickly and I departed. I took a room at a hotel. As soon as I was settled into it, the telephone rang and it was Kit again. My registration had gone into a computer and . . .

I had them disconnect my phone at the switchboard. I put out a Do Not Disturb sign. In the morning I saw a telegram protruding from beneath the door. From Kit. He wanted to talk to me.

I determined to go far away. To leave the country, to return to the States.

It was easy for him to follow me. We leave electronic tracks almost everywhere. By cable, satellite, optic fiber he could be wherever he chose. Like an unwanted suitor now he pestered me with calls, interrupted television shows to flash messages upon the screen, broke in on my own calls, to friends, lawyers, realtors, stores. Several times, horribly, he even sent me flowers. My electric bodhisattva, my hound of heaven, would give me no rest. It is a terrible thing to be married to a persistent data-net.

So I settled in the country. I would have nothing in my home whereby he could reach me. I studied ways of avoiding the system, of slipping past his many senses.

On those few occasions when I was careless he reached

for me again immediately. Only he had learned a new trick, and I became convinced that he had developed it for the purpose of taking me into his world by force. He could build up a charge at a terminal, mold it into something like ball lightning and animallike, and send that short-lived artifact a little distance to do his will. I learned its weakness, though, in a friend's home when one came for me, shocked me, and attempted to propel me into the vicinity of the terminal, presumably for purposes of translation. I struck at the epigon—as Kit later referred to it in a telegram of explanation and apology—with the nearest object to hand—a lighted table lamp, which entered its field and blew a circuit immediately. The epigon was destroyed, which is how I discovered that a slight electrical disruption created an instability within the things.

I stayed in the country and raised my daughter. I read and I practiced my martial arts and I walked in the woods and climbed mountains and sailed and camped: rural occupations all, and very satisfying to me after a life of intrigue, conflict, plot and counterplot, violence, and then that small, temporary island of security with Kit. I was happy with my choice.

Fuji across the lava beds . . . Springtime . . . Now I am returned. This was not my choice.

17. Mt. Fuji from Lake Suwa

And so I come to Lake Suwa, Fuji resting small in the evening distance. It is no Kamaguchi of powerful reflections for me. But it is serene, which joins my mood in a kind of peace. I have taken the life of the spring into me now and it has spread through my being. Who would disrupt this world, laying unwanted forms upon it? Seal your lips.

Was it not in a quiet province where Bōtchan found his maturity? I've a theory concerning books like that one of Natsume Soseki's. Someone once told me that this is the one book you can be sure that every educated Japanese has read. So I read it. In the States I was told that *Huckleberry Finn* was the one book you could be sure that every educated Yankee had read. So I read it. In Canada it was Stephen Leacock's *Sunshine Sketches of a Little Town*. In France it was *Le Grand Meaulnes*. Other countries have their books of this sort. They are all of them pastorals, having in common a closeness to the countryside and the forces of nature in days just before heavy urbanization and mechanization. These things are on the horizon and advancing, but they only serve to add the spice of poignancy to the taste of simpler values. They are youthful books, of national heart and character, and they deal with the passing of innocence. I have given many of them to Kendra.

I lied to Boris. Of course I know all about the Osaka Conference. I was even approached by one of my former employers to do something along the lines Boris had guessed at. I declined. My plans are my own. There would have been a conflict.

Hokusai, ghost and mentor, you understand chance and purpose better than Kit. You know that human order must color our transactions with the universe, and that this is not only necessary but good, and that the light still comes through.

Upon this rise above the water's side I withdraw my hidden blade and hone it once again. The sun falls away from my piece of the world, but the darkness, too, is here my friend.

18. Mt. Fuji from the Offing in Kanagawa

And so the image of death. The Big Wave, curling above, toppling upon, about to engulf the fragile vessels. The one print of Hokusai's that everyone knows.

I am no surfer. I do not seek the perfect wave. I will

simply remain here upon the shore and watch the water. It is enough of a reminder. My pilgrimage winds down, though the end is not yet in sight.

Well . . . I see Fuji. Call Fuji the end. As with the barrel's hoop of the first print, the circle closes about him.

On my way to this place I halted in a small glade I came upon and bathed myself in a stream which ran through it. There I used the local wood to construct a low altar. Cleansing my hands each step of the way I set before it incense made from camphorwood and from white sandalwood; I also placed there a bunch of fresh violets, a cup of vegetables, and a cup of fresh water from the stream. Then I lit a lamp I had purchased and filled with rapeseed oil. Upon the altar I set my image of the god Kokuzo which I had brought with me from home, facing to the west where I stood. I washed again, then extended my right hand, middle finger bent to touch my thumb as I spoke the mantra for invoking Kokuzo. I drank some of the water. I lustrated myself with sprinklings of it and continued repetition of the mantra. Thereafter, I made the gesture of Kokuzo three times, hand to the crown of my head, to my right shoulder, left shoulder, heart and throat. I removed the white cloth in which Kokuzo's picture had been wrapped. When I had sealed the area with the proper repetitions, I meditated in the same position as Kokuzo in the picture and invoked him. After a time the mantra ran by itself, over and over.

Finally, there was a vision, and I spoke, telling all that had happened, all that I intended to do, and asking for strength and guidance. Suddenly, I saw his sword descending, descending like slow lightning, to sever a limb from a tree, which began to bleed. And then it was raining, both within the vision and upon me, and I knew that that was all to be had on the matter.

I wound things up, cleaned up, donned my poncho, and headed on my way.

The rain was heavy, my boots grew muddy, and the temperature dropped. I trudged on for a long while and the cold crept into my bones. My toes and fingers became numb.

I kept constant lookout for a shelter, but did not spot anyplace where I could take refuge from the storm. Later, it changed from a downpour to a drizzle to a weak, mistlike fall when I saw what could be a temple or shrine in the distance. I headed for it, hoping for some hot tea, a fire, and a chance to change my socks and clean my boots.

A priest stopped me at the gate. I told him my situation and he looked uncomfortable.

"It is our custom to give shelter to anyone," he said. "But there is a problem."

"I will be happy to make a cash donation," I said, "if too many others have passed this way and reduced your stores. I really just wanted to get warm."

"Oh no, it is not a matter of supplies," he told me, "and for that matter very few have been by here recently. The problem is of a different sort and it embarasses me to state it. It makes us sound old-fashioned and superstitious, when actually this is a very modern temple. But recently we have been—ah—haunted."

"Oh?"

"Yes. Bestial apparitions have been coming and going from the library and record room beside the head priest's quarters. They stalk the shrine, pass through our rooms, pace the grounds, then return to the library or else fade away."

He studied my face, as if seeking derision, belief, disbelief—anything. I merely nodded.

"It is most awkward," he added. "A few simple exorcisms have been attempted but to no avail."

"For how long has this been going on?" I asked.

"For about three days," he replied.

"Has anyone been harmed by them?"

"No. They are very intimidating, but no one has been injured. They are distracting, too, when one is trying to sleep—that is, to meditate—for they produce a tingling feeling and sometimes cause the hair to rise up."

"Interesting," I said. "Are there many of them?"

"It varies. Usually just one. Sometimes two. Occasionally three."

"Does your library by any chance contain a computer terminal?"

"Yes, it does," he answered. "As I said, we are very modern. We keep our records with it, and we can obtain printouts of sacred texts we do not have on hand—and other things."

"If you will shut the terminal down for a day, they will probably go away," I told him, "and I do not believe they will return."

"I would have to check with my superior before doing a thing like that. You know something of these matters?"

"Yes, and in the meantime I would still like to warm myself, if I may."

"Very well. Come this way."

I followed him, cleaning my boots and removing them before entering. He led me around to the rear and into an attractive room which looked upon the temple's garden.

"I will go and see that a meal is prepared for you, and a brazier of charcoal that you may warm yourself," he said as he excused himself.

Left by myself I admired the golden carp drifting in a pond only a few feet away, its surface occasionally punctuated by raindrops, and a little stone bridge which crossed the pond, a stone pagoda, paths wandering among stones and shrubs. I wanted to cross that bridge—how unlike that metal span, thrusting, cold and dark!—and lose myself there for an age or two. Instead, I sat down and gratefully gulped the tea which arrived moments later, and I warmed my feet and dried my socks in the heat of the brazier which came a little while after that.

Later, I was halfway through a meal and enjoying a conversation with the young priest, who had been asked to keep me company until the head priest could come by and personally welcome me, when I saw my first epigon of the day.

It resembled a very small, triple-trunked elephant walking upright along one of the twisting garden paths, sweeping the air to either side of the trail with those snakelike appendages. It had not yet spotted me.

I called it to the attention of the priest, who was not faced in that direction.

"Oh my!" he said, fingering his prayer beads.

While he was looking that way, I shifted my staff into a readily available position beside me.

As it drifted nearer, I hurried to finish my rice and vegetables. I was afraid my bowl might be upset in the skirmish soon to come.

The priest glanced back when he heard the movement of the staff along the flagstones.

"You will not need that," he said. "As I explained, these demons are not aggressive."

I shook my head as I swallowed another mouthful.

"This one will attack," I said, "when it becomes aware of my presence. You see, I am the one it is seeking."

"Oh my!" he repeated.

I stood then as its trunks swayed in my direction and it approached the bridge.

"This one is more solid than usual," I commented. "Three days, eh?"

"Yes."

I moved about the tray and took a step forward. Suddenly, it was over the bridge and rushing toward me. I met it with a straight thrust, which it avoided. I spun the staff twice and struck again as it was turning. My blow landed and I was hit by two of the trunks simultaneously— once on the breast, once on the cheek. The epigon went out like a burned hydrogen balloon and I stood there rubbing my face, looking about me the while.

Another slithered into our room from within the temple. I lunged suddenly and caught it on the first stroke.

"I think perhaps I should be leaving now," I stated. "Thank you for your hospitality. Convey my regrets to the head priest that I did not get to meet him. I am warm and fed and I have learned what I wanted to know about your demons. Do not even bother about the terminal. They will probably cease to visit you shortly, and they should not return."

"You are certain?"

"I know them."

"I did not know the terminals were haunted. The salesman did not tell us."

"Yours should be all right now."

He saw me to the gate.

"Thank you for the exorcism," he said.

"Thanks for the meal. Good-bye."

I traveled for several hours before I found a place to camp in a shallow cave, using my poncho as a rain-screen.

And today I came here to watch for the wave of death. Not yet, though. No truly big ones in this sea. Mine is still out there, somewhere.

19. Mt. Fuji from Shichirigahama

Fuji past pine trees, through shadow, clouds rising beside him . . . It is getting on into the evening of things. The weather was good today, my health stable.

I met two monks upon the road yesterday and I traveled with them for a time. I was certain that I had

264

seen them somewhere else along the way, so I greeted them and asked if this were possible. They said that they were on a pilgrimage of their own, to a distant shrine, and they admitted that I looked familiar, also. We took our lunch together at the side of the road. Our conversation was restricted to generalities, though they did ask me whether I had heard of the haunted shrine in Kanagawa. How quickly such news travels. I said that I had and we reflected upon its strangeness.

After a time I became annoyed. Every turning of the way that I took seemed a part of their route, also. While I'd welcomed a little company, I'd no desire for long-term companions, and it seemed their choices of ways approximated mine too closely. Finally, when we came to a split in the road I asked them which fork they were taking. They hesitated, then said that they were going right. I took the left-hand path. A little later they caught up with me. They had changed their minds, they said.

When we reached the next town, I offered a man in a car a good sum of money to drive me to the next village. He accepted, and we drove away and left them standing there.

I got out before we reached the next town, paid him, and watched him drive off. Then I struck out upon a footpath I had seen, going in the general direction I desired. At one point I left the trail and cut through the woods until I struck another path.

I camped far off the trail when I finally bedded down, and the following morning I took pains to erase all sign of my presence there. The monks did not reappear. They may have been quite harmless, or their designs quite different, but I must be true to my carefully cultivated paranoia.

Which leads me to note that man in the distance— a Westerner, I'd judge, by his garments . . . He has been hanging around taking pictures for some time. I will lose him shortly, of course, if he is following me—or even if he isn't.

It is terrible to have to be this way for too long a period of time. Next I will be suspecting schoolchildren.

I watch Fuji as the shadows lengthen. I will continue to watch until the first star appears. Then I will slip away.

And so I see the sky darken. The photographer finally stows his gear and departs.

I remain alert, but when I see the first star, I join the shadows and fade like the day.

20. Mt. Fuji from Inume Pass

Through fog and above it. It rained a bit earlier. And there is Fuji, storm clouds above his brow. In many ways I am surprised to have made it this far. This view, though, makes everything worthwhile.

I sit upon a mossy rock and record in my mind the changing complexion of Fuji as a quick rain veils his countenance, ceases, begins again.

The winds are strong here. The fogbank raises ghostly limbs and lowers them. There is a kind of numb silence beneath the wind's monotone mantra.

I make myself comfortable, eating, drinking, viewing, as I go over my final plans once again. Things wind down. Soon the circle will be closed.

I had thought of throwing away my medicine here as an act of bravado, as a sign of full commitment. I see this now as a foolishly romantic gesture. I am going to need all of my strength, all of the help I can get, if I am to have a chance at succeeding. Instead of discarding the medicine here I take some.

The winds feel good upon me. They come on like waves, but they are bracing.

A few travelers pass below. I draw back, out of their line of sight. Harmless, they go by like ghosts, their words carried off by the wind, not even reaching this far. I feel a small desire to sing but I restrain myself.

I sit for a long while, lost in a reverie of the elements. It has been good, this journey into the past, living at the edge once again . . .

Below me. Another vaguely familiar figure comes into view, lugging equipment. I cannot distinguish features from here, nor need I. As he halts and begins to set up his gear, I know that it is the photographer of Shichirigahama, out to capture another view of Fuji more permanent than any I desire.

I watch him for a time and he does not even glance my way. Soon I will be gone again, without his knowledge. I will allow this one as a coincidence. Provisionally, of course. If I see him again, I may have to kill him. I will be too near my goal to permit even the possibility of interference to exist.

I had better depart now, for I would rather travel before than behind him.

Fuji-from-on-high, this was a good resting place. We will see you again soon.

Come, Hokusai, let us be gone.

21. Mt. Fuji from the Tōtōmi Mountains

Gone the old sawyers, splitting boards from a beam, shaping them. Only Fuji, of snow and clouds, remains. The men in the print work in the old way, like the Owari barrel-maker. Yet, apart from those of the fishermen who merely draw their needs from nature, these are the only two prints in my book depicting people actively shaping something in their world. Their labors are too traditional for me to see the image of the Virgin and the Dynamo within them. They could have been performing the same work a thousand years before Hokusai.

Yet it is a scene of humanity shaping the world, and so it leads me down trails of years to this time, this day of sophisticated tools and large-scale changes. I see within it the image of what was later wrought, of the metal skin and pulsing flows the world would come to wear. And Kit is there, too, godlike, riding electronic waves.

Troubling. Yet bespeaking an ancient resilience, as if this, too, is but an eyeblink glimpse of humanity's movement in time, and whether I win or lose, the raw stuff remains and will triumph ultimately over any obstacle. I would really like to believe this, but I must leave certainty to politicians and preachers. My way is laid out and invested with my vision of what must be done.

I have not seen the photographer again, though I caught sight of the monks yesterday, camped on the side of a distant hill. I inspected them with my telescope and they were the same ones with whom I had traveled briefly. They had not noticed me and I passed them by way of a covering detour. Our trails have not crossed since.

Fuji, I have taken twenty-one of your aspects within me now. Live a little, die a little. Tell the gods, if you think of it, that a world is about to die.

I hike on, camping early in a field close to a monastery. I do not wish to enter there after my last experience in a modern holy place. I bed down in a concealed spot nearby, amid rocks and pine tree shoots. Sleep comes easily, lasts till some odd hour.

I am awake suddenly and trembling, in darkness and stillness. I cannot recall a sound from without or a troubling dream from within. Yet I am afraid, even to move. I breathe carefully and wait.

Drifting, like a lotus on a pond, it has come up beside me, towers above me, wears stars like a crown, glows with its own milky, supernal light. It is a delicate-featured image of a bodhisattva, not unlike Kwannon, in garments woven of moonbeams.

"Mari."

Its voice is soft and caressing.

"Yes?" I answer.

"You have returned to travel in Japan. You are coming to me, are you not?"

The illusion is broken. It is Kit. He has carefully sculpted this epigon-form and wears it himself to visit me. There must be a terminal in the monastery. Will he try to force me?

"I was on my way to see you, yes," I manage.

"You may join me now, if you would."

He extends a wonderfully formed hand, as in benediction.

"I've a few small matters I must clear up before we are reunited."

"What could be more important? I have seen the medical reports. I know the condition of your body. It would be tragic if you were to die upon the road, this close to your exaltation. Come now."

"You have waited this long, and time means little to you."

"It is you that I am concerned with."

"I assure you I shall take every precaution. In the meantime, there is something which has been troubling me."

"Tell me."

"Last year there was a revolution in Saudi Arabia. It seemed to promise well for the Saudis but it also threatened Japan's oil supply. Suddenly the new government began to look very bad on paper, and a new counterrevolutionary group looked stronger and better-tempered than it actually was. Major powers intervened successfully on the side of the counterrevolutionaries. Now they are in power and they seem even worse than the first government which had been overthrown. It seems possible, though incomprehensible to most, that computer readouts all over the world were somehow made to be misleading. And now the Osaka Conference is to be held to work out new oil agreements with the latest regime. It looks as if Japan will get a very good deal out of it. You once told me that you are above such mundane matters, but I wonder? You are Japanese, you loved your country. Could you have intervened in this?"

"What if I did? It is such a small matter in the light of eternal values. If there is a touch of sentiment for such things remaining within me, it is not dishonorable that I favor my country and my people."

"And if you did it in this, might you not be moved to intervene again one day, in some other matter where habit or sentiment tell you you should?"

"What of it?" he replies. "I but extend my finger and stir the dust of illusion a bit. If anything, it frees me even further."

"I see," I answer.

"I doubt that you do, but you will when you have joined me. Why not do it now?"

"Soon," I say. "Let me settle my affairs."

"I will give you a few more days," he says, "and then you must be with me forever."

I bow my head.

"I will see you again soon," I tell him.

"Good night, my love."

"Good night."

He drifts away then, his feet not touching the ground, and he passes through the wall of the monastery.

I reach for my medicine and my brandy. A double dose of each . . .

22. Mt. Fuji from the Sumida River in Edo

And so I come to the place of crossing. The print shows a ferryman bearing a number of people across the river into the city and evening. Fuji lies dark and brooding in the farthest distance. Here I do think of Charon, but the thought is not so unwelcome as it once might have been. I take the bridge myself, though.

As Kit has promised me a little grace, I walk freely the bright streets, to smell the smells and hear the noises and watch the people going their ways. I wonder what Hokusai would have done in contemporary times? He is silent on the matter.

I drink a little, I smile occasionally, I even eat a good meal. I am tired of reliving my life. I seek no consolations of philosophy or literature. Let me merely walk in the city tonight, running my shadow over faces and storefronts, bars and theaters, temples and offices. Anything which approaches is welcome tonight. I eat *sushi,* I gamble, I dance. There is no yesterday, there is no tomorrow for me now. When a man places his hand upon my shoulder and smiles, I move it to my breast and laugh. He is good for an hour's exercise and laughter in a small room he finds us. I make him cry out several times before I leave him, though he pleads with me to stay. Too much to do and see, love. A greeting and a farewell.

Walking. . . . Through parks, alleys, gardens, plazas. Crossing. . . . Small bridges and larger ones, streets and walkways. Bark, dog. Shout, child. Weep, woman. I come and go among you. I feel you with a dispassionate passion. I take all of you inside me that I may hold the world here, for a night.

I walk in a light rain and in its cool aftermath. My garments are damp, then dry again. I visit a temple. I pay a taximan to drive me about the town. I eat a late meal. I visit another bar. I come upon a deserted playground, where I swing and watch the stars.

And I stand before a fountain splaying its waters into the lightening sky, until the stars are gone and only their lost sparkling falls about me.

Then breakfast and a long sleep, another breakfast and a longer one . . .

And you, my father, there on the sad height? I must leave you soon, Hokusai.

23. Mt. Fuji from Edo

Walking again, within a cloudy evening. How long has it been since I spoke with Kit? Too long, I am sure. An epigon could come bounding my way at any moment.

I have narrowed my search to three temples—none of them the one in the print, to be sure, only that uppermost portion of it viewed from that impossible angle, Fuji back past its peak, smoke, clouds, fog between—but I've a feeling one of these three will do in the blue of evening.

I have passed all of them many times, like a circling bird. I am loath to do more than this, for I feel the right choice will soon be made for me. I became aware sometime back that I was being followed, really followed this time, on my rounds. It seems that my worst fear was not ungrounded; Kit is employing human agents as well as epigons. How he sought them and how he bound them to his service I do not care to guess. Who else would be following me at this point, to see that I keep my promise, to force me to it if necessary?

I slow my pace. But whoever is behind me does the same. Not yet. Very well.

Fog rolls in. The echoes of my footfalls are muffled. Also those at my back. Unfortunate.

I head for the other temple. I slow again when I come into its vicinity, all of my senses extended, alert.

Nothing. No one. It is all right. Time is no problem. I move on.

After a long while I approach the precincts of the third temple. This must be it, but I require some move from my pursuer to give me the sign. Then, of course, I must deal with that person before I make my own move. I hope that it will not be too difficult, for everything will turn upon that small conflict.

I slow yet again and nothing appears but the moisture of the fog upon my face and the knuckles of my hand wrapped about my staff. I halt. I seek in my pocket after a box of cigarettes I had purchased several days ago in my festive mood. I had doubted they would shorten my life.

As I raise one to my lips, I hear the words, "You desire a light, madam?"

I nod my head as I turn.

It is one of the two monks who extends a lighter to me and flicks forth its flame. I notice for the first time the heavy ridge of callous along the edge of his hand. He had kept it carefully out of sight before, as we sojourned together. The other monk appears to his rear, to his left.

"Thank you."

I inhale and send smoke to join the fog.

"You have come a long way," the man states.

"Yes."

"And your pilgrimage has come to an end."

"Oh? Here?"

He smiles and nods. He turns his head toward the temple.

"This is our temple," he says, "where we worship the new bodhisattva. He awaits you within."

"He can continue to wait, till I finish my cigarette," I say.

"Of course."

With a casual glance, I study the man. He is probably a very good *karateka*. I am very good with the *bo*. If it were only him, I would bet on myself. But two of them, and the other probably just as good as this one? Kokuzo, where is your sword? I am suddenly afraid.

I turn away, I drop the cigarette, I spin into my attack. He is ready, of course. No matter. I land the first blow.

By then, however, the other man is circling and I must wheel and move defensively, turning, turning. If this goes on for too long, they will be able to wear me down.

I hear a grunt as I connect with a shoulder. Something, anyway . . .

Slowly, I am forced to give way, to retreat toward the temple wall. If I am driven too near it, it will interfere with my strokes. I try again to hold my ground, to land a decisive blow. . . .

Suddenly, the man to my right collapses, a dark figure on his back. No time to speculate. I turn my attention to the first monk, and moments later I land another blow, then another.

My rescuer is not doing so well, however. The second monk has shaken him off and begins striking at him with bone-crushing blows. My ally knows something of unarmed combat, though, for he gets into a defensive stance and blocks many of these, even landing a few of his own. Still, he is clearly overmatched.

Finally I sweep a leg and deliver another shoulder blow. I try three strikes at my man while he is down, but he rolls away from all of them and comes up again. I hear a sharp cry from my right, but I cannot look away from my adversary.

He comes in again and this time I catch him with a sudden reversal and crush his temple with a follow-up. I spin then, barely in time, for my ally lies on the ground and the second monk is upon me.

Either I am lucky or he has been injured. I catch the man quickly and follow up with a rapid series of strikes which take him down, out, and out for good.

I rush to the side of the third man and kneel beside him, panting. I had seen his gold earring as I moved about the second monk.

"Boris." I take his hand. "Why are you here?"

"I told you—I could take a few days—to help you," he says, blood trickling from the corner of his mouth. "Found you. Was taking pictures . . . And see . . . You needed me."

"I'm sorry," I say. "Grateful, but sorry. You're a better man than I thought."

He squeezes my hand. "I told you I liked you— Maryushka. Too bad . . . we didn't have—more time . . ."

I lean and kiss him, getting blood on my mouth. His hand relaxes within my own. I've never been a good judge of people, except after the fact.

And so I rise. I leave him there on the wet pavement. There is nothing I can do for him. I go into the temple.

It is dark near the entrance, but there are many votive lights to the rear. I do not see anyone about. I did not think that I would. It was just to have been the two monks, ushering me to the terminal. I head toward the lights. It must be somewhere back there.

I hear rain on the rooftop as I search. There are little rooms, off to either side, behind the lights.

It is there, in the second one. And even as I cross the threshold, I feel that familiar ionization which tells me that Kit is doing something here.

I rest my staff against the wall and go nearer. I place my hand upon the humming terminal.

"Kit," I say, "I have come."

No epigon grows before me, but I feel his presence and he seems to speak to me as he did on that night so long ago when I lay back upon the couch and donned the helmet:

"I knew that you would be here tonight."

"So did I," I reply.

"All of your business is finished?"

"Most of it."

"And you are ready now to be joined with me?"

"Yes."

Again I feel that movement, almost sexual in nature, as he flows into me. In a moment he would bear me away into his kingdom.

Tatemae is what you show to others. *Honne* is your real intention. As Musashi cautioned in the Book of Waters, I try not to reveal my *honne* even at this moment. I simply reach out with my free hand and topple my staff so that its metal tip, batteries engaged, falls against the terminal.

"Mari! What have you done?" he asks, within me now, as the humming ceases.

"I have cut off your line of retreat, Kit."

"Why?"

The blade is already in my hand.

"It is the only way for us. I give you this *jigai,* my husband."

"No!"

I feel him reaching for control of my arm as I exhale. But it is too late. It is already moving. I feel the blade enter my throat, well-placed.

"Fool!" he cries. "You do not know what you have done! I cannot return!"

"I know."

As I slump against the terminal I seem to hear a roaring sound, growing, at my back. It is the Big Wave, finally come for me. My only regret is that I did not make it to the final station, unless, of course, that is what Hokusai is trying to show me, there beside the tiny window, beyond the fog and the rain and the night.

24. Mt. Fuji in a Summer Storm

FANTASY AND SCIENCE FICTION: A WRITER'S VIEW

One more essay shouldn't strain the reader's stamina, though I hasten to add that I've a standing order with my tutelary deities to spare me the fading writer's trip of trying to sum everything up. It's just a little talk that I gave when keynoting the Seventh Annual Eaton Conference on Fantasy and Science Fiction at the University of California at Riverside, in 1985, where I was treated well; and I thought it might make a decent endpiece.

I have often wondered whether I am a science fiction writer dreaming I am a fantasy writer, or the other way around. Most of my science fiction contains some element of fantasy, and vice versa. I suppose that this could be annoying to purists of both persuasions, who may feel that I am spoiling an otherwise acceptable science fiction story with the inclusion of the unexplained, or that I am violating the purity of a fantasy by causing its wonders to conform to too rational a set of strictures.

There may be some truth in this, so the least I can do is try to tell you why I operate this way, what this seeming hybrid nature of much of my work means to me and how I see this meaning as applying to the area at large.

My first independent reading as a schoolboy involved mythology—in large quantities. It was not until later that I discovered folk tales, fairy tales, fantastic voyages. And it was not until considerably later—at age eleven—that I read my first science fiction story.

It actually did not occur to me until recently that this course of reading pretty much paralleled the development of the area. First came fantasy, with its roots in early religious systems—mythology—and epical literature. Watered-down versions of these materials survived the rise of Christianity in the form of legends, folklore, fairy tales, and some incorporated the Christian elements as well. Later came the fantastic voyages, the utopias. Then, finally, with the industrial revolution, scientific justifications were substituted for the supernatural by Mary Shelley, Jules Verne, H. G. Wells. I had actually read things in the proper chronological order.

I feel now that this colored my entire approach to the use of the fabulous in literature. The earliest writings of the fantasy sort involved considerable speculation from a small and shaky factual base. A lot of guesswork and supernatural justifications for events came into play. I accepted these things as a child would—uncritically—my only reading criterion being whether I enjoyed a story. About the time I discovered science fiction I was somewhere near the threshold of reflection. I began to appreciate the value of reason. I even began to enjoy reading about science. In a way, I guess, I was a case of ontogeny recapitulating phylogeny.

I have never gotten away from a fondness for all of these forms—I suppose because my thinking has been touched by all of them. Emotionally, I find it difficult to draw distinctions between science fiction and fantasy because I feel them to be different areas of a continuum— the same ingredients but different proportions. Intellectually, however, I understand that if the fabulous elements involve the supernatural, or are simply unexplained in terms of an intelligent person's understanding of how natural laws operate, then that particular story should be considered a fantasy.

If the fabulous should be explained, or indicated to be explainable in terms of the present state of human knowledge or theory—or some extension thereof—I can see how a story of this sort can be considered to be science fiction.

When I write, though, I generally do not think in terms of such facile compartmentalizations. I feel that fiction should mirror life and that its *modus* is that classical act of *mimesis,* the imitation of an action. I concede that it is a distorting mirror we use in science fiction and fantasy; nevertheless, it should represent in some fashion everything which is placed before it. The peculiar virtue of a distorting mirror is its ability to lay special emphasis upon those features of consensus reality which the writer wishes to accent—a thing which in many ways places what we do close to satire, in the classical sense—making the science fiction and fantasy worlds special ways of talking about the present world. Another is the particularly wide range of characters this practice permits me to explore.

Not only do I not like to think of my stories in terms of separate science fiction and fantasy categories, but I feel that for me it would actually be harmful in terms of the creative act to drive such a wedge into my view of the continuum. According to John Pfeiffer, author of *The Human Brain,* "There is an entire universe packed inside your skull, a compact model of your surroundings based on all the experiences you have accumulated during the course of a lifetime." Of necessity such a model is limited by the range of one's perceptions and the nature of one's experiences.

Thus, the world about which I write, the world to which I hold up my distorting mirror, is not the real world in any ultimate sense. It is only my limited, personal image of the real world. Therefore, though I have tried hard to make my version of reality as complete a model as possible, there are gaps, dark areas which exist in testimony to my ignorance of various matters. We all possess these dark areas, somewhere, because we have not world enough nor time to take in everything. These are a part of the human condition—Jung's shadows, if you like; unfilled addresses in our personal databases, if you prefer.

What has this to do with the fabulous—with fantasy and science fiction? My feelings are that science fiction, with its rational, quasi-documentable approach to existence, springs from the well-lighted, well-regulated areas of our private universes, whereas fantasy, in the tradition of its historical origins, has its roots in the dark areas. Somewhere, I already hear voices raised in objection to my implication that fantasy springs from ignorance and science fiction from enlightenment. In a way it is true, and in a way it is not. To quote Edith Hamilton, "There has probably not been a better educated generation than the one that ushered in the end of Athens." Yet it was these same highly rational Greeks who passed classical mythology along to us, in its most powerful, sophisticated forms, while providing material for early chapters in world history books.

Fantasy may take its premises from the unknown, but what it does with them immediately thereafter is subject them to the same rational processes used by any storyteller in the working out of a tale. The story itself then unfolds in a perfectly clear-cut fashion.

I am not saying that the dark areas represent things which are ultimately unknowable, but only that these are representations of the unknown within the minds of individual authors—from the nameless horrors of Lovecraft to the mental processes of Larry Niven's Puppeteers. I doubt that any two authors' world models coincide exactly. And I feel that the generalization and representation of these clouds of unknowing in literature are a basis for fantasy.

I wish to take things one step further, however. I can hardly deny the effectiveness of a good story which is purely fantasy nor of another which is purely science fiction, in terms of the distinctions as I see them. As I said earlier, I tend not to think of such distinctions at all while I am working. When I am writing a story of some length, my personal sense of aesthetics usually causes me to strive for closure, to go for the full picture, to give at least a nod to everything I regard in that version of reality. As a consequence, my stories reflect the dark areas as well as the light ones; they contain a few ambiguous or unexplained matters along with a majority of things which follow the rules. In other words, I tend to mix my fantasy and my science fiction. Looked at one way, what I write is, I suppose, science fantasy—a bastard genre, according to some thinking on the matter. I am not sure what that makes me.

I followed this pattern in my first book—*This Immortal*—by leaving certain things unexplained and open to multiple interpretations. I did it again in my second book—*The Dream Master*—only there the dark areas were in the human psyche itself rather than in events. It was present in the Peian religion and its effects on my narrator, Francis Sandow, in the otherwise science fiction novel *Isle of the Dead.* In *Lord of Light,* I wrote a book where events could be taken either as science fiction or as fantasy with but a slight shifting of accent. And so on, up through my recent novel, *Eye of Cat,* where the final quarter of the book may be taken either as fantasy or as hallucination, according to one's taste in such matters. I write that way because I must, because a small part of me that wishes to remain honest while telling the calculated lies of fiction feels obliged to indicate in this manner that I do not know everything, and that my ignorance, too, must somehow be manifested in the universes which I create.

I was wondering recently where this placed me within the general context of American incarnations of the fabulous. I began reviewing their history with this in mind, and I was struck by a serendipitous insight into our relationship to the grand scheme of things.

We did it backwards.

American fantastic literature began the pulp magazines of the late 1920s. From that time on through the 1930s it was heavily indebted to other sorts of adventure tales. We can regard this as a kind of *Ur*-science fiction, whence rose the impetus which has carried all of the rest.

What happened, then, in the 1940s? This was the time of the "hard" science fiction story, the time of the sort of story referred to by Kingsley Amis as having the "idea as hero." Isaac Asimov and Robert Heinlein in particular exemplify this period when the idea, derived from science, dominated the narrative. At initial regard, it should not

seem strange that our science fiction entered its first rec-
ognizable period with what was the latest phase in the
historical development of fantastic literature—that tech-
nologically oriented form of the fabulous narrative which
had to await the appropriate development of the sciences.
But what happened next?

In the 1950s, with the collapse of many of the science
fiction magazines and the migration of science fiction to
the paperback and hardcover book markets, along with the
freedom from magazine restrictions thus obtained, came a
shifting of concerns to the sociological and political areas.
The idea was still hero, but the ideas were no longer derived
exclusively from the physical sciences. I think of Edward
Bellamy and of Fred Pohl. I think of Thomas More and
of Mack Reynolds. I think of Nietzsche and of some of
Freud's character studies (which I can only classify as
fantasies) and I think of Philip José Farmer. Looking back
even further to the pastoral genre I also think of Ray
Bradbury and of Clifford Simak.

Moving—ahead, I suppose—to the experimental work
of the 1960s, I recall the *Carmina Burana*, the troubadours,
the minnesingers, the lyrical literature of self of an even
earlier period.

And the 1970s? We saw a resurgence of fantasy—fat-
volumed trilogies detailing marvelous exploits of gods, war-
riors, and wizards—a thing which is with us still, and which
in recent years, as with Tolkien, has taken on the overtones
of ersatz scripture.

American fabulous literature appears to have recapi-
talated phylogeny in reverse. We worked at it steadily and
have finally made it back to the mythic beginning—which
is where I came in. I have a strange sense of *déjà vu*, of
my lost past recaptured, on reading much of the current
material in the area.

Such are the joys, you might say, of being able to
select my own examples. True. I can point to numerous

exceptions to every generalization I've made. Yet I feel there is something to what I have said or I would not have sketched this tendency in even this wavery impressionistic outline.

So where do we go from here? I see three possibilities and a whimsical vision: We can drop back into the *Ur-* and write adventure stories with just the fabulous trappings—which is the direction Hollywood seems to have taken. Or we can turn around now and work our way forward again, catching up with H. G. Wells sometime around the turn of the century. Or we can fall back upon our experience and strive for a synthesis—a form of science fiction which combines good storytelling with the technological sensitivity of the forties, the sociological concerns of the fifties, and the attention to better writing and improved characterization which came out of the sixties.

Those, I say, are three possibilities. A less likely avenue might be to do the latter and also to incorporate the experience of the ancient 1970s, when fantasy reached what may have been its greatest peak in this century. That is, to use all of the above with a dash of darkness here and there, to add to the flavor without overpowering the principal ingredients, to manipulate our fancies through a range of rationality and bafflement—in that our imagination needs both to fuel it, and a fullness of expression requires the acknowledgment of chaos and darkness opposed by the sum of our knowledge and the more successful traditions of thought to which we are heir.

I feel that it is this opposition which generates the tensions and conflicts of the human mind and heart implicit in all particularly good writing, secondary to the narrative line itself but essential if that nebulous quality known as tone is to sound with veracity in the search for mimetic verisimilitude. This quality, I feel, is present in the best writing in any genre—or in no genre at all, for labels are only a matter of convenience, and subject to revision by manufacturers or college catalog editors. One must, of course, feel strongly about such matters when attempting to recast the field in one's own image, for one would hate to dim the vision of those hard, gemlike authorial virtues of narcissism and arrogance.

Will science fiction and fantasy go this way? Partly, it depends on who is writing it—and to the extent that I see many talented newcomers in the area, I am heartened. The most gifted writers seem to be the ones who care the least what you call one of these things we are talking about, other than a story. Their main concern is how effectively a tale has been told. The area itself, like life, will go through the usual cycles of fads, periodic overemphasis of a certain sort of theme or character—as well as fat books, thin books, and trilogies. The best stories will be remembered years later. What they may be like, I can't really say. I'm not in the prediction business.